Love & (Mellow) Drama

Love Trials II

Manali Desai

Ukiyoto Publishing

All global publishing rights are held by

Ukiyoto Publishing

Published in 2023

Content Copyright © Manali Desai
Cover Design by Aviral Kumar

ISBN 9789360162160

All rights reserved.
No part of this publication may be reproduced, transmitted, or stored in a retrieval system, in any form by any means, electronic, mechanical, photocopying, recording or otherwise, without the prior permission of the publisher.

The moral rights of the author have been asserted.

This is a work of fiction. Names, characters, businesses, places, events, locales, and incidents are either the products of the author's imagination or used in a fictitious manner. Any resemblance to actual persons, living or dead, or actual events is purely coincidental.

This book is sold subject to the condition that it shall not by way of trade or otherwise, be lent, resold, hired out or otherwise circulated, without the publisher's prior consent, in any form of binding or cover other than that in which it is published.

www.ukiyoto.com

To my 'dramatic' husband

Thanks for not being mellow

Happy Birthday! This is my very thoughtful (can be interpreted as useless) gift to you just like one of the many you've bestowed upon me. Now this will truly be an 'unforgettable' day, year after year.

Also,

Here's a reminder that

Everything that's right in your life is my doing, and

Everything that's wrong in mine is yours

P.S:

Me - 7

You - 0 (or is it 1.5?)

It doesn't matter as long as I'm winning

Note: For those of you who are new here, that's the count of the number of books I've written so far vs the number of books my husband has read out of those. His birthday is 9th April which coincides with the publication day of this book (9/04/2023)

Acknowledgments

My real-life family and friends: Thanks for tolerating me.

My (non-writer/non-reader) virtual friends: Thanks for helping me see the good and the bad of my writing (Maybe this book will help change your opinion of the 'bad')

My reader friends: Thanks for reminding me that you've had enough of my existing books and need a new one regularly (are two books a year, okay?) And also for recommending me books that helped me in the process of writing this one.

My writer friends: Thanks for showing me how it's done (sometimes also how it's not done!)

"It might be that movies are not close to real life. But for some, they're what makes life bearable, and sometimes, even better."

- Varun Agarwal

Contents

Prologue	1
Dancing Tunes	4
Absence Makes the Heart Go…?	10
Goodwill, or God's Will?	19
Who's That Girl?	25
A Friend Indeed	30
Deva Shree Ganesha	34
Dance, Romance?	43
Women, Woes…What?	56
Finding 'foot' ing	64
Not-So-Well Begun	70
Kissing the Pain Away	79
Festival of (True) Colors	90
Moving On (or Holding On?)	97
The Little Things (In Big Countries)	105
He Said, She Said	111
Change(d)	118
Locked Down	129
Back to Square One	144
Before & After (The Happily Ever After)	159
She Rose	172
The Daily Wave	178
(Not) The End - Epilogue	180
The Love & (Mellow) Drama Map	188
The Love & (Mellow) Drama Playlist	189
Glossary of Terms/Phrases	195

About the Author

Prologue

"Life can be boring or exciting, depending on how you choose to live each moment."

- Gayatri Kulkarni

October 2014

"Jaa Simran Jaa....Jee le apni zindagi..."[1]

The girl spoke louder than the actor who uttered the dialogues on screen. Her voice carried so much emotion that one would think it was her own life story being portrayed in the movie.

She was bouncing in her seat and cheered for the female actor who began chasing the train which was slowly moving away from the platform.

"C'mon Simran, run faster. Yes, girl. You can do this."

Her enthusiasm made those around her look at her, either in amusement or irritation.

As soon as the actress was able to board the train and be in the arms of her beloved, she jumped out of her seat.

Pheweep!

Pheweep!

Pheweep!

She whistled, clapped, and cheered on, blowing kisses toward the onscreen couple as they set off together into the sunset.

The end credits of the film rolled in alongside a song from the movie. Most of the crowd had begun to disperse and move out of the cinema hall. But the girl was looking at the screen with wide, unblinking eyes.

"Gayu. It's over now. Let's move."

Another girl, who seemed to be her companion for the movie, tugged at her arms and made to drag her.

"No no, Simi. Please wait. This is my favourite bit."

---

[1] *A dialogue from the Hindi movie Dilwale Dulhania Le Jayenge which roughly translates to "Go live your life to the fullest, Simran"*

The screen showed a scene of a mustard field where the female protagonist comes running.

"Quick go to the other end of the hall quick. Be my Raj for today, Simran."

"Gayu, seriously. Do we really have to do this? Wasn't coming to watch an almost two-decade old movie to a shady theatre like this, enough?"

The girl merely folded her arms over her chest in response while the off-screen Simran fumed. The other girl continued to look at the screen with anticipation and then at her friend with impatience.

"The things I do for you Gayatri Kulkarni….seriously…I wouldn't be surprised if I end up in jail someday." Simran muttered as she walked over to the other side of the movie hall.

On the screen, the female protagonist had found the source of the sound that enticed her to the fields. It was a familiar tune of a mandolin she had come to associate with her beloved. Soon she spotted him and they looked at each other like long lost lovers. He stopped playing the mandolin and spread his arms wide, inviting her for an embrace.

The girl shrieked at this moment and began running towards her friend, copying the movements of the female protagonist on screen, who also ran into the arms of her darling. Both embraces, the on and off-screen were completed at the same time and the screen went blank.

"Are we done, Miss Gayatri, or shall I say Miss Melodrama? Can we please go?"

"Oh, shut up! Don't pretend like you didn't enjoy that!"

Both girls made their way out of the hall, one exasperated and the other giggling away.

"Sir, we need to clean the hall before the next show. Please move out."

A tall figure who had silently been observing all the drama whilst leaning against the wall of the exit door, moved out. He chuckled and shook his head in disbelief.

"There he is. Oi! Varun, we've been waiting for over ten minutes. Where did you disappear, man?"

"Nothing, I was just looking for something." Saying so he looked endearingly at the retreating petite figure that had held his attention for the past three hours.

***

Dancing Tunes

"When your goal is to take centre stage, why dance like no one's watching?"

-Gayatri Kulkarni

January 2016

"Our next participant is someone who has captivated the hearts of the judges right from her audition. Hailing from Mumbai, this girl has the makings of the next Madhuri Dixit. Not my words; that's what one of our judges said. Without further ado, let's call on to the stage... Miss Gayatri Kulkarni...."

The hall broke into a tumultuous applause as a petite girl made her way to the stage. She was dressed in a traditional Maharashtrian attire. The red nauvari saree accentuated her fair complexion and hourglass figure. She smiled with radiance and bowed down to the judges and audience. She was nervous, but also excited. She looked on at the judges with a confidence she'd never felt before; definitely not in the audition round. A conversation she had right before going in that day, came to her mind on its own accord.

"Gayu, please remember not to give this so much importance...it is only something..."

"Yes, aai. I know. Can you be happy about it for once, please?"

"Okay fine, but you have to remember my condition. Now go in and give your best."

"So, Gayatri. How does it feel to qualify in the top 25?"

One of the judges asked Gayatri, bringing her out of her contemplation.

"Ma'am, dance is the only thing that makes me feel confident. It makes me feel like I have an identity. So reaching this level in the competition means so much more than an acknowledgement of my dancing skills."

"Very well then Gayatri. Let's see what you've got in store for us today."

This was her moment. She did feel a little nervous about having her family in the audience, but once the music came on, her mind went blank about everything else. The lyrics of *Pinga* reverberated across the hall in a few moments. With it began a show of movements that most had never seen before. Gayatri's back was turned to the audience and her hands were folded at the small of her back in the form of a swan. As the music and lyrics started, she moved one of her hands away from her body as if mimicking the movements of a wave. She then did the same with her other hand and slowly swayed her body in a similar manner, from top to bottom. Thumping her feet to match the tune of the song, she turned around gracefully and looked the audience in the eye. Her body turned, twisted, and swirled in a manner that had everyone entranced. She smiled in a mysterious and charming way while maintaining eye contact. So alluring were her moves and the playfulness in her eyes, that each person looking at her felt like she was looking directly at them and performing only for their eyes.

The song slowly reached its crescendo and most of the audience was already up on their feet, clapping, cheering, and some of them even whistling. Gayatri swirled around the length and breadth of the stage with her head towards the ceiling and her eyes closed as if in a trance. In a least expected move, she lifted one leg up and continued to swirl with one foot on the stage while the other one was pointed towards the top of the stage at a ninety-degree angle. There was an audible gasp from the audience and even the judges. One of the judges covered her mouth with her hands as if she could not believe what she was seeing.

Without losing her balance or stopping her bodily movements, Gayatri did a 180-degree spin and then a split to end her performance as the music came to a stop.

There was pin-drop silence in the auditorium for a few seconds as Gayatri stood up and took a bow. She smiled nervously wondering if she had failed. But after some murmurs, an applause so loud broke out that Gayatri's shrieks of delight were hardly registered. The judges and the audience were on their feet. Most of them were also chanting "once more" while continuing to clap with vigour.

Gayatri's eyes filled with unshed tears.

THIS!

This was what made it all worth it. Her eyes moved over the audience searching for familiar faces and landed on her family. Her elder brother Sharad was up in his seat, whistling and clapping loudly. Her mother looked pleasantly surprised and gave her a thumbs up. Gayatri looked right and left of Sharad and her mother, but could not locate her father. She wondered where he could be and what might have happened to make him miss her performance. She looked questioningly at Sharad, but before he could react, Gayatri's attention was back on the stage because the applause had finally settled a bit.

One of the judges, a well-known actor of the 90s from Bollywood and a dancing queen herself, was walking towards the stage. Gayatri looked at her in confusion and with some surprise. Once the distance between them was minimal, Gayatri was enveloped in a hug by the said judge. Breaking apart after a few seconds but still with her arms around Gayatri's waist, she said, "You made me a proud Maharashtrian with that performance. I have said this before and I will say it again, you are the next Madhuri Dixit in the making. The dancing and entertainment industry awaits you with open arms, darling."

Gayatri was now crying in earnest, out of sheer happiness. Was this really happening? Sharad whistled loudly. Her mother was wiping away a tear with the edge of her dupatta. Where was her father though?

The judge hugged her again. This time, she whispered only for Gayatri's ears, "A proposal awaits you backstage. I hope you will take it. Your father is with the team already."

Gayatri's mind was abuzz with apprehension and excitement. What could the proposal be? Is that why her father was not with Sharad and her mother? So lost was she in these thoughts that the comments from the other judges hardly registered in her mind. She merely nodded, smiled and bowed down in gratitude to their words of praise.

Soon she walked off the stage with the sound of applause for her performance still following her. She was not at all surprised to find her father waiting for her. What surprised her though, was that instead of the beaming pride she expected to be written across his face, there was a deep frown.

Before she could make head or tail of it, her father said, "This madness has to stop now, Gayatri! We let you indulge this far and that's enough. We're not some millionaires to be able to afford such whims and fancies."

Saying so, he held her by the hand and started pulling her away from the people around them; mostly team members of the reality show. Some participants like Gayatri were also there but they merely hung around to witness the drama unfolding.

"Let her make her own decision sir…."

"Gayatri please infuse some sense into your father and explain how big an opportunity this is…."

A few of the team members shouted out as Gayatri was dragged away by her father. She tried to resist but that only made her father grip her hand more tightly.

"Baba, at least tell me what's….."

Gayatri began but was silenced by the threatening look her father gave her.

Sharad and her mother stood at a little distance from them, near the exit of the auditorium. Seeing the look on his father's face, Sharad walked out immediately saying, "I'll bring the car around."

"What happened ji…?" Uma, Gayatri's mother, in her typical manner, was about to start her questioning barrage. But, Shishir, Gayatri's father, raised his hand and made a gesture indicating they'll continue the discussion later.

"Tch, this dance of yours has always caused more problems than anything else." Uma muttered irritatingly while making her way towards their car.

Once they were all seated inside their humble Maruti Alto, Sharad took off. Not a second had passed since the car was out of the auditorium premises, and both the parents exploded.

"Please tell me what has happened?"

"We have let this dancing thing get too far."

Sharad gave Gayatri a sympathetic look and gestured for her to stay calm. Shishir glared at his wife. She glared in return too but sensing defeat, she crossed her arms in front of her chest in mute defiance and turned her face to look out the window. Looking directly at Gayatri now, Shishir began to narrate the events that had led to all this.

"You know why they called me backstage? The show organisers apparently had a proposition for us, rather for you Gayatri. First, they asked me what kind of background we have and did we have any financial problems. When I said we belong to the middle class and were able to get by well, albeit, with some struggle sometimes, their faces fell."

Shishir paused for a while to look at Uma, who still stubbornly continued to look out the window. Shishir sighed and continued, "Then they asked me if anyone out of the four of us had any ailments. I told them that Uma and I have some age-related issues but otherwise nothing much to worry about."

Uma let out an audible 'Hmmphh' at this.

Shishir rolled his eyes and went on, "Anyway, the team members exchanged worried looks, and then one of them said, *'Sir, let me be very honest with you. Your girl has talent and though we would like to take her ahead in the competition, we won't be able to do so unless there's some strong backstory, like a financial or emotional struggle.'* One of the other team members whispered something in his ear at this point. The one who had spoken to me continued, *'But, we do have another alternative for you. And let me tell you, we're only doing this because we genuinely see potential in Gayatri. Not all the participants who have reached this stage in the competition have been given this offer. Please consider this as an investment in your daughter's future and her dream.'*

Shishir paused to take a breath and continued, "By this time I could already smell something fishy and did not like the route the conversation was taking. Nonetheless I nodded and he went on, *'The show runs on TRPs and funds invested by producers. But most of the time that is not enough. So, if you could provide some aid in that direction, it could help Gayatri's chances of going forward in the competition.'*

"Why didn't you just give him one tight...?" Uma realised that the kids were with them and stopped herself in time.

Shishir shook his head and went on, "I was already walking away by this time but the guy continued anyway, *'Sir, it's just a small amount to pay for your daughter's and even your family's stable future. The competition will open up so many opportunities for her that you can't even imagine. All that will cover up your investment in less than six months.'*

Shishir finished his long monologue, huffing and muttering angrily with a few broken bits audible, "Am I Ambani or what?" and, "An investment he says? My foot!"

Shishir looked at Uma and there was a silent exchange of words between the parents that the children could not comprehend.

"See, Gayatri. We understand that you love dancing, that's why we indulge you, albeit a little reluctantly. But let me make two things very clear. One, I can't and won't support this 'hobby' or whatever it is. Certainly not in a manner that makes it the focus of all our lives. Neither do I have the financial standing to do so, nor do I understand how something like that can possibly benefit you or any of us. Secondly...."

"There's no need to be so politically correct about this. I already told her what this will lead to if she fails..." Uma cut her husband off and continued.

"But, aai. I have not failed!" Gayatri cried out in anguish.

Uma gave her daughter such a threatening look that she was silenced right away.

"Shut up and listen to me, okay? Your path ahead is now clear. Focus on your boards and score decently. Your aim is to make the cut-off into Sharad's college and course. You will pursue the same degree as him. I am aware of how politics also interests you, so do not give me that look, young lady."

"That is only because..." Gayatri butted in angrily. She was tired of having to prove, yet again, how important dancing was for her.

"We do not care for the reasons anymore! You will get a degree that's promising enough. Once you have enrolled in the course, you can keep pursuing this 'dance' thing as an extracurricular activity in cultural events and stuff." This time it was Shishir who finished his wife's verdict.

Gayatri had no choice but to stay mute. She could cut off her mother, but she wasn't yet brave enough to interrupt her father.

"Have we made ourselves clear?" Shishir gave his younger offspring a hardened look.

Gayatri nodded and looked out the window, cursing her fate for being born to parents who were neither affluent nor supportive.

Fine! I'll score the best marks and get into this forsaken course. But I'm not going to give up dancing at any cost.

She was determined to prove them wrong anyway.

***

Absence Makes the Heart Go…?

"If two people really want to be together, nothing and no one can come in their way."

- Varun Agarwal

March 2016

Itnnaaa mazaaaa kyuuu aa raha haiii, tune hawa mein bhaang milayaa[2]

Avni Mehta sang along loudly to the lyrics as she swayed in abandon to its catchy tune. The Holi celebrations at Pashmina Serene were on, in full swing. Being a posh residential complex did not stop its residents from letting their hair loose on festive days, especially a festival like Holi. This Indian festival is the epitome of foregoing all your inhibitions and Bollywood songs like the current one which had Avni going berserk, only added to the overall madness. She was wearing a white kurta coupled with a white salwar; both of which currently looked like a painter's canvas. The Holi colours had turned her clothes and almost every visible part of her body, into a mélange of various shades.

Accompanied by his younger brother, Abhi, Varun Agarwal walked into the premises where the festive celebrations were on. Immediately his eyes fell on Avni and a smile spread across his face.

"Hey, Abhi. Come join us!"

Avni ran towards Abhi and before he could react, she dragged him towards the spot where she had been dancing. From the table nearby, she grabbed a palmful of colours that were on display and rubbed it across his face and neck.

"Happy Holi!!!" Saying so she ran away, not giving Abhi a chance to reciprocate.

Her laughter could be heard over the din of the loud songs. Not one to give up easily, Abhi too grabbed an armful of colours in both hands and set off after her. The two were now chasing around like a bunch of kids, shrieking as if their tails were on fire. Soon Abhi caught up with Avni and grabbed her by the waist, taking full revenge for her mischief.

---

[2] Lyrics from the song *Balam Pichkari* from the Hindi movie *Yeh Jawaani Hai Deewani* which roughly translate to," Why am I having so much fun. Have you mixed bhaang in the air?"

Varun observed their antics from the side-lines and laughed. Abhi caught him in the act and whispered something in Avni's ear.

Oh! This is not good

Varun knew right away he was the next target but he was no match against the two. While Abhi ran towards Varun from the front, Avni ambushed him from behind. Abhi rubbed the colours over his brother's face laughing mirthfully, while Avni grabbed his waist from behind making sure their prey could not escape. As Avni continued to hold him firmly, Abhi grabbed a hose pipe from nearby and aimed it at the duo.

"Buro na maano Holi hai[3]" Abhi shouted loudly as Avni cackled and Varun struggled to get back his bearings. He felt Avni's grip loosen from his waist but before she could move away, he grabbed her with one hand. As she tried to wriggle free, with his other hand, Varun jostled the hose pipe out of Abhi's grip.

"No, not the pipe, Varun. No!!!!"

"You should have thought of that before you attacked me, you little devil."

Avni's pleas were drowned in the force of water from the hose pipe. Varun had the good sense to aim the pipe at Abhi in just a few seconds. Laughing at the state they had got each other in, the three hugged tightly. They were, after all, meeting after a year.

The Mehtas and the Agarwals had been neighbours for a decade. While the Agarwals had two sons, the Mehtas had one daughter. No surprise to anyone that the three became thick friends pretty soon, especially Avni and Abhi, who were closer in age. Among the three, Varun was the eldest, and decidedly the most level headed. But that did not hinder him from engaging in mischief with the younger two, albeit not without some persuasion.

Once the trio broke apart, Abhi and Avni began swaying their bodies to the tune of the music still blaring out loudly. Soon they were joined by other residents of the complex, including their parents. They all took turns to apply colours on each other's faces. Their circles separated as the elders went to join their age group and the kids to theirs. Varun couldn't help

---

[3] *In India, people say this while celebrating the Holi festival and applying colors or spraying water on each other. It roughly translates to, "Don't feel bad. It's Holi after all."*

but notice that most people, especially the men, seemed keen on making Avni the target of their colour applying and water spraying antics. She, of course, was oblivious to it all, immersed in the madness around herself completely. Avni's focus was anyway on the hook steps and the lyrics of whichever song played out one after another over the loudspeaker. Abhi matched her enthusiasm in singing out the lyrics and her dance steps. The two seemed very much like the childhood besties that they were.

Varun was also enjoying the festivities in his own way. Though not a wallflower, his dance movements were visibly not as fluid or carefree as that of most others in their little circle. At the moment, all his attention was on the girl, rather woman, who had been giving him sleepless nights for the past couple of years. He still could not believe she was here in flesh and blood.

Pyaase dil ko aaj mila hai sagar[4] he sighed in satisfaction while not letting his gaze away from his beloved even for a second.

The Mehtas had moved to Nashik last year, owing to a job transfer of Avni's father, Arvind Mehta. The timing could not have been worse, because, after building up much courage, Varun had finally confessed his feelings to Avni. Surprisingly, there was no resistance from her, but in her trademark tongue-in-cheek manner she did say, "Der se aaye par durust aaye[5]" while bursting into laughter and hugging him tight. Just like that, the two were in a relationship. Apart from the little disagreements every now and then, they were quite the #couplegoals or as Abhi called it 'diabetically sweet'. Things took an unexpected turn when Arvind's transfer call came in. In just a month, Abhi lost his best friend and Varun, his girlfriend.

There was certainly a dent in the blissfulness of their ten-month old hitch-free relationship. But against what they had heard from friends, Varun and Avni were determined to make long-distance work. Agreed things hadn't quite been as smooth, what with his MBA preps and her college admissions. They just could not manage to talk to each other for more than ten minutes before some or the other task called for attention and their video or audio call had to be cut. But Varun didn't let their lack of

---

[4] *Lyrics from a Hindi song which roughly translates to, "Today the thirsty heart has found the sea."*
[5] *A popular saying which means you are coming with a perfect result especially after a long struggle or endeavour to achieve sth.Furthermore it can be seen as success or Victory of a person who was putting his/her effort to succeed sth passionately for a long time.*

communication become a reason for a lack of love. He assumed Avni would understand this. But apparently it wasn't so. Every now and then, she would ping him at odd hours saying how she was missing him or how her patience was wearing thin because he hardly replied to such messages from her. Things got better when they both secured admission in the institutes they were aiming to get into. But then they made new friends and there was always one or the other assignment to work on. They had been getting into quite a few arguments lately, especially about Avni's friends.

Not friends. A friend. Singular.

All that was in the past now, because looking at her now, it felt just like yesterday when she had said goodbye to the city of dreams. When he had held her in his arms and kissed her like there was no tomorrow as she said, *"Alvida Kehnse se phir milne ki umeed marr jaati hai*[6]*"*

"Are you going to do something about that look on your face?" Abhi's question made Varun realise he had been almost drooling. Abhi had spoken into Varun's ear such that no one would notice, least of all the subject of their discussion. Varun looked at his younger sibling quizzically, wondering what he was aiming at.

"Oh for God sake, do I have to spell out everything? Just go home, I'll take care of the rest. I don't know who awarded you Student of the Year. I definitely think the professor has a soft corner for your looks; because it definitely doesn't seem like you have any brains. Honestly tell me, it was a female professor, isn't it?"

Varun laughed as he nodded his head. Then giving Abhi a side hug he walked out of the party and made his way home. As he waited for the elevator in the building foyer, he noticed Abhi had lifted Avni into his arms and thrown her into the inflatable water pool.

"Abhi you moron, I'll have to change now. What the hell!"

Varun smiled to himself as he very well understood Abhi's ploy. Avni made her way grumpily to where Varun was waiting. He noticed that she

---

[6] *A Hindi phrase which is a popular dialogue from the movie Kabhi Alvida Na Kehna, which roughly translates to, "Saying bye kills the hope of meeting again."*

had a stole wrapped around her upper body, which she removed once she stepped inside the building premises.

"Oh, there will be blood now Mr. Abhi.. think lending me this stole will save your ass… you just wait and watch…"

Varun took in her wet figure which dripped from head to toe. Where previously she had looked like a dry-coloured canvas, now she appeared like a water coloured one. He felt himself going weak in the knees realising that her clothes were almost see-through now. He could make out the perfect roundness of her breasts, her thin waistline, and even her shapely thighs. The whole water-dipping prank by Abhi hadn't left much to the imagination about Avni's figure and walking out had been a smart move on her part; and lending her the stole a gentlemanly one on Abhi's. Varun looked away as he felt movements in a body part he was sure would lead to embarrassment in public. Currently, she was running her hands through her hair trying to soak out as much water as possible. Despite turning his face the other way, Varun couldn't help but chuckle at her still ongoing rambling. Avni stopped in her tracks when she realised she had walked into some company.

She glared at him while continuing her tirade, "Oh, you think it's funny? Now I'll be the perfect model for cough and cold meds for the next two weeks. Be prepared for this." She then went into a fake coughing spree and pretending to hold a medicine strip in her hand, went, "Vicks ki goli lo khich khich door karo."[7]

Varun laughed heartily as he reached out to her and enveloped her in a tight hug. Before he could stop himself or she protested, he planted a quick kiss on her forehead.

"I've missed your drama the most…"

"Oh, don't lie, I know what you've missed the most" Looking around to ensure it was just them, Avni placed her hand on his inner thigh, moving up slowly toward her original target. She looked at him hungrily with a twinkle in her eyes which left him wanting to do much more than only kissing her forehead. Just then the elevator dinged indicating its arrival, breaking them apart.

---

[7] *A Hindi product tagline for Vicks candies which roughly translates to, "Take a tablet of Vicks and get rid of irritation/hoarseness of throat."*

They held hands while stepping into the lift but never breaking eye contact. Avni moved towards Varun, winking and biting her lower lip as she closed the small distance between them. Varun cleared his throat and with his eyes pointed toward the upper left corner of the elevator.

"Oh well, there goes your Fifty Shades fantasy."

He snorted, "Darling that's all you. My fantasies are much more x-rated than making out in an elevator."

She punched him hard on the shoulder in response and mumbled, "One track mind," as he leaned towards her ear and whispered, "And how would you know what track is that?"

The effect that had on her skin sent him into a frenzy. He could see the goosebumps on the back of her neck and on her arms as she turned away to hide the colour in her cheeks.

Once they reached their floor, Varun literally jogged towards the Agarwal residence to open the door. He stood at the entrance and bowing down to Avni, said, "Atithi Devo Bhava[8]" while she pushed him inside and kicked the door shut in a haste.

Before she could turn around, Varun pushed her into the closed door, pinning her arms against it with his left arm, locking her in place. He breathed into her ears, while his right hand brushed aside the hair on her back onto her shoulder. Slowly he moved his fingers around the neck, once again causing the hair on her back to rise in anticipation. She moaned as his hands moved down to her back, making its way to her waist and then forcing her to turn around, and facing him.

There was a challenging and thirsty look in her eyes; the one that always drove him crazy. He threw away the stole in her hand to a corner, never breaking eye contact, kissed her on the neck, sending shivers down both their bodies. His hand tugged at the waistband of her salwar, pulling it down with impatience as she mumbled a satisfactory 'mmm'. His other hand was tangled deep in her hair, forcing her face closer to his. Their breaths became deeper and heavier as anticipation hung heavy in the air with every inch of gap being closed between their lips. He winked before finally planting his thin lips over her luscious ones. Losing all sense of time and place, he moved his tongue hungrily over her upper lip and then

---

[8] *A Hindi phrase which roughly translates to, "A guest is akin to God."*

on her lower one, deriving pleasure from her body writhing below his. She mumbled something incomprehensible while leaning more towards him and making her own way down the front of his kurta and to his bare chest. Her tongue now found its way into his mouth, moving in a way that shocked him with the amount of pleasure it sent down to all body parts, especially the one that was now up in attention, demanding more. She broke the kiss, looking into his eyes while moving her lips to his bare chest, licking, sucking and then biting so hard that an involuntary moan escaped Varun's mouth.

He stopped her then, and while kissing her cheeks, picked her in his arms while making his way to the bedroom.

As soon as he laid her down on the bed, a noise broke the silence of the house. He couldn't place it at first but then the familiar tune of *Mein tenu Samjhawan ki*[9] reached his ears. The guilty look on Avni's face didn't miss Varun's sharp eyes even as the shock began to sink in. This was their song; the song that had been her ringtone for *him*, at least that's what he believed until that moment.

"Varun, I can…"

Not wanting to hear her explanation, he walked towards her phone, looked at the name of the person calling, and threw the handset towards her on the bed. It missed her face by a few inches and she flinched a bit. But he didn't care about chivalry or politeness at the moment.

"So, I was right, wasn't I?"

"Varun, you're taking it all wrong…"

His threatening look silenced her. "I should have guessed when you refused to separate the phone from yourself even for a second" He walked towards her and thrust the phone into her hand, "Unlock it right now!"

He scrolled through the messages and read them out loud, "*Darling, I miss you. Holi is so boring without you'*. Darling, are we now? What do you have to say about this darling? *'Thinking about our long drive on that rainy day. Let's do it again once you're back.'* Oh, this one is my favourite, *'You deserve someone who is with you and near you and not someone who only promises to be by your side.*" He slipped a look at her and relished at the panic-stricken look on her face. She grimaced further when he mimicked her and went on, *'There is nothing*

---

[9] *Lyrics of a Hindi song*

going on between me and Mihir, trust me Varun' 'Why can't you understand my need to have a friend I can trust? I could not find it in me to go on without you and Abhi by my side every day. Mihir was the only one who helped fill that space in my heart and life' Huh! So this is how he filled that space?"

Avni looked at him pleadingly and opened her mouth to say something. But Varun raised his hand to stop her.

"You know what. I don't even want to give you the chance to justify it. I'm done. We're done. Please save yourself some dignity by not coming in my way for the rest of your visit."

Before his mind and body could overpower his decision, he walked out of the room, slamming the door behind him. The loud howling and pleading of Avni followed him till he made his way to his bedroom, but he was determined not to pay it any heed or go console her in any manner.

For the next couple of days, he limited his movements within the house to his bedroom and the dining area. He ate alone, avoiding meal times with the family and their guests. He stayed out of the house most hours of the day citing assignments and project work as excuses, which on most occasions was true too. But they were all living under the same roof, so complete ignorance was quite impossible. However much he didn't want to, updates about their guests reached his way, either from his parents or from Abhi.

"The sale of their apartment has gone through. The papers should be drawn by tomorrow," Radha Agarwal, his mother, said casually, while serving him hot rotis during dinner one day.

"Avni left a while ago. I hope everything's fine between you two. She was crying relentlessly, pleading with me to talk to you," Abhi informed Varun one evening while dropping by into his bedroom.

To it all, he merely nodded or grunted to show that he had heard what was relayed to him.

A few days after Avni left, Shyam Agarwal, Varun's father, asked him, "Are you free tonight? Someone has to drop the Mehtas at VT station."

He nodded at the time but later excused himself citing some project work that required him to be out.

When Abhi returned that night after dropping off their guests, he seemed to be in a bad mood. Varun had thought about sharing his woes with him, but one look at his younger sibling's face was enough to tell him that Abhi had other things on his mind.

Varun wasn't sure when he would be able to tell Abhi. But one thing he was sure of. He would not be trusting another woman with his heart any time soon.

***

Goodwill, or God's Will?

"Believing that only good things will happen to you is like hoping that your ice cream never melts, even in summer and when kept outside the freezer"

- Gayatri Kulkarni

April 2016

"Yes, yes, Mithibai only. The same course as Sharad's, Political Science…"

"Aai please! The board results aren't even out yet and…"

Uma Kulkarni silenced her daughter with one look and it was Gayatri's cue to stay out of the conversation. She looked around and wondered for the umpteenth time what she was doing there. Agreed that she didn't have much to do in the interim period while she awaited her HSC board results and her college began. But she could think of ten things she desired to indulge in instead of spending it at this rather elaborate celebration of Ramnavmi.

Her entire family was at the Wadala Lord Rama temple to join in the festivities organised by the Agarwal family. Their younger son, Abhi Agarwal, was Sharad's closest friend. Their mothers too had met a few times. Hence an invitation had been extended to the Kulkarnis to be a part of this event put together by them. Knowing her mom, Gayatri had anticipated Uma's antennae to be upright, taking this as the perfect opportunity to broadcast their family's apparently perfect life in front of anyone with eyes and ears. What Gayatri hadn't expected though was the movie in focus to be 'Humari Beti'[10]. Not wanting to be a part of this charade, Gayatri tuned herself out. She was anyway least interested in the group of women who were now indulging Uma with follow-up questions about Gayatri's studies and career.

Walking away a bit, she took in the interiors of the grand temple. The decor done in and around it for the occasion had literally taken her breath away. She had been especially awed by the huge rangoli outside the temple entrance. It depicted key moments from the Hindu epic Ramayana. Flowers were strewn across the intricate and colourful design adding to

---

[10] *Hindi words which roughly translate to 'our daughter'*

its charming aura. The earthen lamps placed on the periphery of the rangoli invited the eyes of all the visitors straight to it. It was no wonder that nobody could enter the temple premises without a look of admiration towards the artistry. Looking at it, Gayatri too had felt glad for giving in to her mother's persuasion to join them.

"Gayatri, how are your dance classes coming along, dear?"

Her reverie was broken by this unexpected question. She had accepted that nobody besides herself, and sometimes her brother, would ever be interested in her passion for dancing. Apparently, Radha Agarwal, Abhi's mother, was different from the other adults around her. She was looking at Gayatri with curiosity, awaiting her response.

"They are going very well, aunty. They asked me to join as a trainer myself. So now I'm not just a student but a choreographer too…"

"That's wonderful…" Radha Agarwal responded encouragingly.

"It has kept her busy during this long break. But once college starts, she'll have to quit, of course."

Uma interjected, putting an end to the conversation.

Radha looked at Gayatri who shrugged her shoulders.

"Maa, we're about to start…"

Abhi Agarwal called out to his mother, indicating that her presence was required to begin the aarti. He smiled at Gayatri and waved to Sharad. She had met him a couple of times and knew him briefly. Gayatri couldn't help but notice that he looked quite dapper in the traditional attire of a yellow coloured kurta. Radha walked to the front and joined her family. As Abhi moved to make more space for her, Gayatri's eyes fell on a towering figure beside him. Her breath caught in her mouth and she gasped audibly.

Well, well. Who do we have here?

Mr. Tall turned towards her and gave a curious smile.

He probably heard your gasp, girl.

She blushed and felt butterflies in her stomach. He was wearing a green coloured kurta with a dupatta around his neck. Gayatri quickly averted her eyes to the idols in front.

Stop behaving like a bimbette!

One of the priests blew the conch shell indicating the commencement of the aarti. Gayatri sighed in relief and joined in merrily, thankful for the distraction. She closed her eyes in reverence while clapping her hands to match the tune. But in all honesty, it was just a tactic to restrain herself from checking out more of Mr. Green Kurta and his gorgeousness. It wasn't helping though, because even with her eyes closed, his smiling face appeared before her.

I wonder how he looks from close quarters.

"Can you not be so obvious?" Sharad whispered in her ear.

Gayatri jerked her eyes open and turned towards him, quickly following his gaze. Her cheeks turned red as she realised her little charade had not gone unnoticed.

"That's Abhi's older brother, Varun. In case you want to give a name to your latest crush."

She kicked Sharad and gave him a spiteful look while sticking her tongue out.

"He isn't single though from what I know." Sharad added. The satisfying tone and mocking look on his face did not miss Gayatri.

This time his reward was a punch on the arm. Sharad winced and went on, "How does it matter to you anyway? Your status is also, 'it's complicated', isn't it?"

Though a bit heartbroken on learning about Mr. Gorgeous's status, Gayatri had to admit that Sharad was right. She rolled her eyes in response to his question and said, "Can we focus on the aarti before we're reminded by Mother India about what amazing kids we are?"

Sharad shrugged while chuckling a bit and turned his face to the front. Gayatri looked around and saw that the temple was filled to its capacity. As the aarti reached its crescendo, her eyes landed on the Agarwal family who stood right at the front. She avoided gazing at the elder brother to circumvent further leg pulling from Sharad. She looked at Abhi instead and noticed that his eyes were fixed on somebody in the crowd.

Seems like I'm not the only one with butterflies in the stomach.

As soon as the aarti ended, Abhi rushed into the crowd with the prasad dish in his hand.

"Jaa Simran jaa, jee le apni zindagi." Gayatri mumbled to herself and sighed.

"Here, please take the prasad."

She turned and found herself looking into a set of brown, expressive eyes. Eyes that currently seemed amused. Eyes that belonged to a body that had a green kurta on it.

When had he walked over?

"Err, thanks…I…umm…"

"Hi Uma aunty, here please take the prasad."

"Thank you, dear. I was going to rush to you before it went kaput, but you're faster than me."

Uma laughed at her own joke and Gayatri was thankful for her mother's vanity. Because her blustering had gone unnoticed and she was sure the butterflies in her stomach were no longer just for her ears. Mr. Brown Eyes smiled at Uma and started to walk away.

As if struck by a sudden thought, he turned around and smiled mischievously. Leaning towards Gayatri and ensuring Uma's attention was elsewhere, he whispered.

"Bade bade deshon mein aisi choti choti baatein hoti rehti hai, Senorita."[11]

Winking slyly, he pointed toward Abhi and walked away, without waiting for her response and leaving her speechless. Not to mention embarrassed. She covered her face and let out a soft whimper, hoping nobody else had noticed her busybody act.

"Come, let's meet the other Agarwals and take our leave."

Still reeling from the encounter, Gayatri followed her mother wordlessly as they approached Radha and a few other women. They were all congratulating Radha on the success of the event and Uma butted in excitedly with her own praises. Gayatri smiled out of courtesy but started looking for a way out. Seeking Sharad she spotted him in a corner with Abhi. There was no sign of Varun though. She sighed in relief but there was also a kind of lingering disappointment.

---

[11] *A dialogue from the Hindi movie Dilwale Dulhaniya Le Jayenge roughly translates to "Such trivial things keep happening in big countries (and one should learn to ignore them)"*

"Hey, are you coming for the movie tonight?"

Gayatri took her phone and read the text she had just received. She was about to type in her response when Uma tapped her on the shoulder.

"Sharad and Shishir have left to get the car out. We'll take your leave now." Uma told Radha.

The whole gang of women took this as some sort of cue. Because all of them collectively made their way toward Abhi. Gayatri had no choice but to follow.

"Hello Abhi, how are you?," Uma asked, and without waiting for his response, she went on, "Did you hear the good news? Gayatri is soon starting out at your college."

Abhi smiled politely and said, "Congratulations. Though I must warn you that it's not as fancy as it is made out to be. Also, no concessions for you on the ragging front."

Gayatri smiled but her mind was elsewhere. She didn't want to miss the beginning of the movie and was sure her friends would whine endlessly if she kept them waiting. Not to mention, if Mr. Green Kurta showed up, he'd probably start mocking her again.

She mumbled, "My friends are waiting for me," and began to walk out. Uma was behind her in a second.

"What friends? Where are you going?"

"I told you about it in the afternoon, aai. I'm going out for a movie with some *Nrityanihar friends.*"

"Okay, fine."

"Who all are coming?"

"The usual lot. Simran, Kartik and a couple of our teachers from *Nrityanihar.* You know them all."

"Oh, did I hear the name Kartik?," Sharad butted in as Uma and Gayatri took seat inside the car.

Gayatri gave him a warning look and said, "Please drop me at Dadar station."

"Sure, but can you pass on a message to Kartik? Tell him I said, *pyaar dosti hai*[12]. I'm sure he'll understand."

Gayatri rolled her eyes and said, "Yeah, fine. Just drive now."

Sharad chuckled and began whistling, but thankfully stayed shut. Predictably though, he was whistling and humming the tune of *Kuch Kuch Hota Hai*.

"It's time to put the 'it's complicated' status to 'single'." Gayatri mumbled to herself. She'd always thought of Kartik only as a friend. But lately, he'd been behaving like a love-smitten teenager, showering her with gifts and calling or texting her all the time. To make things worse, he had admitted to Sharad that it was only for Gayatri that he'd joined *Nrityanihar* dance classes. She knew it was only a matter of time till he asked her out. To be honest, she had been enjoying the attention too and didn't have the heart to ask him to stop. She was determined to clear it out today though.

Her mind had already been made up about it beforehand. She tried convincing herself it had nothing to do with a certain tall stranger she had just met.

Oh, don't blame yourself. He caught up on your DDLJ reference and the butterflies in your stomach haven't rested since.

***

---

[12] *A dialogue from the Hindi movie Kuch Kuch Hota Hai which roughly translates to, "Love is friendship"*

Who's That Girl?

"They really should call your past lovers axe instead of ex. Or maybe an axe murderer?"

- Varun Agarwal

May 2016

"So, how's college?"

"Nothing much. We're preparing to welcome the new batch at Mithibai, who dropped off their forms today…"

"Great, actually, the placements at Welingkar seem really promising this year.."

The question was thrown out without addressing anyone's name, so both the Agarwal sons began to answer at the same time. Shyam Agarwal raised his eyebrows and looked over at his wife. Radha shrugged her shoulders and with a sigh, turned to the boys, "Let's begin with you first, Varun."

The four of them were having dinner together. They were seated at a mahogany dining table. Its glass top gleamed under the three yellow bulbs hanging below the pendant lights over the table. The wooden legs had intricate motifs and were sturdy enough to hold the weight of the thick glass atop it. The glass itself was translucent and appeared a different shade depending on the time of the day. Currently, it looked golden yellow. On most days, the table saw only the four Agarwals using it. Nonetheless, it did have a capacity for seating as many as twelve people. It could be described as rather elaborate and in any other setting, it would seem much too big. But in a household as grand as theirs, it fitted in just fine.

Varun gave a nod to his younger sibling and continued, "I know that I already have the offer from Mehta uncle. But I do want to see how I fare in the campus placements too. It's always better to know your potential outside your circle too. That's what you've always taught us."

Shyam looked at his son sharply and relented after a thoughtful pause, "Hmmph! That's right. Good call. I guess it's better to keep friends and business separate. Anyway, Arvind has Avni too in case he wants to extend the offer to someone else."

Varun got the feeling that his father knew of the exact reason why he was reluctant to take up Arvind Mehta's offer. After the Holi debacle, Varun had stopped talking to Avni completely. In fact he had deleted her contact and blocked her on every possible platform. Whatever updates he got about the Mehtas was via his parents. He knew Avni had been trying to reach out, courtesy of Abhi.

"Look, just talk to her man. She keeps asking about you and ends up crying almost every time."

"Listen, Avni and I are done, okay? I don't want your equation with her to get clouded because of my opinions. But, just know that she did something, which in my dictionary, is unforgivable."

Post that, Abhi never even mentioned her name in his presence. One day, when he received a call from Arvind Mehta, Varun knew Avni had something to do with it. Why else would Mehta uncle, with whom he had hardly exchanged ten sentences over the years, call him? With a sigh, he answered the call and what happened in the next few minutes made him sick and grateful at the same time.

"Hello, Varun dear. How are you?"

"I'm fine, uncle. How are you and aunty?"

If Arvind noticed that Varun hadn't asked about Avni, he let it be. But Varun didn't miss the slight exasperation on the other end, before Arvind went on, "We're *all* fine too dear. I'm calling to ask if you'd be interested in joining as a Junior Manager at my firm. You know I'm retiring in a couple of years and will be focusing full-time on the business. I will need all the help I can get and with an MBA from a prestigious institute like Welingkar to your credit, you'd be a great add-on."

"But, uncle.."

Apart from his government job, Arvind Mehta ran a distillery production and distribution business. It was a mid-sized but reputable and successful set-up. Varun knew working there would be a great opportunity to learn and grow. In any other circumstances, he would have been elated. But he knew the offer had come out of desperation, and not to acknowledge his abilities.

"There's no pressure to decide right away of course. Please take your time. You can let me know whenever you've made your choice." Arvind pressed, sensing Varun's hesitation.

"Sure, uncle. Can I let you know after the campus placements? I don't want to promise you and then back out."

"Sure, dear. I understand of course. Your Bina aunty and Avni will be delighted to know you're considering the offer."

"Thank you, uncle. I really appreciate it. I am sure it will be a great experience. Do pass on my regards to aunty."

There was a sigh from the other end before Arvind said, "Okay then, I guess we'll talk soon. Bye."

"Bye uncle."

That had been a few weeks ago. Varun hadn't got back with his answer to Arvind yet. But he knew his decision already. He only wanted a better offer in his hand before turning down Arvind's.

"And what about you, Abhi?" Shyam's question brought Varun back to the present.

"We're preparing to welcome the new batch. Most of them dropped their forms off today. I'm hoping to find at least a couple of capable ones to join the cultural committee."

"Gayatri was there too?" Radha asked curiously

Varun's ears perked up in interest. The girl had been frequenting his thoughts since their brief encounter at Ramanavami. He couldn't quite gauge what he found attractive about her. He felt a warm sensation building up inside him as he recalled how she had turned red after he whispered the DDLJ dialogue into her ear. Thankfully, Abhi's response jerked him to his senses.

"Yes, she was there too. I'm actually quite surprised at her choice of this course.."

"What do you mean?," Varun butted in.

"She was in the top 25 at *Dance Beat*. She has trained in many forms of dance, the latest being contemporary. I've seen her videos and she's got immense talent. But her parents believe dancing cannot be pursued as a career. So they made her follow in Sharad's footsteps..."

A look of understanding passed between the siblings saying *Thank the stars our parents let us be, despite disagreements.*

Abhi went on, "In fact, umm…" He looked at Varun a little apprehensively, before continuing, "She reminds me a lot of Avni actually…" He stopped immediately, seeing the fire in Varun's eyes and quickly changed the topic.

"We also have a girl from Chandigarh joining us, Ayesha Banerjee. I saw her marksheet and certificates and am pretty sure she has the potential to be an asset for the department." He paused a bit and continued with a sigh, "I got into a tiff of sorts with her…"

Varun looked at his younger brother curiously, an amused smile playing across his lips. There was a definite blush on Abhi's face as if Varun had caught him red-handed.

"Well, well. Looks like someone is smitten…" He thought to himself.

Before he could voice it out though, Radha said, "I hope you've not caused trouble. That's not the way to treat newcomers, especially someone new to the city."

She looked over at Shyam for support who said, "Yes, remember that your mother was once new to the city too."

Abhi nodded and dinner was soon over. But his sibling's words lingered on in Varun's mind, haunting him a bit.

She reminds me a lot of Avni.

"So, tell me about this Ayesha, little brother." He put his arms across Abhi's shoulder in a bid to get his mind off that disturbing thought. They walked over to Abhi's bedroom and settled down on the king-size bed. Varun looked around, and not for the first time, wondered how two bedrooms with the same size and structure could be so different from each other. While Abhi's was glam and trendy, Varun's room had a more minimalist and warm look.

"I actually met her twice before today, and well it's been a bit of a rocky start. You remember I was a bit off on the day when I dropped off the Mehtas? That's when I first met her."

As Abhi began narrating his tale, Varun had a feeling that Ayesha Banerjee was going to come up in a lot of conversations in the Agarwal household in the coming days.

"Then I met her again at the Ramanavami celebrations…"

Hey, that's the day you met the Kulkarni girl too. You know, the one who is just like…

He shut his mind from going down that line of thought and focused on what Abhi was saying.

***

A Friend Indeed

"If you've got what you want, you're living the best life. If you've not got what you want, you've still got to make it your best life with whatever you get."

- Gayatri Kulkarni

May 2016

"Hey, why don't you come over this time? I'll ask aai to prepare your favourite *puran poli*[13]."

Abhi's face instantly lit up. Gayatri looked at Sharad and a look of relief passed over their faces. Abhi had been in a sullen mood for some time and seeing him smile was a respite for them all.

"Sure, that sounds good." Abhi gladly accepted Sharad's proposition.

The three of them were walking back to Vile Parle station from Mithibai College. Abhi and Sharad, who were in the second year of the B.A Political Science (Hons) at Mithibai College, had finished their lectures for the day. The two of them were classmates and fast friends. Sharad had visited Abhi's place a couple of times but Abhi was yet to drop by at the Kulkarni residence.

Gayatri was at Mithibai that day too for submitting her admission form into the same course. The whole procedure had gone quite smoothly for her, thanks to Abhi and Sharad's rapport with the college admin staff. Gayatri had befriended a girl, *Ayesha Banerjee* at the college gate. She looked a little lost and Gayatri couldn't help asking if she needed any guidance. Incidentally it turned out that Ayesha was there to submit her form for the same course. Gayatri immediately took a liking to her and guided her towards the boys who had been waiting for her inside the campus. Unfortunately, Abhi had gotten into a tiff with Ayesha because some of her documents were missing and her form could not be submitted. Since then Abhi had been pensive.

"We'll plan out a few things related to the ice breaking session for welcoming the juniors." Sharad suggested, trying to keep Abhi's mood up.

---

[13] *Puran puri, Puran poli, Holige, Obbattu,* or *Bobbattlu, Poley, Bakshamulu,* is an Indian sweet flatbread that originates from Southern India.

On cue, Gayatri looped her arm through his, "Have I told you you're the best brother a girl can get?"

"Nice try, kiddo. The activity remains a surprise for you too." Sharad replied, ruffling her hair.

Abhi chuckled seeing a visible pout appear on Gayatri's face who stuck her tongue out.

They reached the station and hopped onto a Borivali-bound slow local train. In about 45 minutes, they were at Bhoomi Residency located in Mahavir Nagar, Kandivali West. The door to the Kulkarni's 2 BHK abode was opened after Gayatri rang the doorbell. Immediately, Uma was upon Abhi like a bee to a flower.

"Abhi dear. So happy to have you with us."

In her head, Gayatri could hear the theme music of *Kyunki Saans Bhi Kabhi Bahu Thi*.[14] Any moment now, she felt that Uma would invite Abhi inside, showing off her happy family and her charming house like *Tulsi Virani*[15].

"Thank you, aunty. Sharad managed to lure me with your puran poli. I've had it once when Sharad got it for lunch during a long day at college."

"You're welcome anytime, dear." She held the door wide open, making an elaborate gesture for them to make an entry. Gayatri smirked, deriving pleasure from her imagination coming true, at least in part.

Once they were seated on the sofa in the hall, Uma offered a glass of water to Abhi and said, "I'll let you kids be" and walked off into the kitchen. After a while, the three of them got up and made their way toward Sharad and Gayatri's shared room.

Gayatri who was the first up, ran in and shut the door of the bedroom before the guys could walk in.

"Oh damn damn damn..." she muttered and breathed out a sigh of relief.

"What the hell Gayu?! Open the door. Now!" Sharad shouted out.

Gayatri's gaze had fallen on the stack of clothes on her bed. A red bra lay on top of the pile. Below it she could also see her pink lace panties. Her

---

[14] *An Indian (Hindi language) TV show from the early 2000s*
[15] *The female lead from the Indian TV show Kyunki Saans Bhi Kabhi Bahu Thi*

mind immediately recalled the tagline *Ye to bada toing hai*[16] and imagined Abhi's face going a similar shade of red or pink on seeing her lingerie strewn around as he set foot in the room. Not wanting the scene to play out in reality, she rushed in and banged the door on impulse. She balled up the clothes and threw them inside the cupboard, while shouting out, "Yeah, just a sec. I'm sorry."

"What is it? Why are you two fighting again?" Gayatri heard Uma's voice and rushed to open the door.

"Sorry, I needed to use the washroom, " she said and looked at the audience outside the room sheepishly.

Abhi gave her a curious look as if doubting her excuse. Gayatri averted his gaze and turned to her mother accusingly.

"Aai, can we buy a laundry bag, please?" Gayatri stepped outside the room dragging her mother along with her towards the kitchen.

The next hour passed in preparing lunch. Gayatri loved puran poli herself, so for a change, cooking didn't seem so tiring. The boys stayed inside the room and came out only when Uma called them for lunch.

"Gayu, you also sit with the boys."

Gayatri raised an eyebrow but didn't say anything. She knew this was being done to impress their guest for the day. Normally, she'd be asked to serve first and later she and Uma would dine together.

When Abhi saw Gayatri take a seat with them, he gave her a wide smile.

She smiled too and soon they began eating as Uma served them the puran polis right off the stove.

"I saw some of your photographs and trophies in the room. Then Sharad showed me a few of your dance videos. You have got a fan in me, mademoiselle" Abhi said to Gayatri and made a bowing gesture.

Instantly, a smile lit up Gayatri's face. Looking at him gratefully she said, "Thank you. That means a lot. I got into the top 25 at *Dance Beat*, but…"

"Yes, actually Gayatri had been aiming to join this course for a while. She worked really hard and made it into the first cut-off list itself." Sharad

---

[16] *A Hindi tagline from Amul Innerwear's TVC which is racy and suggestive of the man wearing the underwear being sexually attractive*

butted in. Gayatri turned to him, irritated, but Sharad was gazing towards the kitchen. She followed his gaze and saw Uma walking out.

Abhi looked from Sharad to Gayatri, confused and a bit amused.

"Array, Abhi. You're not eating. What happened, is it not good dear?"

"No no, aunty. They are delicious. Thank you."

She smiled and put one puran poli into Sharad's plate.

"Another one coming right up…" she told Abhi and walked back to the kitchen with a sprint in her step.

"Phew! That was close. Listen, buddy. Gayatri's dancing is a bit of a touchy subject with my parents. And this one was about to get into her *Gadadhari Bheem*[17] mode. You see Gayatri couldn't go ahead in the show and was kind of made to opt for this course over a career in dancing." Sharad rallied off once Uma was out of earshot.

Abhi turned to Gayatri with a sorry face. She just shrugged her shoulders and said, "It's fine. I do enjoy politics too so I'll be okay. Anyway, I'll pursue dancing once I start earning enough. I'm already kinda making a bit from it but nothing steady so far."

"That's amazing. I'd love to dance with you someday, Gayatri."

"I'd like that too. Also, friends call me Gayu. *Mujhse Dosti Karoge?*"[18] She smiled warmly, extending her hand towards him for a shake while Sharad rolled his eyes.

Abhi ignored him and took her hand into his.

"Okay, Gayu. I have a feeling we'll be more than friends." Saying so he winked and she found herself blushing. Not because of what he said, but because his wink and the way he said *more than friends* made her remember the other Agarwal; the one who had made her blush similarly not so long ago.

---

[17] *In the Hindu epic Mahabharata, Bheem is the second among the five Pandavas. He is often associated with the emotion of anger/temper and his weapon (a club). The term Gadadhari Bheem is used to refer to someone who is in battle mode, extremely angry, or in the mood to fight/argue.*

[18] *Hindi words which translate to, 'Will you be my friend?'. The reference here is being drawn from a Hindi movie with the same title*

Deva Shree Ganesha

"What doesn't kill you makes you stronger? Nah! Having things your way despite the odds, makes you stronger."

- Varun Agarwal

September 2016

"Hey, Abhi. The florist has sent some designs for the Ganesh decor. Can we have a look and finalise?"

"No, Gayu. I'm telling you. I'm genuinely asking you because we need you…"

Varun had just walked into his brother's room to discuss something. But he stopped short when he realised Abhi was on the phone with someone.

"Did he say Gayu? Is that who I think it is? When did she become *Gayu*? And why does that nickname sound familiar? Varun was curiously. Along with the curiosity, there was an unexplained warmth. He also suddenly felt an itch to hit his younger sibling on the head.

"Is it because he's talking to her?" He was about to walk out of the room when Abhi turned around from the window. He had been standing and conversing on his cell phone while taking in the view of the city from the French window of their 18th floor apartment. On seeing Varun, he mouthed, "Give me 5 minutes, okay?"

Varun shrugged and settled down on the bed. The matter he needed to discuss with Abhi was urgent so he decided it was better to wait then come back later. Like every year, the Agarwals were getting a Ganpati idol at their home for the festival of Ganesh Chaturthi. It had taken some persuasion but Abhi had finally convinced them to get an eco-friendly idol this time. Varun was onboard right away and Radha had been convinced in a few days too. But Shyam had taken his time, weighing in the size, design and decor options and finally caving in only a week before the idol was to be brought in. Bappa's arrival at the Agarwal residence was now just a couple of days away.

"See, I know the skit was Ayesha's idea but I know that you helped too. So I'm asking you because of your contribution and not for her…" Varun heard Abhi's one-sided conversation over the phone. Suddenly, Abhi stopped speaking and an animated feminine voice came in from the other end. A few seconds later, Abhi laughed out loud, "Fine! Have it your way. I'm just glad you agreed. I'll see you tomorrow, okay? Bye now!"

With a smile still lingering on his face, Abhi whistled as he walked over to the bed and settled down next to his brother. The victorious look on his face made Varun's eyebrows shoot up inquiringly.

"I see you've got your ways of convincing the females to do your bidding. That poor girl…"

Abhi let out such a loud and unexpected laugh that the shock of it made Varun move away a bit.

"Oh, Gayu is no 'poor girl' let me assure you. I was only trying to include her because she and Ayesha are such good friends and the two of them together in the cultural committee will only help us do better work."

Varun could sense an underlying, layered intention. "Umhmm, you'll have to tell me what this conversation was about to convince me." He punched Abhi on the shoulder to probe further. His interest was piqued more because of Miss *Gayu*.

"Ayesha had this idea of doing a skit in the college neighbourhood to promote the idea of eco-friendly Ganesh idols. At least the idols that we bring at home," Varun's sly smile made Abhi stop and add hastily, "Shut up! I know that look and yes, it was her idea that inspired me to get an eco-friendly idol for our home too."

"Well, well, well Mr. Lover Boy. I take back my words then. It's Ayesha who has you doing her bidding."

"Shut up, bhaiya. It's nothing like that. I think it's just a crush. Anyway, since she was the only girl on our committee I suggested we include Gayatri too. Ayesha had anyway told us of Gayatri's suggestions to include some dancing and singing in the skit too. So I was just asking Gayatri to join. But she was being her usual drama queen. She's somehow convinced that I'm only doing this for Ayesha and to make her feel comfortable rather than to acknowledge Gayatri's own contribution."

Ignoring his increased heartbeats at the mention of Miss Kulkarni's name, Varun intervened, "Doesn't seem like she's too far from the truth, is it?" Varun found himself admiring the girl's tongue-in-cheek.

"Okay, maybe a bit true but not completely. You haven't seen Gayu's dance or you'd know why she'd be a bonus to the committee anyway."

Laughing at his brother's admission, Varun couldn't help imagining Miss. Drama Queen's lithe figure in motion, setting the stage on fire.

"Wait, let me show you rather than just telling you." Abhi thrust his cell phone into Varun's hand, bringing him out of his venereal thoughts. A video was playing on the screen. It took him a few seconds to recognize the couple dancing quite steamily to *Bang Bang*.

"That's from our fresher's party. Gayatri and I performed together. Just look at the way she dances."

"Hmmm…" was the only response Varun could utter as he was consumed by feelings of awe, arousal and above anything, envy. His fists clenched as he watched the video with a poker face, observing Abhi's hands moving from Gayatri's arms, to her waist and then her neck.

Controlling the itching in his hands to strangle Abhi, he thrust the phone back into its owner's hand while mumbling, "Yeah, you're right."

"See, I told you. Anyway, you wanted to discuss something, bhaiya?"

Abhi's question helped Varun shake off the unexplained rage building inside him.

"Yes, the florist has sent a few designs for the mandapa. Let's show it to maa and papa, and finalise it, shall we?"

After half an hour, following some discussions and deliberations, the four Agarwals were able to settle on a design they all liked equally. It was a mix of lilies, orchids, chrysanthemums, roses, and marigolds. These would be festooned in front of a pink and white drape, forming a border around long, thin and wavy strings of white satin ribbons with round-shaped mirrors.

"Maa, we never invite people outside Pashmina. Why not invite a few friends of mine and Abhi's too this time?"

Abhi turned sharply towards Varun, with raised eyebrows, but there was a definite look of gratitude too.

"Why not? We can surely accommodate 5-6 more people. What do you say?" Radha turned towards Shyam to confirm, who nodded his assent.

A look of triumph passed between the brothers.

When they got up to walk back to their rooms, Varun slumped his hand over Abhi's shoulder.

"Do I need to remind you to invite both the girls? I'm sure you know the drill by now." Varun winked and dodged Abhi's punch.

"Good night, kiddo. You're welcome." He laughed as he sauntered off into his room while Abhi waved dismissively and disappeared into his.

Varun got into bed with a wide smile, satisfied about helping his brother's story move ahead. Deep down though, he knew he'd done it for his own selfish motives.

As sleep took over, the silhouette of a certain dancing senora took over all his senses. In a few seconds, *Bang Bang* started playing in the background but this time it was him and not his younger sibling who got to play partner to her.

For the next couple of days, Varun helped out with the setting up of the idol and decor. But his mind kept conjuring up an image of a dancing couple which was giving him sleepless nights; rather nights full of pleasant and undiscussable dreams.

"So, do we get to meet the girl of your dreams tonight?" He asked Abhi when they were done preparing for the Ganesh aarti. The thought that it was the same question he should be asking himself, made him chuckle.

To Varun's utter disbelief, Abhi blushed, "Yes, she's coming with Sharad and Gayatri. They should be here in some time."

Varun controlled his own facial expressions on hearing mademoiselle's name and thumped Abhi on the back.

"Boys, please take your positions. We'll start in a few minutes." Radha called out.

The four Agarwals stood in front of the Ganesh idol and smiled at the incoming guests. A few of Varun's Welingkar batchmates came in and he nodded at them. But there was no sign of the ones the brothers awaited the most.

"Okay then, we'll start now." Shyam's commanding voice broke out. Reluctantly and with sullen faces, Varun and Abhi turned their faces away from the door. Abhi blew out the conch shell and in a chorus they all began to chant the aarti.

Shendur lal chadhayo achchha gajmukhko
Dondil lal biraje sut gauriharko
Hath liye gudladdu sai survar ko
Mahima kahe na jay lagat hoo padko
Jai jai shri ganraj vidhyasukhdata
Dhanya tumara darshan mera man ramata
jai dev jai dev

As they finished the first stanza, a movement at the door caught Varun's attention. His heart knew it before his eyes registered her entry. With downcast eyes, she entered behind her brother and was followed by another girl. The three of them hurriedly made their way to the back. Varun could only make out her pastel green kurti and a netted dupatta as she rushed towards the tail of the crowd. And then he lost sight of Miss Dancing Toes completely. As he turned his face to the Ganesh idol, he caught a glance of Abhi looking in the same direction as him.

Once the aarti was over, Abhi took the prasad plate and ran towards the back. It was like watching a bee flying off to a freshly bloomed honey bearing flower. Varun chuckled and controlled his own urge to follow suit. Despite his jumping nerves, he casually moved towards the group where Abhi was headed. That's when he took in Miss Kulkarni's full outfit. The pastel green kurti he had caught sight of earlier, had bell sleeves that accentuated her slender arms. The kurti and the matching salwar clung to her curves at the right spots, making Varun marvel at her hourglass figure. Her netted dupatta had diamonds strewn across it, which shone as she fidgeted with her hair, tucking them behind her ears. The silver bangles on her arms jingled melodiously when she moved her hands to adjust her dupatta. Her head slowly turned from the Ganesh idol towards their approaching figures. As she nodded and waved enthusiastically at Abhi with a wide smile, the green jhumkas on her ears dangled around wildly.

"I could watch her all day." Varun thought to himself, mesmerised by her aura.

"Glad you guys could make it. This is my brother Varun."

Abhi's statement brought him out of the trance Miss Kulkarni seemed to have cast on him. He turned to Ayesha and Sharad, hoping his face didn't bely his true emotions.

"Hello. Nice to see you again, Sharad. Hi Gayatri. I believe I saw you at the Ram Navami aarti. Hey Ayesha, glad to finally meet you."

Sharad, Ayesha and Gayatri, all nodded at Abhi and waved hello to Varun. As Gayatri looked at him with the most adorably curious expression, he was afraid his heartbeats would give him away. He was sure he would embarrass himself if he stayed there any longer. Quickly taking their leave, he walked off towards his own batchmates from Welingkar. As he moved away, Varun was sure he heard Gayatri mutter out an 'Ouch'.

Did she say something about me?

The thought made him smile curiously. He had to use all his self-control not to turn around and find out if his doubts were true. With the smile still pasted on his face, Varun distributed the prasad among his three batchmates, Anusha, Abhay and Vikas, whom he had invited. He thanked them for coming. When he was at the gate seeing them off, he noticed Abhi introducing his friends to Radha and Shyam.

"Thanks for inviting us. You have a beautiful home."

Varun turned towards Anusha, and smiled distractedly at her compliment. He mumbled a quick "Thank you" while wishing for them to leave quickly. Once they were all inside the elevator and the door closed, Varun ran back in quickly.

"Maybe next time, aunty. Because we need to reach home for another Ganesh aarti at a neighbour's house. I keep dropping in frequently, anyway." Sharad was telling Radha.

"Wait, don't go just yet." Varun wanted to cry out when Abhi said, "At least you can stay Ayesha. Let these two busy siblings go."

A sly smile came over Miss Pastel Kurti's face as she passed on a knowing smile to Abhi and Ayesha.

"Aha! So my brother's crush is not one-sided it seems." Varun thought to himself.

"Maybe next time. There's an aarti at one of my neighbour's places too."

Varun noticed a dark look cross over Abhi's face, who quickly masked it with a sigh and nodded reluctantly.

Sharad and Abhi hugged each other before he moved out. He then hugged Gayatri and said, "Thanks for coming, bombshell."

Bombshell? Wow, they're close!

Gayatri chuckled and hit Abhi playfully before exiting. Varun was at the gate and a look passed between him and Miss Green Kurti. She smiled naughtily and there was a definite blush on her face as she walked towards the elevator. Abhi walked out with Ayesha and Varun waved a bye to them, walking back into the house with a heavy heart.

He had conflicted feelings about his brother's closeness to *Miss Bombshell*.

He felt dejected about not being able to have even one conversation with her.

But more than that, he was confused about the way his mind and body reacted to her presence.

"Varun and Abhi, please help your father clear out all the mess here. I'm heading to the kitchen. We're already past our dinner time." Radha instructed Varun and Abhi and walked off from the prayer room towards the kitchen.

"That girl Ayesha, is she the girl from Chandigarh you were talking about?" Shyam directed a question to Abhi.

"Yes, papa. She's the girl I was..." Abhi's phone rang before he could finish what he was saying. "Sorry, I have to take this." He excused himself as he answered the call and walked away a little.

"Can one of you come and help me a bit here?" Radha called out from the kitchen. Shrugging his shoulders, Shyam made his way to do his wife's bidding.

Varun sighed and started picking up flowers, papers and food crumbs off the floor.

Ting tong!

He was wondering about who might have called Abhi and whether it could be Miss Kulkarni when the ringing of the doorbell broke his chain of thoughts.

"I'll get it" He called out as he walked over to check on the visitor.

As he began to open the door, the fragrance hit his senses before he saw who it was. It was a sweet rosy smell, inviting him to get lost within its embrace. Then came the jingling of bangles, followed by a flurry of pastel fabric, and he knew right away who the intruder was.

"Abhi, see what happens when I concentrate on your love story rather than focusing on… " She began speaking even before the door was completely open and stopped mid-sentence.

A few seconds passed while they stared at each other; Varun with curiosity and Gayatri with shyness.

"Erm…"

"Hmm?"

He was enjoying her discomfiture as she determinedly looked anywhere but at him while fidgeting continuously with her dupatta.

"Did you forget something?" He asked in an attempt to take the conversation further.

"Yes, my heart." The second the words left her mouth, she stuck her tongue out and hit herself on the forehead with her palm. It was such a cute gesture that Varun laughed out loud and was tempted to engulf her in a hug.

Clearing her throat, and with a defiant expression on her face, she went on "I mean, my clutch. It is my heart because it has my phone and dance class ID."

Varun's eyebrows shot up in disbelief and amusement as she continued with an annoyed look, "It's a beige coloured one with a floral pattern of multicoloured gems."

Remembering his manners Varun said, "Wait here. I'll get it for you."

He walked into the house and found the said clutch near the Ganesh idol. Grabbing it quickly he sprinted back to the door, before any of his family members came out and started inquiring.

Avoiding a crowd, are we? His inner self taunted him but he ignored it.

"Here you go." He said to her while handing over the clutch. Their hands brushed lightly while the exchange happened. She jerked hers back immediately but not before an undeniable spark shot through his palm reaching to his toes.

Did she feel that too? He wondered as she finally looked at him and smiled gratefully.

"Thank you," She said, opening the clutch and removing her phone. She shuffled some more and shut the clutch after a few seconds, assured that the treasure within was intact.

"Does this mean we have a *dil ka rishta*[19] now?"

The laughter that rang out of her mouth was music to his ears.

"Please don't sing the song now. It's not even a good one." She spoke in between bouts of her continued laugh.

"Gayu? I thought I heard you. What's up?"

Varun and Gayatri looked at each other sheepishly, before she answered Abhi's question. None of them had realised when he walked up to the door.

"I forgot my clutch. Anyway, I got it now. Bye."

As she turned around, Varun instinctively started singing *Ruk ja o dil deewane puchu to mein zara*

She turned back to look at him and blushed so deep, Varun was reminded of cotton candy.

"And she would make for a delicious one." He shut out that thought and waved her goodbye as she got into the elevator. The elevator closed and made its way down while she waved at both of them and hummed *Dil to akhir dil hai na,*

meethi si mushkil hai na.

"What was all that about?"

Instead of answering, Varun simply laughed and pushed his brother inside their house, closing the door behind them. He knew from experience that matters of the heart need to be handled with care.

And if he was not mistaken, a certain girl with a beige clutch had just made her way into what he had assumed to be an irreparable heart, against his will.

---

[19] *Hindi words which translate to 'heart to heart connection'. Varun is referring to Gayatri statement about forgetting her heart aka her clutch and making a joke on whether they now have a heart connection because he handed her the heart back.*

Dance, Romance?

"For some dancing is a hobby, for some a way of life, and for a few a part of their identity."

- Gayatri Kulkarni

September-October 2016

Umad ghumad ghoome

Re machle re mora man

Goonje re balam ke bol

"Alexa, pause."

An authoritative feminine voice rang out in the activity hall of Mithibai college. The music that had been playing out loud over the speaker came to a halt.

"Abhi, you are not doing the twirl properly. See my right foot here." Gayatri twirled around putting weight on the right foot and then the left as she returned to her original position after taking a full circle twirl.

"Hail our master, Miss Kulkarni." Abhi panted as he slumped into the nearest chair.

"Shut up! Guys, we aren't done yet. C'mon, Abhi. Look at how quickly Ayesha learnt it."

"Hey, that's not fair." Ayesha said defensively.

"Oh, c'mon. Is this a competition now?" Abhi blurted out, sounding a bit aggressive.

Gayatri gave both Ayesha and Abhi a murderous look as she barked out loud, "Alexa, play."

The song resumed and Gayatri dragged Abhi to the floor while guiding him to follow her dance steps. She was teaching them garba[20] as Ayesha wanted to learn the Gujarati folk dance. Abhi asked to join them citing the reason that he had got passes to a Navratri event and needed to hone his garba skills.

---

[20] *A traditional Gujarati folk dance and song*

"Oh pfft. What a load of lies. You're just looking for an excuse to be with Ayesha." Gayatri responded when Abhi asked if she could teach him too.

They decided to use the activity hall in their college during their lecture breaks and after college hours to learn some basic steps. As it turned out, that hardly took any time because both Abhi and Ayesha were quick learners. Gayatri decided to take it up a few notches and teach a few complex steps too. She compiled a playlist of popular Navratri songs and was using these to conduct her dance sessions with her new and enthusiastic learners.

This was their fifth and last day of teaching and learning. Tonight would be the first night marking the beginning of the Navratri festival which would go on for the next ten days. Gayatri had enjoyed passing on her knowledge of this dance form to someone other than her formal students. After college started, she tried to continue her part-time gig at *Nrityanihar*, but one week into the course she knew she couldn't manage both her studies and her job. It had in fact been a while since she got a chance to dance at all. The only times she recalled were when she performed on her first day of college at the ice-breaking session. The freshers were asked to introduce themselves through something creative. She had of course chosen to dance to her all-time favourite song *Diva* by Beyonce because no other song described her personality better. Then there was the freshers' party where she performed with Abhi on *Bang Bang*. Other than these, there were the small bits of dance in their street play for Ganesh Chaturthi, which hardly counted.

This Political Science course was taking up more of her time than she had anticipated; what with all the assignments, being a part of the cultural committee, and traveling back and forth from home to college. The only good thing was that she was quite enjoying the course. Though she would never say it to her mother out loud, Uma had been right when she said politics was indeed something that interested Gayatri.

"Alexa, stop!"

Sharad walked in and shouted out, bringing forth loud groans from the three people inside the hall.

"I see Gayatri is passing on her dramatic skills too. Smile, people. I come bearing gifts." He announced, flourishing out four packets from a bag and passing them around.

"Just what I needed. Thanks, bhav." Gayatri said as she sniffed the vada pav in her hand and dug into it greedily.

After eating, they continued dancing for another half an hour before calling it a day. As they were packing up, Gayatri caught Abhi looking at Ayesha with determination and could almost guess what was coming.

"Umm, Ayesha. Do you have any plans for tonight?"

"No, not really. Why?"

Gayatri couldn't help but smile curiously at their obvious attraction toward each other.

"I have an extra pass for the Navratri celebration at The Bombay Presidency Radio Club. Would you like to join?"

Ayesha turned to him with an apologetic look. A few moments of awkward silence passed while Abhi waited for an answer. Sighing, Gayatri shook her head and took the matter into her hands.

"I have already invited her to Kora Kendra, Mr. Slowmo. But, she has turned down the offer saying *it is happening in my own colony and I don't want to travel so far.*"

Sharad couldn't help laughing out loud at his sister's perfect mimicry of Ayesha's voice. Abhi, however, looked heartbroken and a little irritated.

Ayesha gave an annoyed look to Gayatri and turned to Abhi, "I am sorry but I'd prefer to be with my parents as they're new to all this too."

"How come you have an extra pass all of sudden, by the way?" Gayatri intervened before things got more uncomfortable. She was intrigued about the unexpected availability of a pass to such an esteemed club. She had never been there but knew that it was a club frequented by the elites of South Bombay. Getting a membership, an entry, or even a pass for festive events like Navratri, was not only difficult, but also an expensive affair. Its USP was its seafront location which offered unhindered views of the Arabian Sea with iconic structures like the Gateway of India and The Taj Mahal Palace being at a walking distance.

"Varun has decided to ditch us and go with his Welingkar friends. Something about it being their last few months together and all that." Abhi said dismissively.

Gayatri's ears perked up on hearing *Mr. Dil*'s name. That's what she had started referring to him as, after the wallet encounter. She had been listening to *Ruk jaa o dil deewane* and *Dil se re* almost twice every day since their embarrassing yet memorable encounter. Every single time the songs played on, a warm smile would spread across her face as she recalled *Mr. Dil*'s mischievous smile and playful eyes. Replaying those moments in her mind made the butterflies in her stomach go haywire.

Presently, she wondered where he was going for the Navratri celebration. Curbing her curiosity, she decided not to probe further because she did not want to put ideas into anyone's head.

And your own too, right? Her mind chided but she pushed the thought aside.

The four of them soon went their separate ways after walking together to Vile Parle station. Once home, Gayatri decided to sleep it off after having a light lunch. The dancing and traveling had tired her more than she cared to admit and she needed her energy up for the evening. It was going to be nonstop dancing for at least four hours every night for the next ten days. The anticipation of it excited her as she snuggled up in bed while listening to her new favourite song *Dil se re*. Soon she was engulfed in dreams, dancing to *Nagada Sang Dhol,* alongside a tall guy with a mischievous smile and twinkling eyes.

In no time, the incessant ringing of her phone woke her up. Checking the time while picking up the incoming call, she realised they would be late if they didn't leave soon.

"Are you sleeping? What the hell Gayu! Please get ready and be there on time." Simran's annoyed voice removed the last remnants of drowsiness from her eyes.

"Oh, shut up. I'll see you soon. Bye!"

Gayatri and Sharad had been attending the Navratri celebrations at Kora Kendra in Borivali for the past five years. The first couple of years, they went with a large group of their school friends. Many of them slowly opted out and chose to either go somewhere else, or with someone else. Kartik, his sister, Simran, Sharad and Gayatri, however, had stuck by each other and still went together for all the ten nights, every year. Kartik and Sharad, as well as Simran and Gayatri had been classmates during their schooling days. The boys however, were older by a couple of years and a few classes ahead of the girls while at school. The four had been thick friends for over a decade; especially the girls with each other and similarly with the boys.

Gayatri cut off the phone and jumped out of bed. At that moment Sharad walked into the room, dressed and all set for the evening. He had worn a multi-colored sleeveless kurta over a yellow dhoti. Both the dhoti and kurta had thick embroidered ethnic designs over it. He looked every bit ready for a night of dance and fun.

"Oho, the Sleeping Beauty is finally up. Kartik has been calling me incessantly asking me to ensure we reach on time. Please get ready fast."

"I won't take much time. You look nice by the way. Now out! I need space." Gayatri pushed him out of the room.

Surprisingly, even for herself, she was out in twenty minutes. Uma looked at her daughter adoringly while taking in Gayatri's maroon coloured blouse, paired with a green and maroon ghagra. A sequin chunari was draped from her right shoulder, covering just one-fourth of the blouse as it moved towards the left side of the ghagra where it was tucked in on the top. She had worn a silver waist chain over the chunari and the top of the ghagra to ensure the dupatta stayed in place. The waist chain was similar in design to her necklace, earrings, bangles, and armlets, all of which had maroon beads and ethnic motifs strewn across them. She had minimal makeup on with maroon lipstick and some rouge on her cheeks.

Looking extremely pleased by what she saw, Uma gave a quick peck on Gayatri's cheek.

"*Khup chan distes.* [21] Take care and enjoy."

Bidding their mother a quick goodbye, the duo rushed out of the house. Hailing a rickshaw, they reached Kora Kendra in half an hour. Normally, the ride would hardly take five minutes but the peak hour traffic slowed them down. On any other day, they'd prefer to walk from their house to Kora Kendra as that was a smarter choice. But going on foot with their heavy Navratri attire would be foolhardy. Paying the rickshaw driver, Sharad and Gayatri quickly walked to the entrance, where a medium-height, rugged-looking guy, stood waiting for them. He was dressed in an attire similar to Sharad's. The only difference being its colour which was orange and his kurta had full sleeves.

---

[21] *Marathi words which roughly translate to, "You look very beautiful."*

The expression on his face suggested that he was annoyed. But the minute he saw them, a broad smile spread across his features. As they moved closer to him, it became clear that he was looking only at Gayatri. The expression he wore dripped affliction and one would think he'd forgotten to breathe or blink. Once they reached him, he cleared his throat and turned to Sharad, "Simi is already inside because she didn't want to miss even one minute. Anyway, here are your passes. Let's get moving."

He thrust a pass each into their hands and swiftly started moving ahead.

"Nice to see you too, Kartik." Gayatri said cheekily as they followed suit and made their way in. The loud music and the energetic aura immediately engulfed them, energising their senses. The Kora Kendra ground in Borivali was the grandest one in the suburbs of Mumbai for the Navratri celebrations. It saw close to 30,000 people every day and more than 2 lakhs in all, over the course of the ten-night celebration. In the past five years, Gayatri and Sharad hadn't missed even one night during Navratri and had managed to bag quite a few awards too.

"It's no Bombay Radio Club. But I'm sure you'll enjoy this too."

Gayatri's ears picked up immediately. She turned around and saw a group of boys and girls passing behind them and forming a circle in an empty space nearby. The group was soon blocked out of view before Gayatri could see their faces as more people rushed by. Gayatri, Sharad and Kartik found themselves engulfed in a sea of people dancing around or rushing towards their friends.

Am I hallucinating? He can't be here, can he?

Gayatri shook her head and gave a sweeping look around the huge ground. In a few seconds, she grabbed Sharad's hand excitedly and sprinted towards the right hand side. She waved to a girl who, on spotting them, rushed forth enthusiastically.

"Simi, nice to see you."

Simran waved away Gayatri's greeting and dragged her to the spot where she had been dancing. It was a small circle consisting of six others who hadn't stopped their dancing feet or hands as the three new joiners matched their steps in no time.

Gayatri lost all sense of her surrounding as she went around the circle clapping her hands and tapping her feet to the beat of the traditional

Gujarati songs. She'd missed the exhilaration that this abandon brought to her senses.

Minutes ticked off as the songs changed, but Gayatri refused to let herself stop. She wanted to make the most of this precious time where she was united with her one true love. She didn't even realise when the circle they were dancing in grew bigger and the people around her changed.

She was twirling around, with one of her hands in the air, halfway to finding her other hand for a clap, when she banged into something tall and sturdy.

"Hey, watch where you're stepping." She yelled at the figure in front of her. While trying to bring some distance between herself and that person, her feet got tangled in the wide girth of her ghagra and she lost her balance. She tried to grab something to avoid falling face down but simply grappled in the air as her body moved downwards. She covered her face with her hands anticipating the fall when a pair of hands encircled her waist, helping her up.

It took her a few seconds to catch her breath, while a tingling sensation rolled off her waist and her entire upper body. She was still panting when she realised both her hands were on someone's chest; a broad and muscular one at that. Not to mention she was in an inclined position and anybody looking at them would feel they were in the middle of a dance step. Breathing heavily, she tried to get into an upright position but felt the grip on her waist tighten. She could feel their heartbeats and their heavy breaths mingling with her own as the grip around her waist loosened and she slowly found her footing on solid ground again.

"Hey, are you okay?" She jerked her eyes open to look at her saviour as she stood up straight and the world didn't seem to be moving in a whirl around her.

What's he doing here? Am I still hallucinating? Did I manifest this?

A million questions buzzed through her mind even as she nodded. 'Raging fire' was the first thought that came to her mind as she gazed into his eyes. They were the exact shade of inferno that scared her during Holi and most Hindu rituals. Right now though, she felt like she would willingly burn herself in the dual pits boring into her. A few moments passed in which he continued to look at her with concern while she tried hard to bring her throbbing heartbeats to a normal pace. She was acutely aware of his hands on her bare waist and her hands still on his chest, and how neither of them seemed willing to pull away.

"I am sorry. I was trying to move out of the circle and didn't realise when I banged into you." His voice sounded anything but apologetic as he continued to gaze at her unblinkingly. She could still feel his breath over the skin on her face making it difficult for her mind to form any thoughts or utter any words of coherence. Her brain commanded her to say 'it's okay' but what came out of her mouth instead was, 'Whaaa… whe….wh….'"

He chuckled lightly and lifted one of his hands from her waist to move away a strand of hair from her face that had come loose from her bun. She shuddered when his fingers grazed her cheek as he tucked the strand behind her ear. With a sly smile, instead of taking his hand away, he brought his fingers back to her cheek, and continued to caress her face, while bringing his face closer to hers.

"Gayatri, are you fine? I saw you stumble and almost fall down."

Kartik's voice brought her to her senses and she pushed herself away from Mr. Raging Fire eyes.

I'm burning in heaven. She almost blurted out, but clearing her throat she said, "Yes, I am fine."

Finally breaking eye contact with mister heaven personified, she took in the concerned looks on Sharad and Simran's faces and the annoyed one on Kartik's, who seemed unconvinced. Muttering under his breath, Kartik moved towards Gayatri and grabbed both her hands. He turned them this way and that, to make sure she wasn't injured. Then he pulled her towards their group, keeping his hand possessively over her shoulder.

"What a surprise to see you here, Varun." Sharad said, breaking the awkward silence.

"Yes, a few of my Welingkar friends live in Borivali and invited me over."

Gayatri noticed that he was looking at Kartik with the most curious expression. His gaze took in Kartik's face and attire, moving to his hand which still lay on Gayatri's shoulders. He stiffened and then shrugged.

"One of my friends said she knows you so we joined your circle sometime back."

He pointed towards a girl, who looked somewhat familiar. Before Gayatri could recall her name, Simran relented, "Oh my God, that's Anusha. Remember her?"

"Gayu, it's that Anusha. The one Sharad…"

Sharad turned visibly red and mumbled, "Yeah, we know her," to Varun while Simran shook with laughter.

"Kartik and Sharad had…." Simran was about to go on but Varun covered her mouth with his hand, dragging her away.

"Kartik, you coming?" It was a clear plea for help. Kartik gave a skeptical look to Gayatri and with visible effort, removed his hand from her shoulder.

"Go on. I'll be there in a while." Gayatri pushed him towards a struggling Sharad while laughing over Simran's antics. She had broken free from Sharad's grip and walked over to Anusha. The two girls chatted animatedly, supposedly catching up while Sharad and Kartik hung back, looking helpless.

"Is she an ex-girlfriend of Sharad's?" Varun's question made Gayatri realise they were alone again. She turned to look at him with surprise. There was amusement in his eyes and the smallest possible smile Gayatri had seen on someone's lips. Tearing her gaze away from his face and oh-so-perfectly fitted clothes, she turned to look at her friends again.

"Well, yes and no. It's a little complicated. She was a classmate of Kartik and Sharad's in school. We were all quite close and Anusha was part of our Navaratri dance group. Over a dozen of us came together on these very grounds for three years on every night of the Navratri festival. Then she had to change schools because her family was moving to a new neighbourhood. We haven't met her since she moved out of the school and our locality. Before she left, the guys wanted to give her a farewell of sorts. They planned a surprise party, inviting all their classmates. Both of them had a crush on her and thought this would be the perfect time to profess their love to her. They even had a bet going on whom she would choose. On the day of the party, before either of them could tell her, she made an appearance at the venue, hand-in-hand with another classmate; a girl. They were…umm…kissing each other…on the lips. It became a surprise party for all three of them."

"How long ago was this? I mean how old were you all?" Varun asked, trying hard not to laugh.

"Sharad and Kartik were 16, Simran and I were 14."

She turned towards him again and went on, "Till date we tease the boys saying *'tumhara pehla pyaar adhura reh gaya is liye tumhe saccha pyaar nahi mila'*[22]."

The laughter that came off his mouth felt like music.

"Yes, Anusha came out fully just last year. She identifies as bisexual though. So maybe the guys still have a chance."

At that moment, Anusha turned from Simran towards the boys, and without preamble, engulfed both of them in a group hug. Kartik and Sharad looked like they wanted the earth to open up and swallow them whole.

It made Gayatri laugh out loud and she replied, "I guess that answers our question."

"That was the last song for tonight. Thank you everyone for joining us on day one of this year's Navratri festivities. See you all again tomorrow."

Their attention turned to the announcement made by the singer on stage. Gayatri groaned, earning a raised eyebrow from the towering figure next to her.

"Eh! Never mind." She said with a petulant expression, trying hard not to stomp her feet on the ground.

"Listen, I'm sorry you missed a quarter of an hour of dancing. Can I make it up to you somehow?"

Gayatri turned towards him with a look of astonishment.

"Hey, Varun. We're heading out before the entrance and parking gets blocked. Are you coming?"

A guy, who Gayatri assumed was one of Varun's friends, walked up to him before she could answer. Varun nodded his head and asked them to make a move, indicating that he'll join them in a bit.

---

[22] *Hindi words which roughly translate to, "Your first love was left incomplete that's why you haven't found true love in life yet."*

Avoiding eye contact, Gayatri turned her face and saw Sharad, Kartik, and Simran making their way toward them. Anusha was walking alongside them too, chatting away chirpily.

"Hmmphh." Varun cleared his throat and said, "So, will you be dropping in here for all ten nights?"

Gayatri nodded, suddenly losing her ability to talk or turn her face to look at him. Her mute response though brought forth a wide smile from Varun, which she felt radiating from his face despite not looking at it directly.

"Hi Gayatri. Such a small world, right? How are you? It's so nice to see you all after so long."

Anusha said while walking up and standing next to Varun.

"Nice to see you too." Gayatri said, finally regaining her ability to speak.

"Guess we'll see you around then." Varun said, looking only at Gayatri and beginning to move away.

"Hey, why don't we exchange numbers so that we can coordinate and dance in a group every day? You know, just like old times!" Anusha enthusiastically suggested, making Varun stop in his tracks.

"Sure, give me your phone. I'll feed in my number and here take mine and save yours." Simran was immediately game.

Varun shrugged, looked at Gayatri's hesitant face and exchanged phones with Sharad, then Kartik. Anusha looked expectantly at Gayatri who realised she was the only one who hadn't participated in the number exchange game yet. Twisting one of her hands nervously on the edge of her chunari, Gayatri put out her other hand which had her phone. She didn't want to look too eager, that's why took her time to pass her phone around. Anusha and Varun jumped forth to grab it from her palm at the same time. Anusha chuckled and passed a knowing look to Varun, letting him take the phone first. He smiled expectantly while handing over his own mobile to Gayatri.

The light brushing of his fingers on her palms made Gayatri's mind replay the moment from not-so-long-so, making her blush. After he was done, Varun passed the phone to Anusha who fed in her number as well.

"Here you go." Anusha said, returning the phone to Gayatri.

"Let me hold that for you." Varun offered, waiting for Gayatri to get done feeding her number into his and then Anusha's phone.

He winked conspiratorially at her as their fingers brushed again, sending shivers down her spine. Thankfully, her mind was diverted immediately as he draped his arm over Anusha's shoulder and said, "You never told me about your 'school' day adventures. Who was this girl you kissed during your own farewell party, huh?"

Anusha rolled her eyes, and waving their group goodbye, dragged Varun towards the exit. Gayatri heard her saying, "I was still discovering my sexuality…"

Looking at their retreating figures, Gayatri felt a pang in her stomach. She couldn't quite figure out if it was jealousy or disappointment, or both. While she was still pondering over her disconcertion, Varun turned around and waved them goodbye, saying, "See you all tomorrow."

He began singing *Keh do ke tum mere dil mein rahoge, keh do ke tum mujhse dosti karoge*[23], before turning back and making his way out.

Gayatri felt herself going pink but it went unnoticed in the crowd which was pushing them from all sides, eager to make a quick exit out of the venue. Walking alongside Sharad, Kartik, and Simran, she mulled over the events of the evening.

Even as they caught a rickshaw and returned home, she kept wondering what the remaining nights of Navratri had in store for her.

"Mera dil bhi kitna pagal hai[24]… it never confirmed how to make up to you" Her phone pinged with a new message notification as she settled into bed after freshening up.

Dilwala dost?[25]

She chuckled at the name that popped up with the message on the screen.

"My dil goes hmmm… maybe I'll keep that as a credit note and ask to encash it when I feel like."

---

[23] *Lyrics from a Hindi movie song Mujhse Dosti Karoge which roughly translate to, "Tell me that you'll live in my heart. Tell me that you'll be friends with me."*
[24] *Reference to a Hindi song from the movie Saajan which roughly translate to, "How mad my heart is"*
[25] *Hindi words which roughly translate to 'good-hearted friend'. Varun is drawing reference from his previous encounter with Gayatri*

You better be careful, girl or you're gonna burn in the raging fire of those eyes. Her brain warned her.

But her heart was already making her recall more *dil* songs to respond with, in the next message.

***

Women, Woes...What?

"Knight in shining armour may be redundant. But Cinderella's shoes remain priceless."

- Varun Agarwal

November 2016

Ding Dong!

"Oh, it's you! I thought..."

"Umm, we have a video doorbell. Try using it sometime, maybe? Save both of us the disappointment and also make papa's investment worth it."

Varun sniggered and thumped Abhi on the shoulder while making way for him to come in.

"Whom were you expecting anyway?," Abhi asked as he took off his shoes and they walked into the spacious living room of their luxurious 3 BHK apartment, together.

Varun sighed as he plonked onto the plush six-seater linen sofa. Abhi settled on the love seat opposite him while looking at his elder brother with the most curious expression.

"Some Diwali presents I ordered for a few friends." He mumbled in a low tone. Looking at Abhi's broadening snigger, he added hastily. "I was hoping to hand them over or have them delivered before we leave for Himachal."

"Friends? Plural?"

Ding Dong!

Varun jumped out of the sofa and ran to answer the doorbell. He was glad of the timing for the interruption, because answering Abhi's question would have led to some follow-up questions. Questions he wasn't ready to reveal answers to. Not just yet.

This time he checked the video before opening the door. Seeing the man with the package he'd been waiting for, he couldn't help doing a mental dance.

"I thought you said 'gifts'. This seems to be *a gift*."

Varun didn't realise Abhi had followed him to the door. He ignored the jibe, and quickly, opening the door, collected the parcel.

Before he could resist, the parcel was snatched from his hand. Abhi sprinted inside with it as Varun thanked the delivery person and closed the door.

"Women's footwear? Interesting!" Abhi was reading the label and shook the box inquisitively as Varun walked over to the couch.

"Did a girl hit you with one and broke it? Is this your way of compensating and saying sorry?" Abhi was now chuckling openly as he moved the package from one hand to the other, prying it away from Varun who was trying to snatch it from his younger brother's hands.

"Give it to me, you brat. Okay, fine. I'll answer your questions. But you have to answer a few of mine too. Deal?"

Abhi laughed out loud while shaking the box, "Okay, fine."

Varun added annoyingly, "And I go first…"

"I don't think you're in a position to bargain here," Abhi said, dangling the box from a height. "It does say 'fragile'. I wonder what'll happen if I accidentally drop it."

"Okay you win. Just hand over the box here please?" Varun said in a defeated tone.

"Aha! See that wasn't so hard, was it?" Abhi bowed and handed over the box to Varun with a flourish, who snatched it and darted straight to his bedroom.

Abhi tailed behind, not wanting to miss out on this golden opportunity to pull Varun's leg.

"You think it's safe from me now? I know all about your secret hiding place for such things. Avni told me about it long back." Abhi declared as he entered Varun's bedroom.

An uncomfortable silence followed, in which Varun's expressions changed from hurt to anger, and then indifference as he shrugged his shoulders.

Abhi hesitated a bit as he broke the stretching quietude, "It's obvious these aren't for maa. So spill the beans now." Varun's slight smile gave him a little confidence and he went on. "Are they for Gayu?"

Varun turned visibly red, and coughing slightly, he said, "Yes. I was anyway going to tell you about them because I would require the Kulkarnis' postal address."

"I knew it!" Abhi punched the air as if he had cracked the mystery of the Bermuda Triangle and went on, "None of you have been forthcoming about what's brewing there. But Sharad told me all about your Navratri adventures, or shall I see *Loveratri?*" He chuckled at his own joke before adding.

"Well, at least he told me as much as he knows. God knows how much he doesn't know yet." Thumping Varun's shoulder, Abhi winked and poked him in the belly. "Ignorance is not bliss here, so can we know the story, please?"

Varun chuckled and went into contemplation for a few seconds before relenting.

"There's nothing much to tell really. We exchanged numbers and have been chatting on and off. "

"I see. So these footwear are for your 'chat friend'. And what are your *non-chat* girl friends getting? What did you buy for Anusha? Leave that, what did you buy for maa?"

"I haven't decided. I'm still looking at stuff," Varun mumbled, refusing to look at Abhi while answering.

As if just realising something, Abhi blurted out excitedly, "Wait a second. Gayatri mentioned something about her sandals getting broken during Navratri. She was going on and on about how she needed new ones before her Diwali trip."

Varun looked as if Santa had snatched the gift he had just been handed over for being 'nice' and declared, "Sorry, you've been naughty, child."

"Yeah, well…" He started hesitantly, "I am kind of responsible for her sandals breaking. So I thought…" Clearing his throat, he went on, "May I have the postal address now please?"

"I've messaged it to you." Abhi replied while fiddling on his phone. Looking at Varun smugly he added, "By the way, I had to ask Sharad for it and now he knows why."

"No, you did not!" Varun reached out to smack his brother but Abhi had already snuck out from the room.

Varun chased after him and threatened, "Oh you wait. I'm going to ask Gayatri all about what's brewing between you and Ayesha."

That made Abhi stop in his tracks and turn around.

"No no no, please don't do that. The Kulkarni siblings are insufferable about it as it is."

"Well, isn't that what they call *jaisi karni waisi bharni*[26]?"

"Fine, you win. Ask me directly whatever you have on your mind. Don't involve Gayu, please."

Curbing the urge to , Varun asked, "Let's start with *how was the movie date?*"

Abhi had a mix of anger and incredulity on his face. Like someone had caught him doing an act he never expected to become public knowledge.

"That gossip monger. I'm going to strangle her. It wasn't a movie date! The four of us went together. Gayatri and Sharad were there too and watching a movie like *Pink* hardly counts as a romantic movie date. We went to celebrate the end of exams and semester. It was a group thing."

Varun couldn't help but laugh at his brother's attempt to camouflage his feelings.

"If you say so," Varun said, ruffling Abhi's hair. "For the record, she didn't tell me anything. I saw an update about it on her WhatsApp status."

"What's going on here? So much noise. Can't let a woman sleep peacefully, these Agarwal men!" Radha had walked out of her bedroom and looked irritated.

"Sorry maa, we were just talking…"

"Maa, we were only discussing the Himachal trip…"

Varun and Abhi began unanimously. Radha simply put up her hand and said, "Do it in your rooms whatever it is."

---

[26] *A popular Hindi saying that roughly translates to, "As you sow, so shall you reap."*

Wordlessly, the brothers turned and tiptoed into Abhi's room, which was nearer. They heard the click of their parent's bedroom door and broke into peals of laughter.

Settling down on the bed, Varun asked, "Are you done with your packing?"

"Yeah, almost. I'm really excited to explore Kasauli. I wish the Mehtas didn't have to cancel though…" He stopped himself right in time because Varun had immediately stiffened.

Shaking his head, Varun said, "I think it'll be good to have just the Agarwals for a change. We haven't been spending much time out of the house together, or talking about anything besides work and studies."

Abhi nodded silently, not daring to disagree or aggravate his brother.

Varun's gaze swept around the room as he got up and declared, "Well. I'm going to take your leave now, little one."

"Important things to pack, right?" Abhi asked with a mischievous glint.

Varun was about to retort when Abhi added, "I meant for the trip, bhaiya. Isn't this what they call *chor ki dadhi mein tinka*[27]?"

Laughing despite himself, Varun waved and walked out.

As soon as he entered his own room and secured the lock, he almost ran to his wardrobe. A smile crept up his face and he felt a tickling sensation in his fingers as he took the box out.

He sighed as he settled with it on the bed. Running his fingers over the top, he recalled the past two weeks and what had led to the box being in his hands now.

After that first night of Navaratri, Anusha created a WhatsApp group, including all of them. It helped coordinate the time and place to meetup at Kora Kendra. For the first few days, the messages exchanged between him and Gayatri had not gone beyond a handful of Dil related songs and a few Good Morning and Good Night forwards. Most of their communication happened in the group itself. Even while meeting in person, they couldn't talk beyond hellos and goodbyes because most of the time Gayatri was completely focused on dancing. And, boy, the girl could dance!

---

[27] *A popular Hindi saying that roughly translates to, "A guilty conscience needs no accuser."*

Varun sighed as he remembered that first night when he'd seen her dancing to the Navaratri tunes. His eyes had landed on her in the crowd, because even amidst so many people, it was hard to miss her graceful moves and obvious passion which radiated off her face and body. He had forgotten to breathe for a few seconds. Instinctively, he felt drawn towards her, and made his way towards the circle where she was dancing.

"Where do you think you're going?" Anusha's words had brought him out of the trance. Sheepishly he pointed towards Gayatri.

"Oh, I know that gang. Good idea, let's join them."

Inwardly, Varun was thankful Anusha hadn't noticed his almost lustful intentions. Outwardly he said, "That's great. Let's go!" while mentally pumping his fist in the air.

Her fall and their almost *kiss* had only deepened his desire to get closer to her. In the following days, he reigned in his feelings and maintained a distance, not wanting to come off as overbearing or forceful.

Destiny had different plans though. On the last day of the festival, Gayatri's fervour to make the most of the night was pretty obvious. She had already bagged more than a handful prizes for most of the nights including 'Best Dancer' and 'Best Costume'. With a pang he also recalled the 'Best Couple' prize that she had won with Kartik. It was hard not to think, *"There's something going on here"* when he clapped for them as they received their certificates and gift vouchers. On the last night, she had a determined look about her and seemed focused on nothing but dance. Her 'hello' too had felt distracted.

Varun had his own worries. Like, not being able to see her every day and more agonisingly, a probable end to their short lived chats.

He wasn't participating much in the dancing and chose to stand on the side lines brooding over the coming 'Gayatriless' days. That's when he noticed a guy sneaking into the circle behind her. At first it felt normal, but after a few minutes, the guy seemed to be deliberately closing in on Gayatri, choosing dance moves that made it possible for him to brush against her. He ignored it at first, but when it happened for the fourth time and the guy's fingers brushed against her waist, lingering on for a few seconds more than required, he lost it. Varun made his way into the circle, barging in between the guy and Gayatri, giving him the stink eye, and ready to punch his guts out if he did something similar again. In the process though, he didn't know he had stepped on something; something soft and hard at the same time, something that poked into his toe annoyingly.

"Arghhhh"

He turned towards the source of the scream. Gayatri was limping and had her right foot in her hand, inspecting what appeared to be a wound. With a pang, Varun looked at his own feet to see what he had stepped on. Apparently, in the whole shuffling and getting in between Gayatri and the creepy guy, Varun's foot had found its way on top of one of Gayatri's sandals. Without either him or Gayatri registering it, the sandal had come off and found its way beneath Varun's foot. Gayatri continued to dance, only for her now bare foot to fall on a piece of pebble which led to a bleeding injury. The pokey thing Varun had felt was the buckle of the sandal which had come off, probably because of the weight of Varun's foot. The only good thing was, the creepy guy's disappearance in the aftermath as the group fussed over Gayatri's wound.

As the night's festivities drew to a close, Varun continued to apologise profusely. Though Gayatri kept assuring him she was fine, the guilty feeling in him was only relieved, at least a bit, when Gayatri was announced as one of the winners.

In the following days, he had been looking for an excuse to get in touch with her. With Diwali coming in, he had found the perfect excuse when his brain conjured up the idea of this gift.

With a heavy sigh, Varun brought himself back to the present and caressed the box in his lap. He tore out a page from a book lying on his bedside and quickly jotted down something. Tearing off the page, he snuck it inside the shoe box. Just for safety, he tucked in a corner where it would not be easily visible. He didn't want the note to land in Sharad's hands, or worse the Kulkarni's parents.

As he taped the box and wrote out the postal address for delivery, he chuckled to himself recalling his words and wondering about her reaction.

Jute lo

Dosti do[28]

---

[28] *Hindi words which roughly translate to "Take these shoes and give me your friendship"*

Sorry, did that sound too filmy? Well, anyway
Sounds better than jute lo paise do[29], I hope.

From,
Dilwala dost

---

[29] *Lyrics from a Hindi from the movie Hum Aapke Hain Kaun which translate to, "Take these shoes and give us the money"*

Finding 'foot' ing

"Sometimes, a vacation is just what you need to get away from three P's of your life: people, problems and projects."

- Gayatri Kulkarni

October 2016 - January 2017

"Nice sandals, Gayu. Did you match them with your clothes or is it the other way round?"

"Would you like them thrown at you or would you rather I smack you with them?"

Ayesha laughed uproariously as she witnessed Abhi and Gayatri's banter over the latter's new pair of sandals. Gayatri threw her a warning look, leading to a staring down between the two girls.

"Umm, whatever silent war is going on here. Can we continue it after we place our orders?" Sharad's voice cut in, breaking the awkwardness that engulfed the group.

The four were seated in the college canteen in between their lectures. The girls had joined the boys a few minutes ago after completion of their lectures for the day, whereas the boys still had one more lecture to go. As soon as Gayatri came in his vision range, Abhi had taken one look at her sandals, and given a sly smile. When Gayatri shrugged and took her seat opposite the boys, Abhi fired her with the question he had obviously been dying to ask.

She was smart enough to catch the implication and an instantaneous retort was shot at his smug face. Sharad's intervention helped break the tension and for a few minutes, peace prevailed as the food order was placed.

"I hear you had a warm welcome back from the Diwali holidays, Gayu." Abhi picked up where he left off once the waiter retreated.

"Ayesha had a far steamier one in comparison. One which I believe you were responsible for."

"Really? And why was that? Spill the beans, Banerjee." Sharad butted in, not wanting to miss out on the gossip.

Gayatri was pleased by her successful ploy to steer the conversation away from herself. More specifically from her new, lately always in focus, sandals. When neither Ayesha nor Abhi relented to Sharad's question, Gayatri happily did the needful.

"I hear wedding bells in the Agarwal and Banerjee household, bhav. It's time to start shopping for new clothes."

Ayesha visibly blanched, whereas Abhi determinedly looked anywhere but at the Kulkarni siblings.

"Nothing of the sort. She's making a mountain out of a molehill. We...I mean, Abhi and I, accidentally kissed." Sharad ed but Ayesha put up her hand and continued. "It was a mistake and nothing happened thereafter. Are we living in the 16th century or what, that one kiss leads to a wedding?" She challenged Gayatri, however it was clear from her tone that she did not wish to discuss the matter.

Thankfully, their food arrived, and the next few minutes passed without any of the girls having to discuss their *supposed* love life. Gayatri couldn't be sure of Ayesha, but she heaved a sigh of relief inwardly.

While hogging on the food, her eyes fell on her feet. The sight of the new sandals immediately brought a smile to Gayatri's face. She could not help herself from reflecting back to when the footwear arrived at her doorstep.

On any other day, she would have shouted out to Uma or Sharad asking, "Who ordered these?" while receiving the delivery. Thankfully Varun's message a few minutes ago informed her of the incoming parcel.

"Answer the door and collect the package yourself." The ping showed up on her phone screen right before the doorbell chimed.

"I'll get it," Gayatri shouted out, running towards the door before anyone else opened it first.

A major plus was that each Kulkarni was busy with the last minute packing for their Diwali trip to Kolhapur. So nobody really paid much attention to the exchange between Gayatri and the delivery person.

"Oh, nothing. Just something I had ordered a few days back."

"Who is it?" Uma's voice floated in from her bedroom just as Gayatri closed the door of their house.

Uma was standing just outside her bedroom now and nodded absently at Gayatri's response. In a rare *no inquisitions* conduct, the mother retreated to her room without asking even a single question. Gayatri took the opportunity to carry the box straight to the bathroom before Sharad or her father decided to grill her about *what* and *why* she had ordered. She shook the box to guess what it contained while securing the bathroom latch. An excited squeal escaped her mouth when her guess turned out to be right as soon as she ripped open the packaging. Immediately, she realised her folly and reigned in her exhilaration.

They're totally my kind of design and colour. How did he manage to crack that? She thought to herself while taking them out of the box.

"Not too flat, not very long heels," she mumbled to herself while inspecting the sandals "Oh, the perfect fit too!"

"That's a relief. I don't have to worry about returning them now." She continued as she strapped them on to both her feet. She twirled around humming to herself in delight as she admired how good the sandals looked on her tiny feet.

Still humming, she took out her phone, clicked a photo of the sandals and sent it to the bestower. As she removed the sandals, her hand fell on the box, sending it toppling down. A tiny piece of paper tumbled out of the box and she picked it up curiously.

Her phone buzzed while she was still laughing over the message in the paper and her amusement doubled reading his response to her digital message.

"Dosti mein [30]no thank you? Maybe I should have put that condition in too. Also, where's my *tohfa tohfa tohfa?*"[31]

"Thank you. Ab dosti kar hi li hai to nibhaani bhi padegi.[32] Hukum kijiye aaka[33], I can only afford one wish though…" She inserted a wink emoji at the end and sent her reply with a smile on her face.

---

[30] Hindi words which roughly translate to , 'in friendship'
[31] Hindi word tohfa meaning gift. The reference here is from a Hindi song with the same lyrics
[32] A dialogue from the Hindi movie Maine Pyaar Kiya which roughly translates to, "I have committed to friendship, have to live up to it
[33] Hindi words which roughly translate to, "Command your order my lord"

"Hey, is everything alright in there? I need to use the washroom!" Sharad's urgent voice and impatient knocking on the bathroom door brought Gayatri out of her dreamland.

She shoved her phone and the chit in her pocket hastily. Grabbing the shoe box and closing its lid, she opened the door to an irate looking Sharad.

"Wait, is that what I think it is?" His expression changed to one of sly curiosity and he snatched the box from her hands before she could react.

"Quite thoughtful, isn't he? I wonder how he knew your taste and size." Sharad said as he opened the box and examined the sandals.

"Didn't you have to use the washroom?" Gayatri snapped while trying to grab the box back from him.

"Oh, c'mon. I have a right to know. How do you think he got our address? Now, tell me. Is this something Kartik needs to worry about? Is Varun a potential competitor in acquiring *Gayu land*?"

"I am warning you, bhav…"

Sharad chuckled mischievously as Gayatri began to chase him around the room in perusal of the shoe box.

"Okay, I can play dirty too," Gayatri said, snatching Sharad's phone from his back pocket, "Let me just drop a message asking Anusha about her Diwali plans."

The box dropped from Sharad's hand as he tried to stop Gayatri from typing on his phone. Gayatri rolled with laughter on her bed as she caught the shoe box and slipped away from Sharad's grip.

"You will do no such thing. Give me my phone back." Sharad shouted.

"If you two are done with your monkey antics, dinner is ready. But you will only get it if you confirm you're done with your packing for Kolhapur."

Uma's authoritative voice was enough to pull the siblings out of their war zone. She was standing at the door of their bedroom with hands on her hips and a *don't mess with me* look.

Sharad mumbled, "Yes, aai. My packing is done. I'll come for dinner in a few minutes. Just need to use the washroom."

He sprinted into the bathroom like a mouse released from its trap. Uma looked questioningly at Gayatri who grabbed her travel bag and wordlessly began to put her clothes into it.

"I will be done in ten minutes, aai."

Uma grunted and walked out, leaving Gayatri alone. She used the opportunity to remove her new sandals from its box and stuff them into her travel bag before such awkward situations popped up again.

In the following days, the sandals became her companion on all days of their Diwali trip. Ever since their arrival, not a day went by without the sandals adorning her feet, even if for just a few minutes. During the trip on many occasions, they became a prop in her photos too and she shared them on her status almost without fail.

Every update was sure to receive a response from Varun. Each time he replied, Gayatri whooped internally because that had been her motive all along. She only put up the photos in the hope of receiving a message from him and finding an excuse to chat. Truth be told, she had been looking for an opportunity to get closer to him but held herself back not wanting to appear desperate. They didn't get much of a chance to get to know each other or even interact beyond hi, hello bye and see you, during Navratri.

The sandal gifting and what followed thus became godsent for her to find a way to talk to him. And talk they did! Their chats sometimes went on for hours, extending late into the night, as they interacted about everything under the sun, right from *how was your day* and *what did you eat today* to sometimes cribbing about how their respective siblings were a pain in the butt.

She knew all about the Agarwals Himachal trip and he knew all about the Kulkarnis Kolhapur trip. So much so that Gayatri even knew about Abhi's increased interaction with Ayesha and vice-versa because Varun had noticed Abhi exchanging messages with her frequently. On her end, Gayatri was apprised of Ayesha's communications with Abhi because they had been calling each other almost every day. Whenever they talked during the short vacation, Gayatri was sure to drop in a question or two about Abhi, which Ayesha found difficult to answer with a straight face.

Then, on their first day back to college, she had walked in on them kissing in the college hallway. She thought they had finally accepted their attraction towards each other and that they would be a couple from then on. But nothing of the sort happened.

"My lunch." A message popped up on Gayatri's phone, bringing her back to the present, in the canteen.

She smiled as she sent her response with a photo of her masala dosa, captioning it 'Same pinch'.

"Ahem."

Ayesha coughed next to her and Gayatri hastily put her phone away.

"No smoke without fire." Ayesha mumbled and Gayatri couldn't help but chuckle. It was the same sentence she had been using on her friend whenever she denied having any feelings for Abhi.

As Ayesha rolled her eyes, Gayatri engulfed her in a side hug and whispered, "If we're hot, of course there'll be fire, babe."

The girls laughed and hi-fived each other as the boys looked on confusingly.

***

Not-So-Well Begun

"Taking the first step or being pushed towards it, what does it matter? As long as you're in the game now."

- Varun Agarwal

February 2017

"Here's your blazer. Phew! So glad it's finally over. I never knew hearing the words 'You've got the job' would bring so much joy."

Varun had walked into Abhi's room to hand over the blazer he had borrowed for a campus interview. With so many frequent on-campus interviews happening every day, his own blazer had become a bit worn so he had borrowed Abhi's. He stopped short after entering the bedroom when he realised Abhi wasn't alone.

Abhi jumped up and thumped Varun on the back. Hi-fiving him and enveloping him in a hug, he whooped loudly.

"Congratulations, bro. Wasn't this the firm you'd been aiming to get into all along?"

Varun nodded while looking curiously behind Abhi's back.

"Oh, so sorry. You remember Ayesha, right?"

She smiled warmly and extended her hand out.

"Nice to meet you again. Congratulations. Which firm is it and when do you have to join?"

"Thank you. It's Ogilvy and I have to join from this June."

"Ogilvy? Wow! That's amazing. What's the profile?"

"For now it's going to be a mix of Junior Copywriter and Junior Social Media Strategist. They'll see where I fit better and decide on a permanent profile by December."

"Sounds challenging and exciting."

Varun grabbed a chair and took a seat opposite the bed, facing Abhi and Ayesha.

"Exciting for sure. Good to see you here. Does this mean what I hear is true then?"

Ayesha cast a furtive look towards Abhi who mumbled, "I don't know what you're talking about."

"You really thought you could hide your relationship update from your much smarter, much more charming, elder brother?"

Ayesha laughed nervously while Abhi burst out, "It was hardly a hidden thing. Don't behave like Sherlock."

Varun ignored the jibe and addressed Ayesha, "I don't know whether to congratulate you or wish you all the best. But if this one gives you a tough time, I promise you we'll make him pay for it as a team."

This time Ayesha laughed out loud, without any inhibitions and hi-fied Varun.

"You're one to talk! Was it that gossip monger Gayu again?" Abhi sounded pissed.

Ayesha suddenly sat upright, looking at Varun closely.

Barely managing to hide the reddening of his cheeks, Varun suddenly felt as if he was on trial. The expectant looks on his jury's face pushed him to confess.

"Well, not just her. Sharad put up a photo of you two, where you were kissing Ayesha on the cheek. If that weren't enough hint, he also captioned it 'The things you endure in the name of friendship'."

Ayesha butted in before Abhi could, "But what about Gayatri? Actually, what I really want to ask is what's happening between you and her?"

"Oh, she's smart." He turned to Abhi and communicated his thoughts with an admirable look. The victorious look on Abhi's face and the following shrug was a clear indication for Varun.

"There's no wriggling out of this." He mumbled to himself.

With a deep sigh he relented, "I guess you know about our Navratri meetings and then the Diwali gift…"

"Which haven't left her feet for even one day…" Abhi interrupted and Ayesha gave him an annoyed look which shut him up.

Feeling slightly better for Ayesha being 'team-Varun', he continued, "If you're asking about our relationship status, it's simply friendship at the moment."

"You Agarwal men are so useless…"

"Hey!" Both the brothers burst out unanimously but Ayesha put up her hand which shut them immediately.

"Prove me wrong then! I dare you to ask her out. You know what, if you pull this through, I promise the two of you a double date with the 'sinful sisters'."

Abhi coughed and Varun looked on at Ayesha with a mixture of amusement and incomprehension.

She gave Abhi a scoff.

"Oh, please. We're well aware of the tag." Then she turned to Varun and explained. "The boys in our department have given the duo of Gayatri and me, that loving, totally acceptable tag, which I strongly believe your little brother had a hand in."

"Always the tone of doubt." Abhi mumbled, but Ayesha ignored him and looked expectantly at Varun.

"What's that song about chicken?" Then chuckling as she remembered, she started humming, "Teri bhuk ka ilaaj chicken kuk-du-ku…"[34]

Abhi laughed and hi-fived Ayesha as the two of them started singing in chorus.

"Alright alright, stop it you two," said Varun, giving in, "I can see how much of an influence Gayatri has on everyone around her. Chicken kuk-du-ku indeed." He shook his head and took out his phone.

"I'll be a little lenient. You can ask via text if you feel uncomfortable calling and asking her."

Varun shot Ayesha an incredulous look as he unlocked the screen and opened WhatsApp. Inwardly though he felt a modicum of relief because getting rejected over text would be a lesser blow to his ego at least.

---

[34] *Lyrics from a Hindi song from the movie Bajrangi Bhaijaan which roughly translate, "The cure for your hunger is chicken, kukdu ku…"*

"If she says no, what do I get?" Varun challenged Ayesha as his fingers hovered over the chat box, wondering how to do this.

"I promise to try and convince her. I am as much of an influence on her as she is." Ayesha winked conspiratorially, making Varun blush slightly.

"Do you need help with how to go about it?" She poked.

"No, thank you. You've helped enough." Varun couldn't help the exasperation in his tone. It only made the couple in his presence laugh at his struggle to do the task at hand.

Looking at him with unashamed curiosity, Ayesha now began to hum *Do mil rahe hai magar chupke chupke*

'Sabko ho rahi hai khabar..''

"Chup ke chup ke."[35]

Rolling his eyes, Varun tuned them out to concentrate on the chat with Gayatri.

"Hi." He began

"Hey, what's up?" She replied almost instantaneously.

"Nothing, being victimized by A^2 and cursing my luck."

"A^2? That's a good one." It was followed by a laughing and winky emoji.

He felt encouraged and went on, "What are you doing?"

"Nothing much. Watching TV with aai and Sharad. Oh, wait. Just got a message from Ayesha. What does she mean by 'Say yes'?"

Varun shot an agitated look and not surprisingly Ayesha gave him a thumbs up.

"Ignore her." He replied, followed by a rolling eye emoji.

Before things got further out of hand, he began typing what he intended to ask. He typed and deleted a few times, not quite sure of the right approach.

In the meanwhile, she messaged, "Now Abhi is saying 'Hi Bhabhs [36]'. What are these two up to?"

---

[35] *Lyrics of a Hindi song Do Dil Mil Rahe hai which roughly translate to, "Two hearts are meeting but secretly. Everyone is coming to know but secretly"*
[36] *A Hindi term Bhabhi shortened to bhabhs. It mean 'sister-in-law'*

"Umm, so the thing is…" he began hesitantly.

"You're all making me really nervous." She replied before he could on.

"Forget A^2. Anyway, so here goes. I don't think it's a secret but I want to confess nonetheless. I like you a lot. I believe I'm not wrong in assuming you like me too. So, if you're free tomorrow or the day after, would you like to go out with me?"

"Did they put you up to this? I'm going to kill them!"

"I'm waiting."

"Is this a prank?"

"It isn't. You need to trust me on that."

When the 'typing' notification hovered around for more than a couple of minutes, he sensed her hesitation and feared the worst. Thinking it best to clarify and put this to an end he typed and sent, "It's okay, I understand. Please don't feel coerced to say yes." Then added another message. "We can plot their murder together. Make it look like an accident."

That one got a quicker response in the form of a laughing emoji.

"I'm in for that….now…ummm… so the thing is… yes, I do like you. But… in fact, there are just too many 'buts'. But it's too soon? But we live so far from each other? But…"

He interrupted with his own thoughts, "There's also.. but we belong to different generations. I know and I've thought about these things more than you. It's not that A^2 pushed me so I'm doing this. Believe me, no one can make me do something I don't really want to do. Abhi knows this well. They were just a catalyst."

"Still…"

He typed in, "Okay" and was about to put his phone away dejectedly when it pinged with another message.

"Fine, yes. Let's do this. But only one date, okay? We'll see where it goes from there."

He never knew a simple yes would bring him so much joy and relief. It felt like someone supplied a fresh wave of oxygen to his failing heart.

He kept his response a simple "Thank you,' and added. "Let me know the date, and time. I can be accommodating about that. But let me choose the place. I'll pick you up. We'll chat later, when A² aren't acting like Big Boss."

"They are insufferable. I'm already dreading college on Monday. We can meet tomorrow. But I insist on you picking me up from the nearest station to the venue. I'll let you know the time in a while." She had added a blushing emoji at the end of that text.

"Okay." Varun replied with a heart face emoji and pocketed his phone.

Somehow, he managed to walk out of Abhi's room without physical injuries. Because what followed after he informed them about Gayatri's acceptance can only be called an attack. Jumping up from the bed, Abhi covered the distance between them in two steps, and began thumping him on the back, quite aggressively in Varun's opinion. He even hit him on the head a couple of times.

Ayesha, though reluctant at first, said, "You're welcome." and landed a few blows on his stomach. Their cheering and whistling didn't stop all the while.

It was only when they heard the front door click that they went back to being human.

"I'm home. Someone help me with the groceries, please." Radha's booming voice rang out and Varun rushed out like a rocket with its tail on fire.

A little later, after Ayesha left post evening tea and snacks, Varun was finally able to take his phone out without the hovering eyes of A².

He hesitated a bit at first, but if they were going on a *date*, he'd have to get her comfortable around him.

"Hi, can we get on a call?"

"Give me five minutes."

His phone rang a while later and her initiative only made him like her more. With elation, he also noted that she had called well within five minutes. Smiling unabashedly, he answered the call and stopping himself from ing, he managed a mellowed "Hi"

"Hi" She answered back.

There was a comfortable silence of a few seconds, where all he could hear were her deep breaths. He could also feel her blush and smile, imagining her exact expression as she sat on the bed, or leaned over the window sill of her bedroom.

"Where are you?" He blurted out wanting to conjure an exact image of hers in his mind.

"At my bedroom window. It's the only place I'm sure no one will hear our conversation."

He chuckled and mumbled a 'hmm'

There were literal goosebumps on his arms as he imagined being next to her at the window, with his arm around her shoulder and her head on his. A deep sigh involuntarily escaped his mouth.

"So…," she began hesitantly. It was a shy, but challenging tone.

He smiled and replied, "Have you been to The Radio Club?"

There was a slight uncertainty as she answered, "No"

"Then let's go there tomorrow."

He expected her response to be a bit more enthusiastic than the simple 'Okay.'

"Is there a problem?"

"Not really."

Then she went quiet, not willing to explain any further. So he probed again, "Please tell me"

He could feel her relaxing, and there was also a hint of a smile in her response. "Not only is it too far, but it's also one of those places where I'm sure I'll feel out of place."

"I see. Okay, I understand. Would somewhere in Bandra be more convenient then?"

"Sure," there was the hesitance again.

"Let's do one thing. I'll send a few options in Bandra. If you don't like any of them, we'll go to the place of your choice. Okay?"

Her responding "Great" sounded much more enthusiastic than any of her responses so far.

There was some chattering noise from her background and she said, "We'll talk later". The call was cut even before his 'Okay' went through.

"Sorry, aai was calling." Her ping came in almost immediately.

"It's okay. I'm sending you the options. Reply when you can."

She sent a smiling and thumbs-up emoji in response. Somehow he still felt her reluctance. He couldn't be sure but had an inkling that his choice of restaurants and dine-outs weren't going to match hers.

Nonetheless, he quickly made a list and sent her a message.

"1. Vista
2. Salt Water
3. Candies
4. Bird Song
If none of these, then you pick one. I'm fine with anything you decide." He had added in a mix of fine-dine and casual eateries, because he was unsure of her preferences. He had a fair idea though and when she replied, "Candies" in just a few seconds, he couldn't control the resulting frown.

Nevertheless he replied "Okay" with a thumbs up and smiling emoji.

Well, isn't that tit for tat? He mused.

Though her choice was not the place he had in mind for their first date, he was still excited.

"I can reach there by myself. There's no need for you to pick me up."

Why does she sound annoyed?

But he wanted to put his foot down on this at least. He replied, "I insist. Please tell me where and when."

"Fine. Bandra station at 5 pm tomorrow evening."
"Great. See you then. Good night." He added a blushing emoji hoping she'd be able to gauge his excitement.

"See you. Good night." She texted back with a star-eyed emoji.

He hugged the phone to his heart while gazing out at the setting sun. Sighing, he turned and lay down in bed wondering how agonizing the next twenty-fours were going to be.

Sabra ka fal meetha[37]. His heart mused and he couldn't help the resultant smile.

---

[37] *A Hindi proverb which roughly translates to* 'The sprouting of patience is sweet.'

Kissing the Pain Away

"Being a damsel in distress may be an outdated and cliched thing. But when it leads to happy endings, who cares how it came about?

- Gayatri Kulkarni

March 2017

"Do me a favour?"

"Let's play Holi…"

"God, can we get serious for a minute?"

"Uff ye holi aayi hai holi, rango me hai pyar ki boli…" [38]

Varun rolled his eyes and struck a hand on his forehead.

"Guys, please!"

Ayesha, who had been laughing at Gayatri and Abhi's antics so far, looked at Varun and shouted out, finally managing to shut up the duo.

Varun looked at her gratefully and let out an exasperated sigh.

"Thank you!" he said, "This double date is turning out to be more of a punishment than a reward, Ayesha."

Landing a punch on Abhi's shoulder, Ayesha pulled his cheeks while chuckling and said, "I'm sorry, I'll control this clown. You control yours, deal?"

"Clown?" Abhi said in mock hurt, placing a hand over his heart.

"You were saying?" Gayatri turned questioningly towards Varun. She would've loved to carry on the drama and though a bit stung, she knew when to stop.

"Sorry, I didn't mean to offend you." Varun looked worried.

"It's fine." She said, smiling at him. "I've been called worse things."

Varun looked at her with raised eyebrows but she waved it off and asked him what favour he wanted.

---

[38] *Lyrics from a Hindi song from the movie Waqt*

"Pass the salt shaker please." Gayatri handed it to him and their eyes collided. Despite their increased communication and having been on a date together, the fire in his eyes melted her heart instantly. Abhi coughed and the brothers exchanged a look as Gayatri and Ayesha gazed at each other confusingly.

"I guess Abhi hasn't asked you yet so I'll do the honours. Ayesha and Gayatri, would you like to join us at Pashmina to celebrate Holi together?"

"I'd love to but can I bring a friend along?," Ayesha was game immediately.

Abhi turned to her, "As long as it's not *Professor Joshi*, the guest is allowed."

Ayesha's eyes were spitting fire as she answered, "You know he left for Delhi! Anyway, it's his sister Nalini. We've grown quite close."

Abhi nodded but Gayatri could sense the tension and opened her mouth to intervene. Before she could utter anything, Varun put a hand on her palm, restraining her words.

"Don't fret. He needs to get over it on his own." He whispered in her ear, leaning in towards her.

The hair on Gayatri's neck and back stood on end. A tingling sensation spread over her entire body as the breath from Varun's mouth blew warm air onto her skin and his lips almost touched the tip of her right ear. The touch of his hand over hers was also doing unspeakable things to her mind. She nodded vaguely, trying hard not to pass out from the pleasure that his closeness brought.

He smiled faintly and with a mischievous glint in his eyes, landed a quick peck on her cheek before moving his face away from hers. Though shocked, Gayatri wasn't displeased by his move and was sure her intensified heartbeats were audible to everyone present in the restaurant. A smug look from a passing waiter made her look the other way demurely.

Girl, who are you and what have you done to Gayatri?

She shook herself out of her dreamland when she noted with a little disappointment that Varun had moved to his original position; a bit too far in her opinion.

Oh, and just when you were craving for more!

She turned to look at him with a hurt expression but all her anger melted away as he winked at her conspiratorially. In a move that shocked even herself, she winked back at him and took in his surprised smile with a responding grin.

She was also acutely aware that Varun hadn't withdrawn his hand from hers yet. His fingers were moving across the top of her hand, caressing her index finger and knuckles in the most endearing manner.

Endearing? It's arousing you, girl! Her lusty self, chided.

"You haven't answered yet, Gayu. Will you be coming too?" Abhi's question brought her to her senses and she jerked her face away from Varun's. It was disappointingly also followed by the separation of their entwined hands.

She hesitated a bit as she confessed, "I would love to…" She looked at Varun guiltily. "But, my parents…"

"Sharad is invited too, of course." Both Varun and Abhi said at the same time.

"Okay, I guess that should stop my parents from asking unnecessary questions." She relented, "Sure, let's do this."

Their food arrived after that and the rest of the double date passed comfortably. They discussed the upcoming Holi celebrations and other random things. After dinner, the boys dropped them outside Sunrise Housing Society, where Ayesha resided. Since the dinner date was sure to go on beyond her curfew hour, Gayatri had told her parents she was staying at Ayesha's place for some project work. Thankfully Sharad hadn't played his usual role of *Naradmuni*[39] and things had gone smoothly; at least so far.

The girls waved the boys a goodbye. Varun gave her a bashful look when Abhi under the pretext of moving from the rear to shotgun, hugged and kissed Ayesha on the cheek. Gayatri mouthed out "It's okay" hoping to make him feel better. As the car drove off, the girls waited at the gate till the departing Honda Amaze turned a corner before finally going out of sight.

---

[39] Narada (Sanskrit: नारद, IAST: Nārada), or Narada Muni, is a sage divinity, famous in Hindu traditions as a travelling musician and storyteller, who carries news and enlightening wisdom. He is also infamous for being a gossip monger and causing thrifts among people.

Ayesha let out a sigh, which made Gayatri push her inside the society premises, while mimicking, "We're only friends, Gayu. There's nothing like that, Gayu," in the tone of her best friend.

Ayesha wasn't one to take it lying down.

"But how can I go out with someone so much older than me, Ayu? It's so uncool," she mimicked back in Gayatri's tone.

They laughed all the way up the elevator till the time the door of Ayesha's house was opened by her mother, Lata Banerjee.

"Seems you girls had fun," Lata inquired, letting the door open for the girls to enter the Banerjee residence.

"Yes, aunty. So glad to finally meet you," Gayatri said, marvelling at Ayesha's resemblance to her mother.

"I was almost beginning to think Gayu is a figment of my daughter's imagination. Glad to know it's a real person." Lata said jokingly and chuckled at her own humor.

Gayatri joined in her laughter and controlled her urge to hi-five Lata.

Meanwhile Ayesha's, "Mom!Kichu ēkaṭā bala [40]." Got conveniently ignored.

After exchanging introductions and pleasantries with Ayesha's father, Lalit Banerjee, the girls moved to Ayesha's bedroom. As expected, Ayesha badgered Gayatri with questions about the first date. Though she was happy to share most of what happened, she kept a few things to herself.

Like, how the kiss made you feel? Her lusty self, awakened again.

"You tell me. How are things with Abhi? He still seems jealous of Viren." She asked Ayesha after she was done narrating her lust story.

Love story girl, love story. She shook herself out of her thoughts as Ayesha began to speak.

"Things are great, actually. But he has to understand I can't just delete Viren out of my life like that, right? Anyway, I'm hoping we'll be fine now that Viren is no longer *Professor Joshi* for us and has left the city altogether." Ayesha said. It felt like she was convincing herself more than Gayatri.

---

[40] *Bengali word which roughly translate to "What nonsense you're saying"*

"The important thing is that you chose Abhi. He has to firstly appreciate that. The rest, whatever he feels, is his problem babe, not yours." She said, giving Ayesha's palm a reassuring press.

Not so long ago, Ayesha's personal life had been nothing less than a Bollywood romcom, where she had confusing feelings about two boys. One was of course, their senior and Sharad's best friend, Abhi Agarwal. The other was Viren Joshi, Ayesha's neighbour, who later also taught them *Changing Nature of the Federal System* for a few months. The girl simply could not figure out which of the guys she liked more, or whether she really wanted to get into a relationship with either of them. Until finally, Abhi had taken matters into his own hands and the two of them aka A^2 had finally ended up together. All through it, Gayatri had seen Ayesha struggling with her feelings and was glad when the drama came to an end. Looking at her best friend now, she was sure Ayesha had made the right choice.

They talked about their course, the upcoming projects and the Agarwal siblings for a quarter of an hour, until their tired bodies could not take it any longer. Bidding each other goodnight, Ayesha turned the lights off and was snoring away within minutes. But sleep eluded Gayatri as she lay there staring at the ceiling and recalling her first date with *Mr. Dil*.

Gayatri reached Bandra at the decided hour waiting for his update. She had dropped him a message after boarding a Churchgate bound slow local from Kandivali. Though she was a bit put off by the prospect of having to wait for him, her excitement at what their first date held in store, helped curb the impatience. She was used to being on the move when trying to reach somewhere in the city of dreams so this pick-up service was making her restless. Getting off the train she made her way outside the railway station. Right on cue, her phone rang as soon as she stepped into the pleasant sunshine.

"Do you know Lucky Restaurant?" He asked straightaway.

She nodded, then quickly realising he couldn't see her through the phone, said, "Yes"

"Great, can I pick you up from there? I'll be reaching in a few minutes."

"Sure, see you." She was about to ask something but the call had ended already.

Pocketing the phone, she turned on the music again and made her way afoot to the popular non-vegetarian eatery which she reached in under five minutes. Gayatri was just taking her phone out to call him, when a car stopped near her, honking to catch her attention. Looking up, she saw him waving at her frantically as other vehicles began to line up behind the car. Gayatri got in quickly and they drove off as she put on the belt and made herself comfortable. A woodsy aroma hit her nostrils as she leaned back in the seat. It was a bit intense for her liking but not completely unpleasant.

"Hi," he said, giving her a side grin while lowering the volume of the music. With unexpected satisfaction, she noted that the song playing was *Dekha Hazaaro Dafaa*.

Well, at least our music choices match, she thought as she replied, "Hi," while returning his smile.

A few minutes of silence followed in which he gave her a sideways glance while she took in his appearance, quite unabashedly. She could only make out his well-fitted dark blue shirt from the seating position he was in. The sleeves were rolled up to his elbows and the taut muscles beneath the visible and covered area of his long arms almost made her drool. He was humming the song and drummed his fingers on the steering wheel cheerfully as he drove; his attention entirely on the road. A chic silver metallic watch with a dark blue dial sat on his right wrist. She was no watch connoisseur but could make out a deluxe product when she saw one and this was surely Rado or some such similar luxury brand. Sensing her eye on himself, he turned to look at her with a cocked eyebrow.

"Worthy of being your date?" He asked, flashing her a mischievous grin.

She gave a nervous laugh but didn't hold back from being candid herself.

"We'll leave that assessment for later. Let it be known that Gayatri gave you a fair chance…"

"Before stomping all over my heart? Uff, tough crowd."

"Well, we can't have a romcom without some heartbreak and conflict now, can we? Nobody wants to watch a movie where the hero isn't worth their time and money." She challenged.

"Oh, but I forgot my gun at home! How will I rescue you from the goons and save the day now?," He said with a glint in his eyes.

"*Bade bade desho mein aisi choti choti baatein hoti rehti hai*, Mister Agarwal. And lucky for you, this heroine comes bearing her own armour." She took out and held her bottle of pepper spray like a gun, making bullet sounds while aiming it at him.

Though he laughed, Gayatri didn't miss the look of admiration he gave her. Before he could respond, they were already outside Candies.

"You can get down. Let's meet here again or you can go wait inside. I'll park the car and join you in a bit."

She nodded and got down as he drove away. The sight of the cafe made her sigh involuntarily as a wave of nostalgia hit her. She had great memories of this quirky cafe from her school days. She had been a part of many dance competitions and cultural events that happened at the St. Andrew's Centre for Philosophy & Performing Arts, which was within a walking distance from Candies. She participated in most of these competitions with a group and had only done a solo performance a couple of times. Whenever there was a group involved, Candies had been their go-to hang-out spot in between and after rehearsals. It even ended up being their celebration spot after the event was done with, because most times they managed to bag one of the top three prizes if it had been a dance competition.

The best part about the cafe, besides the pocket-friendly yummy food and the picturesque decor, was that one never failed to find a sitting spot despite it being almost always crowded. Spread across a three-floored Portuguese-style villa, with indoor and terraced seating, the cafe had ample space to easily host over a hundred patrons at a single time. The memory of the good times spent here brought a smile to Gayatri's face as she walked towards the cafe's entrance. Rather than stepping in, she thought it'd be better to wait for Varun on one of the many benches strewn across the entryway itself. Gayatri itched to dance to the tune of the music reverberating from the cafe. But thought it better to sit and soak in the sunlight streaming in through the leaves that formed a beautiful green tunnelled canopy leading towards the cafe's door. On instinct, she removed her phone, took a photo of the entryway, and shared it on the WhatsApp group of *Nrityanihar*. Most of the members in it had been a part of her ensemble performances at St. Andrew's. She was responding to the instant responses the photo received, looking at her phone screen with a grin on her face, when a tap on her shoulder brought her back to the present. She looked up to find Varun looking at her inquiringly, shaking off the quiver that ran down her body as his fingers grazed her bare skin.

"Welcome back to the real world. I called out a couple times but…," he quickly pulled his hand away from her shoulder and nodded towards the phone in her hand.

"Sorry, this place has a lot of memories with my dance group and I just shared a photo with them." She justified apologetically.

He seemed a bit pissed but gave a curt nod and led the way inside the cafe.

Probably not a good idea to use the phone if Mr. Grumpy keeps showing around. She decided, following him while pocketing her mobile.

She already knew what she wanted, and quickly pointed out the items from the glass display to the man behind the counter. Varun was looking at her with an amused expression. Clearly, he didn't know his way around the Candies menu.

"It's a self-service cafe and you need to place the order by picking the items from the display here," she said pointing toward three huge glass display counters where different food items were laid out, "Then you pay for it at the next counter, after which they prepare or heat up the items and you collect them from the last counter," Gayatri finished explaining to a curious looking Varun as she pointed to the far corner where an open kitchen counter and one more counter with a person who appeared to be the cashier, was seated.

She then helped him choose some of the popular items like the chutney sandwich, mini samosa, mac & cheese pasta, and the lemon tart. When his face went like he was going to throw up, she laughed and suggested jam tart instead of lemon tart and he heaved a sigh of relief.

At the pay-out counter, they got into a bit of argument when he refused to go Dutch. She only agreed on the condition of going solo the next time around.

At once, his eyebrows shot up and with a twinkle in his eyes, he said, "So there's a next time already? Seems like I'm a worthy enough hero for buying a ticket!"

"If you don't let the viewer buy the ticket, they can't say paisa wasool[41]," she answered while sticking her tongue out. Immediately realizing this wasn't Sharad, Kartik, Abhi, or any of the men who were used to her idiosyncrasies, she regretted her impulsiveness. Embarrassed by her literal tongue-in-cheek, she mumbled under her breath and moved to the collection counter.

After making the payment, Varun joined her at the food collection counter in a few minutes. The warmth and butterflies his proximity brought didn't help with her already heightened level of discomfort of not being able to divide the expense of this date. Probably sensing her awkwardness, he offered, "Why don't you grab us a table? I'll join you in a while with our order."

Though her manners dictated otherwise, she grabbed the opportunity to put a little distance between them. A self-pep talk and a breather for getting her jumpy nerves under control was the need of the hour or she was sure her *date* would be running for the hills soon, shouting out, "Unhappy meal, unhappy meal–with a dissatisfying human toy". She nodded and made her way towards the stairs leading to the upper floors. Then remembering he wouldn't know his way around or not know where to find her, she turned and said, "I'll be at the Candies Sky Terrace, the top floor open terrace area."

His eyes scrunched up a bit and he turned to look outside the cafe door for a few seconds. With a slight hunch in his shoulders he turned back to her and nodded imperceptibly. She could sense his disapproval, but hey, wasn't she already making a compromise by letting him pay? She shrugged and determinedly made her way up the stairs before she lost her defiance to his deploring eyes.

Once at the terrace, she chose a table for two below a shady tree. Hanging her purse on the chair, she took her seat and enjoyed the cool breeze that caressed her face and hair. After a few minutes, Varun appeared on the staircase leading to the terrace, laden with two food trays. Realising how heavy they must be, she jumped up from the seat and made towards him to help out. The floor however was a little slippery and in her haste, she slipped and fell face down on the mosaic tiles in a position she was sure would make a great body outline at a murder scene.

---

[41] A Hindi term used to define an experience or a commodity as being worth it's price

She heard an uproarious laughter from above her, followed by hurried footsteps making way towards her sprawled figure. Before she could turn over and get up, a strong grip around her waist helped her get into a sitting position.

Varun was on his knees, looking at her with a mixture of amusement and concern as he asked, "Are you okay?"

She simply nodded, not wanting to add to her embarrassment, and tried to get up by taking the support of a nearby table. She winced as a mild pain shot across her legs. Great! The mishap had left emotional as well as physical damage. She was just cursing herself for not being more careful, when he scooped her up in his arms, leaving her shocked and breathless. A little scream escaped her but he ignored it and said in a mock hurt tone, "People might get other ideas you know". With her arms entwined around his neck and shoulders, the distance between them was mere inches and she could feel his breath on her face and neck. It was how his arms felt across her waist that made her hide her face in his chest though. Because if she continued to look into his eyes, she was sure the lusty witch within her would conquer and claim their conquest on his lips. Going by his heartbeats and how they felt against her skin, she knew their rapid beating meant he was equally affected by the proximity between their bodies. Sighing deeply, he slowly made his way with her in his arms toward the table she had picked for them.

As he lowered her into the chair, their eyes met again; one a shy pair of greens that went downcast, the other, a pair of browns, hungry and seeking permission. He gripped her chin with one hand forcing her face upwards again, while the other hand caressed her right cheek. His eyes held a promise and the caressing was so beguiling that it blocked her mind to everything else but the pleasure they evoked. She closed her eyes in abandon, her lips parted as she let out a moan. Even with her eyes closed, she felt their proximity grow lesser and she felt his lips on hers, pecking her top lip and then the lower one in the most gentle manner. She found her hand finding its way into his hair even as she opened her mouth more, inviting him deeper. That was all the signal he needed, as his lips became suddenly demanding and changed track from being hesitant and unsure. He ran his tongue over her top lip and as she shuddered with delight, he did the same to her lower lip, before biting them and thrusting it inside. Her hand moved from his hair to the top of his shirt, her fingers finding their way to the exposed skin on his neck and chest. He let out a groan and suddenly pulled himself away, leaving her feeling suddenly bereft.

She realised only a few seconds later that they weren't alone on the terrace anymore. A group of friends had walked up the stairs and made way to a nearby table as Varun got up and took the seat opposite her.

Though the rest of that date had not been as awkward as she'd thought, the memory of that kiss and its lingering tickle had hung around.

The following days and the second date tonight had only made her fall for *Mr. Lip Locked*, deeper and stronger. With a smile on her face, she closed her eyes and was enveloped by a pair of strong arms.

She didn't want to imagine what a festival like Holi could lead to, where they'd be left to the mercy of wet clothes and complete abandon.

***

Festival of (True) Colors

"They call it a 'crush' for good reason; because their reality, ultimately, might end up crushing your heart."

- Gayatri Kulkarni

March 2017

"Is Avni here?"

"Umm, no… why?"

Abhi looked around to make sure Varun wasn't around as he answered his mother's loaded question.

"Oh, those sandals. I think I've seen her wearing similar ones. Never mind." Radha shrugged and entered the Agarwal residence.

"They're mine," Gayatri answered timidly, camouflaging the conflicting emotions rapidly rising in her heart and mind.

"So, shall we move out?" Abhi intervened. "We can wait for Varun near the elevator."

Abhi, Gayatri, and Ayesha were at the door of the Agarwal residence. They had been waiting for Varun and were about to step out when Radha walked in carrying some sweets.

"Yes, almost everyone's already gathered," Radha informed. "Your father is there with Sharad and Ayesha's neighbour I believe? They're helping him make some final arrangements. I'll be there in a bit with the remaining snacks and sweets."

Gayatri nodded absently while still reeling from Radha's slip as she put on her footwear. It was hard not to think back to some questions she'd been wondering about, whose answers were finally falling into place because of Mrs. Agarwal's accidental revelation. Ayesha sensed Gayatri's disconcertment and put a hand around her shoulders as the girls moved out, sheepishly followed by Abhi.

"Listen, Gayatri. Don't bother about what maa said." Abhi said consolingly. "Bhaiya doesn't even talk about her, let alone talk *to* her."

"Hmm," was all she could manage to respond with. All of a sudden, she felt like rolling up inside the quilt on her bed in her home. The prospect of playing Holi, facing so many people, smiling and pretending her mind wasn't going crazy, felt taxing.

"Did someone die or what?" Varun's question brought Gayatri out of her internal discord.

She looked up at him with a nervous smile. Despite her inner turmoil, she couldn't help the twinge in her heart at the sight of him. He had put on a pair of simple white kurta and pajama. Gayatri had always wondered how his towering 6'2" frame somehow looked even more eminent in Indian attire. Not for the first time, she found herself thinking how the difference in their heights was just another of the many differences she'd thought of as being problematic.

He's soooo tall. I'm realllyyyy short
He's 24. I'm (only) 18
He's rich. I'm well… not that rich
He'll soon start working. I'm still studying

As if on cue, her mind began counting them all off again. It was the sight of his eyes boring into hers that ultimately stopped the barrage of derailing thoughts.

His *raging fire* eyes, the ones she'd come to associate and match with the growing desire they felt for each other, were currently looking at her with concern. She shrugged and looked away, fearing her own eyes and face might belie her outward calmness.

The elevator dinged, indicating its arrival, saving them all from the prospect of responding to Varun's question.

"Where is Sharad?" Varun asked nobody in particular as they filed into the elevator.

"Oh, you'll find out soon." Ayesha relented with a little gleam in her eyes.

Varun cocked his head, looking from her to Gayatri. The memory of Sharad's behaviour from earlier that day instantly elevated Gayatri's mood. Her *Always so reserved* elder brother had taken on a different mode today and she was enjoying the change. She looked at Ayesha, winked conspiratorially, and broke into giggles, refusing to answer the curious glances from the Agarwal siblings.

The four of them got out of the elevator and walked towards the area where the Holi celebrations already seemed to be in full swing. The lyrics of *Tip Tip Barsa Paani* became louder with each step and they were soon amidst a horde of people dancing and running around. Most of them were already soaked, sporting colourful faces and clothes. Unanimously, their eyes landed on Sharad who was chasing someone with a fistful of colours in both palms. His target was soon within reach and he smeared her face in seconds, even as the girl squealed.

Gayatri and Ayesha rushed forth in her support, pushing Sharad away from her. Soon it was boys vs girls as the three boys took fistfuls of colours and the girls grabbed the nearby water guns. Each group targeted the other and threw the colours and sprinkled water from the guns onto whoever came within their reach. After all of them were done taking a satisfying revenge, and laughing their hearts out, Ayesha did the introductions.

"Guys, this is Nalini, my neighbour."

"Nalini Joshi, right?" Varun asked curiously.

When she nodded, he went on excitedly, "Viren Joshi's sister? From King George?"

Nalini nodded, looking utterly confused, while Varun regarded her incredulously.

"That's why your face looked familiar. I'm sure people have told you how alike you siblings look. What a small world. You probably don't know this. Your brother and I were in the same class throughout our school years from kindergarten to the tenth grade."

Just then the song changed to *Balam Pichkari*. Though curious to know more about this unexpected connection between Varun and the Joshis, Gayatri didn't want to miss the one song she could never skip dancing to during Holi.

Before she could stop herself, her feet began tapping and she was swaying to the tune while singing out the lyrics loudly.

Itna maazaaa kyuunnn aa raaha hai

Then she looked at Varun, dragged him towards her and continued dancing and singing *Tune hawa mein bhaang milaya.*

He guffawed and joined in willingly, matching her steps and singing the lyrics.

Ho teri malmal ki kurti gulabi ho gayi
Manchali chaal kaise nawaabi ho gayi, toh?

A familiar abandon took over Gayatri as she laughed out loudly while twirling, turning and twisting her body, forgetting all about her earlier anxieties. Varun's hands were perched on her shoulder and then her waist, the brushing of his fingers on her bare skin making her giddy.

As the song was reaching its end, she felt a gust of something hit her stomach, its force pushing her back a few steps. It took her a few seconds to realise she had been attacked by the pressure of water from a hose pipe.

She turned furiously to find the culprit and wasn't at all surprised when her eyes fell on the mirthlessly laughing figure of Abhi. He then turned the pipe and aimed it at Ayesha, who had anticipated his move and in a bid to escape the onslaught, bumped into Gayatri. Because the floor was slippery, the girls went tumbling down, Ayesha on flat ground, and Gayatri into the nearby inflated pool.

A screaming laughter escaped Gayatri's lips as she tried to push herself out of the water. Her arms flailed about, failing to reach the pool's edge or hold on to it for support. She kept laughing even as a pair of arms grabbed her from around the waist and pulled her out. Immediately, her teeth began chattering of their own accord and her body too began to shiver because of the change in temperature. A cloth was thrown over her shoulders and she wrapped herself tightly inside it, thankful for some warmth.

"Okay, let's get you out of here." A familiar voice whispered in her right ear, dragging her towards the building entrance. She was acutely aware of the warmth that penetrated her because of the arm over her shoulder and another one around her waist.

She faintly registered him turning around and saying, "I'll drop her home and be back in a while."

"But I still want to play." She protested, trying to wriggle out of Varun's grip. He held her in place, his arms around her waist tightening possessively, and brushing against the slightly exposed skin in the process. Once inside the building premises, he stopped in his tracks, and turned her so they were facing each other now, instead of being side by side. His one arm was still on her shoulder, while the other was moving in slow circles over the skin on her waist. Her breath hitched and her teeth momentarily forgot to chatter because of the cold as she placed her hand on his broad chest to keep herself steady. His hand moved from her shoulder, trailing up the right side of her neck, reaching her cheek and playing around with the hair strands over her ear, then moved down again before reaching her chin and tilting her face up.

The raging fire in his eyes was an inferno, melting her insides. He cleared his throat, bringing them both out of the trance.

"I know you're not done," he said, leaning in closer, and whispering in a rasping voice. He planted a kiss on the top of her ear before moving his face away and looking into her eyes.

She gasped and he chuckled while clarifying, "I meant with playing Holi. I know you still want to play. But you'll catch a cold if you don't take a hot shower and change now. You're already shivering, your clothes are dripping and…" moving closer again. "I don't want others to see what's meant for my eyes," he finished while giving her an appraising look from top to bottom, halting for a second longer at her heaving bosom, before turning away and pressing the elevator button.

She nodded, trying to keep her wobbly knees from giving away. Was she trembling because of the cold or was it his words that made her unsteady? Gayatri wasn't sure. In fact, she didn't care anymore, as she gazed into his eyes which were burning with desire. They moved into the elevator, refusing to break their staring game or let go of each other's entwined hands. Once the doors closed, she winked mischievously while standing on tiptoe and kissing him on the right cheek. She was about to repeat the feat on his left cheek, when he held her face and twirling her around, pointed towards the top left corner of the elevator.

Leaning down, he whispered in her ear, "Smile, you're on camera."

She immediately let go of his hand and moved away, keeping a distance between them. He chuckled and looked at her smugly, winking flirtatiously while thumping his back against the elevator wall. Leaning over it in a carelessly lazy posture, he continued to look at her hungrily. All too soon, the elevator dinged and Gayatri almost sprinted out, running towards the Agarwal residence. She heard his chortle and hurried footsteps following close behind and was a little disappointed when instead of taking her into his arms, he went straight to the door of their house and maneuvered the lock open. He turned to her with a flourish, inviting her in with open arms and a smug expression.

She squared her shoulders, masking her dismay from earlier, and walked in without giving him a glance. Once inside, she headed towards the couch, where she picked up her bag and turned to head to the guest bathroom. She should have expected the bumping into his broad chest. She should have known he would tail her and block her path. But as his breath mingled with hers, she found herself going weak in the knees anyway.

"I thought you weren't done?" He asked with a wink and that smile that she had come to know very well.

Still a little put off by his earlier nonchalance, she thumped his chest and tried to push him away. That only made him wrap his hands around her waist, pulling her into a tight embrace. Before she knew what was happening, he lifted her in his arms. A little scream escaped her mouth as her hands went around his neck to avoid falling down. That's when their eyes finally met. All her anger went off like a light being turned off and another one being turned on just as fast; the one that was sending waves of anticipated pleasure across her body. He moved from the hall towards his room, never taking his eyes off her and closing the distance between their faces, which was minuscule, to begin with. When they were so close that Gayatri could count the number of tiny hairs on his two-day-old stubble, she closed her eyes in surrender, her hand already threading its way into his thick, wavy hair. He let out a moan before pressing his lips onto hers, sweet and gentle at first, hungry and demanding in a few seconds. He kicked the door of his bedroom open, and refusing to let the kiss break, set her down and then pushed her into the wall, all the while exploring her lips, first the upper one and then the lower one. He bit hungrily on the pout of her lower lip, making her moan in pleasure. She felt him smiling as her hands moved from his hair, to his face, neck and then inside his kurta, playing with the hair on his chest. He grunted, pushing her further into the wall and grabbed her right leg, wrapping it around his waist. One of his hands was in her hair, grabbing them tight while keeping her face tilted up towards his mouth. His tongue was now rolling around her lips teasingly before forcing her mouth open wider as he thrust it in and did things that made her mewl in delight. His other hand was on the leg wrapped around his waist, the fingers moving up and down the insides of her thighs, slowly reaching up to her core.

Tamma tamma loge

Tamma tamma loge tamma

Tamma tamma loge

Tamma tamma loge tamma

The ringing of her phone broke Gayatri's lustful spell. Varun's lips were still on hers, but she suddenly realised where she was. She tried to break away but Varun's hand moved from her hair and came next to her arm, against the wall, blocking her way out. His lips were now on her neck, trailing kisses from the right to the left.

"Varun, my phone. I need to answer it," she pleaded, despite her body demanding otherwise.

"Ignore it," he said, biting her collarbone. It took all her strength to push him away. She ignored the hunger in his eyes which got replaced with irritation as she ran to her phone.

"Always the phone, first Avni and now you…", he burst out angrily.

All the air was sucked out of her being.

So, I was right! It was always about her.

Seething in anger, she answered the phone and told Sharad she'll be down in a few minutes.

"It's also time for us to leave," she added before cutting the phone. Ignoring Varun's pleas, she walked into the bathroom and changed into dry clothes.

She made her way out of his room, removing Varun's hand from the top of her palm, trying to stop her in her tracks.

"Gayu, listen to me at least. I'm sorry, okay? My anger got the better of me…"

Without turning to look at him, she said, "I shrugged off all the questions and signs but it's pretty clear now. I'm sorry but I can't be a replacement for your ex."

His *No, you're getting it all wrong, Let's talk about it first,* all fell on deaf ears as she opened the door of the house and exited with a determination she'd never before felt in her life.

***

Moving On (or Holding On?)

"For most men, weddings are a chance to indulge in bird watching. For some, it becomes bird preying."

-Varun Agarwal

July 2017

"Aunty, it's very simple. See, pretend you have a roti dough ball in your hand and now roll the dough round and then squish it flat."

"Oh yes, you're a genius, beta. See, am I doing it okay now?"

"Very good aunty. Let's do it with the song now."

Dhak-Dhak Dhak-Dhak Dhadke Ye Dil

Chhan Chhan Bole Amritsari Choodiyan

Raat Badi Hai Mastaani

Toh Dilbar Jaani Kar Le Gallan Goodiyan

"Alexa, stop."

"Okay, let's take it from the beginning now. Everyone, positions please. Mehta uncle and aunty on the right, Radha aunty and Shyam uncle, over here, behind me, on the left. The other couples behind them."

"Alexa, play."

Main Daalun Taal Pe Bhangra

Tu Bhi Gidda Paa Le

Chal Aisa Rang Jamaa De Hum

Ke Bane Sabhi Matwaale

"Alexa, stop."

"Mehta uncle, you're not looking at aunty. Try to remember the first time you saw her and bring that expression on your face."

"Well, that's not a good memory. Worst day of my life to be honest," he said good-humouredly, earning a punch from his wife as the other couples guffawed unanimously.

"Sheesh, papa. If anything it was your best and mom's worst day I'm sure."

It was a voice Varun was achingly familiar with. Currently, it was making Gayatri's frown deeper every time it said something; it belonged to Avni Mehta.

Varun could see Gayatri had a retort ready for Avni's comment about the Mehta couple. A showdown between these two women would not bode well so close to the upcoming event.

"Okay, let's take five everyone. I'm sure you're all a bit tired," Varun, who had been observing the whole scene from the side lines, intervened.

The older couples scattered out sighing in relief. Some went straight to the water stall and some plopped their tired bums into the nearby chairs. The Agarwals, and their friends, and families were gathered at Pashmina Serene's activity hall. They were all practicing for the sangeet ceremony of Varun and Abhi's first cousin, Rishi. The wedding was in four days and the sangeet a day before that. When Meera, Rishi's mother, asked Radha if she knew a good choreographer for taking care of the sangeet dance performances, Radha immediately recommended Gayatri's name.

Before Varun or Abhi were made aware or could intervene, Meera had already contacted Gayatri and hired her as the sangeet choreographer.

"Maa, you could have asked us. Now the poor girl is obliged. She might have said yes under duress, not wanting to offend you," Abhi confronted Radha once he came to know about it from Gayatri.

"Nonsense, I know she has re-joined *Nrityanihar* and is actively seeking such freelance assignments," Radha was quick to defend her preference.

Varun could only mutely accept the situation and pray it didn't turn ugly. Because of course Meera chachi and Ashok chachu had invited the Mehtas. Varun had been dreading Gayatri and Avni's upcoming encounter ever since. He even had a couple of nightmares where he ended up playing referee between the two women, trying to pull them apart and stop them from pulling each other's hair off.

Thankfully, since the choreography sessions began a couple of days ago, Avni hadn't shown up. Today, she had walked in with a strut, the one Varun only knew too well. Seeing her in flesh after over a year had brought back all the hurt. And though it was hard to admit, he could see some truth in Gayatri's accusations.

Yes, the two did look and behave a lot alike.

When he saw them side by side, it only made him look away in guilt.

"But why aren't we using the hook step from the song itself?," Avni's voice made him turn back to them.

Even from this distance, he saw Gayatri's body go stiff. Putting on a forced smile, she responded, "Bina aunty was finding it difficult. So I changed it to make it simpler for everyone to grasp."

"Oh yes! Thank you for that dear. Even I couldn't do that step and that roti-making trick was genius," Radha butted in, all praises for Gayatri. The women had returned to the makeshift stage and the men were clambering out of the chairs too.

Avni's lips twitched and her face turned an ugly shade of red. But she quickly nodded her assent and changed the topic.

"Aww, aunty. That's so sweet. I've missed your praises like that showered on me." She gave Radha a side hug which was returned by the older woman.

Gayatri walked over to the others and began arranging them in the dance formation. Though she was hiding it well, Varun sensed that she was put off by Avni's comment. He walked over, intending to apologize. She noticed him but averted her eyes as she helped Bina and Arvind memorize the steps they had learned so far.

"Can we talk for a bit?" He asked hesitantly once she was within earshot.

"Yes, of course. If it's about yours and Abhi's dance performance, I've shared a video with Abhi. You can have a look to recall the steps." She answered without looking at him and continued to help Bina get one of the steps correctly.

"No, it's not about that. And in private, please?" He pleaded.

"Alexa, play," she shouted out "You guys practice and go over the steps we've learned so far, I'll be back in a minute."

The older couples started dancing as Gayatri smiled at the result of her hard work. Then she turned around, sighed, and indicated Varun to lead the way. They walked to the right side, a little away from where the others practiced. The strained silence between them was bearable only because the music and lyrics drowned it out.

Varun stopped in his tracks and looked at her, gathering his strength. Her eyes were focused on something behind him and he wasn't surprised when he turned around and found Avni looking at the pair of them rather wistfully. Grimacing, he turned back and focused on Gayatri. Better dealing with one problem at a time.

"Look, I'm sorry about what happened at Holi. I realise I was in the wrong and maybe what you suspect isn't completely untrue. Maybe I was and am still hurting over Avni and you happened to walk in at the right, or shall I say, wrong time…"

She put her hand up, stopping him midway while still looking at Avni.

"Honestly, it doesn't matter. Maybe I was a rebound. Maybe you only saw her in me. I don't care. That's your problem to resolve. I accept your apology and wish you the best. Let's just promise to stay cordial to each through the remaining two days. Now, I need to get back to my job."

Just like that, she turned around and walked back towards the dancing group. Varun couldn't help but admire the change in her as he saw her retreating figure. There was a definite self-assuredness around her, where previously there had been a certain shyness. Though he recalled her always being upfront, in the last few days, he had observed her being sassier than before.

They weren't talking to each other, but she hadn't blocked him out virtually. Not yet at least. Through her social media and courtesy of Abhi and Ayesha, he was abreast with what was happening in Gayatri's life. He knew she was performing better than ever in her course. He knew she had re-joined *Nrityanihar* as she was determined to make dance a part of her routine again. He knew she had finally agreed to go on a date with Kartik.

That last bit pinched. A lot. It rubbed salt on his wounds left behind by not one, but two women.

This has to end.

He walked to the other side, where another part of his hurtful past stood.

"Hi, Avni."

Aghast, she looked here and there, as if to make sure she'd heard him right and he was really talking to her. Her reaction was so predictable that he let out an involuntary chuckle.

"You heard it right. I'm talking to you." She looked happy but also a bit fearful so he added, "And I'm not here to confront or argue either. So relax."

There was that smile. The one he found endearing.

"How are you?"

"I like her. Good choice."

They both said at the same time and Varun's eyebrows shot up inquiringly.

"What? I've kept a tab on your life even if you haven't bothered. I'm sorry things ended the way they did for us and well… for breaking your trust." She looked genuinely remorseful. "I know you must be curious so I'll update without you having to ask. Mihir and I started seeing each other a while back. You refused to talk to me and I tried so hard to get in touch in every manner possible. Anyway, he was there to support me through it all and everything just fell in place after that. When he asked me out a month back, it felt like the natural next step to say yes."

Varun would be lying if he admitted that didn't hurt. But surprisingly it wasn't earth shattering. If anything, he felt a little relieved.

"That's great. Congratulations." He said heartily.

"Congratulations to you as well. Ogilvy huh? You must be glad you didn't cave in to my father's very tempting and forceful offer," there was a mischievous glint in her eyes. His relief went up a notch when she punched him and he felt not goosebumps, but only a warm familiarity.

When he laughed, she joined in too.

"Yeah, I'm liking the work so far. Who knows? Maybe in the future if I get bored, I might reconsider working in a distillery rather than in an agency."

"May I join in the fun?," Abhi's cheerful voice broke in as he walked into the hall and stood next to the duo.

Avni let out a squeal and hugged him. The two caught up on each other's lives as Avni probed him about Ayesha and Abhi happily relented.

Meanwhile, Varun looked wistfully at them and then at the dancing figure on the stage. All the while wondering if he was only meant to be a bridge for women finding out he wasn't the right man for them.

"Okay uncles and aunties. Time for you to rest. You can keep practising without me after that. Abhi and the other people performing to *Tenu Leke* and *Aashiq Surrender Hua*, come on. Hop on to the stage."

Abhi sprinted forth and jumped onto the stage, followed by Varun and the other cousins, including the groom, Rishi.

"Rishi in the centre. Abhi here." Gayatri grabbed Abhi's arm and positioned him behind Rishi.

"Heeriye Sehra Baandh Ke Main Toh Aaya Re

Doli Baarat Bhi Saath Mein Main Toh Laaya Re"

Abhi began singing the lyrics, catching hold of Gayatri's palm and twirling her around. She resisted and looked miffed at first, then gave in while laughing heartily.

Looking around to ensure the oldies were out of earshot, she gave him a little push and said with a wicked smile, "And whose doli will go to Ayesha then, Mr. Flirt?"

"Mad woman, Ayesha is just an excuse to stay close to you. You'll always be my first and forever love." Abhi said, placing one hand over his heart and looking bashful.

Gayatri landed a punch on his shoulder and gave out a little laugh.

"Drama queen. C'mon now. Take your position and behave." She said while moving away from him.

Varun observed their antics and felt a little pang at their easy camaraderie. He was just wishing for such a comfortable equation between them as well, when her wandering eyes landed on him. For a second, he saw his own expressions of longing mirrored in them, before it turned to indifference. Maybe he had totally imagined it, but it felt good nonetheless.

Squaring her shoulders, she said, "Varun, if you could take the position here please."

Her hand was pointing at a space a few feet away from Abhi. Varun shrugged and moved there, deliberating keeping some space between them. She probably misunderstood his move because an irritated 'tch tch' escaped her mouth. Rolling her eyes, she grabbed his elbow and moved him to the intended spot. Immediately, a spark ran through his body and he jerked his head down to look at her. There was no mistaking the hitch in her breath and the yearning in her eyes this time. How could he be reading it wrong from so close? The green of her irises, the ones he had come to associate with long pastured fields; the ones that always made him feel like he was running through or laying down on endless land while soaking in the infinitely stretching sky, were boring into his eyes, with a mixture of regret, anger and wistfulness.

"Alexa, play." She shouted, jerking her hand away, averting her eyes and quickly distancing herself from him.

As the starting notes began playing, she called out again, "Alexa, reduce volume."

"Let's start from the top." Her voice took on a commanding tone. "Rishi, you will have your back turned towards the audience. Tap your feet and move your hands, first the right one, then the left one, from top to bottom while clicking your fingers. Until the first *Hey Ya*. At that you turn your face to the right side, without turning your body. Like this." She turned around, with only the right side of her face towards them and half her face visible. "On the second *Hey Ya*, you do the same for the left side. Then you turn around with a jump as the third *Hey Ya* comes and the actual lyrics begin. Clear?"

As Rishi nodded enthusiastically, she looked towards the rest of the group, "You all will be facing the audience, your eyes should be on the bride in the front row while the initial lyrics which sound like a mantra plays. Lip sync to them while moving your hands as if you're doing an aarti," she stopped here and turned to Abhi, "Have the props been arranged?" She went on as he nodded, "Okay, so you will have actual aarti plates in your hands. You will be holding them as you take your positions before the song begins. Once the first two lines are done, keep them aside and do the jap[42] step as *Shubhmangal Savadhan* plays out."

Her audience looked confused, so she elaborated, "Remember the hook step from *Bhool Bhulaiyaa*? Cut out the flute playing thing from that and do only this one where he is chanting with his fists half closed."

Varun knew Gayatri was an amazing dancer, but it was his first time seeing her in the choreographer mode. As he looked around at his cousins,

---

[42] *Hindi term which means prayer*

smiling and nodding their faces while apprehension dawned on them, he marvelled at her ability to make the steps so simple for every age group.

"You continue doing that while swaying your body as if in a trance, till Rishi turns to face the audience." She finished her instructions and shouted out, "Alexa, pause."

"Shall we all do it with the music and lyrics now?" When everyone nodded enthusiastically, she shouted out. "Alexa, play from the start."

Everyone did as they had been taught while Gayatri moved between them, correcting their postures.

As luck would have it when the lyrics *Doli Baarat Sajake Dulha, Cha Raha Hai* played out, she was next to Varun.

Their eyes collided; raging fire against pasture fields. He smiled while moving his hands in a circular motion around her face, mouthing out a sorry, pretending as if he was praying for her forgiveness. When he forgot to do the jap step as *Shubhmangal Savadhan* came on, she reached out to him, holding his gaze and guided him to the next step.

Her hands were on each of his elbows. He could have bet his much-loving job on her feeling the same way he did. It couldn't be that the scintillating feeling on his skin was one-sided. She mouthed out 'It's okay' as a smile played across her lips and a blush was visible on her cheeks.

She quickly let go and turned to go to the front. As she began teaching them the next steps, Varun couldn't help but notice that she wasn't avoiding looking his way anymore. The stiffness and cold aura felt reduced too.

Maybe all wasn't lost yet.

Maybe I'm not the bridge after all.

He found himself daydreaming despite knowing she was dating someone else now.

***

The Little Things (In Big Countries)

"It might be that movies are not close to real life. But for some, they're what makes life bearable, and sometimes, even better."

- Varun Agarwal

October 2018

"How long have you been doing this?"

"For about five years."

"And why, may I ask?"

"Oh c'mon. You're not a cinephile so obviously you would find this ridiculous. This is an iconic movie holding the record for the longest running film in a theatre."

"So you watch it every year?"

Varun found it hard to ignore the scoff on Anusha's face. Curbing the urge to shake her and reminding himself to be chivalrous, he replied as politely as possible, "Not just any random day. Only on the movie's anniversary."

She snorted out a derisive laugh while adding, "I can smell something fishy here and just because I want to know more about this weird obsession, I'll join you."

Varun was out for dinner at Swati Snacks with Anusha, Abhay and Vikas. They were meeting after a long time. In fact for the first time in person post passing out from Welingkar and starting their individual professional journeys. After a sumptuous meal consisting of the most popular dishes at the restaurant, the group were about to disperse when Anusha asked everyone what their weekend plans were and suggested they could do something together. That's when Varun told everyone he was catching the morning show of *Dilwale Dulhaniya Le Jaayenge* at Maratha Mandir. He extended an invitation to whoever was willing to join him.

"I have other plans." Abhay backed out apologising, while looking thoroughly displeased.

"I have a social event to attend as well." Vikas said.

But Anusha wanted to know more and after getting her curiosity curbed, or rather piqued, agreed to join him.

They dispersed for the night and met up the following morning outside the iconic theatre. Varun was collecting their tickets from the counter when he heard Anusha squeal.

"What a small world! What are you doing here? I thought I was the only one with a crazy cinephile friend."

A peal of laughter and a scoff were followed by Anusha's statement. Varun's ears perked up in disbelief and pleasant surprise. He knew that laughter. It had been tinkling in his ears for months, along with those pasture fields eyes.

"Oh, you're not alone. Apparently, today is the movie's anniversary and this woman has been coming to watch it on this date for many years. The things we do for friendship!"

This was another familiar voice he'd grown to like in the past year. But it was what this second voice had just declared that made Varun turn around, shocked and with a hope, he felt growing every second. Did she say *many years*? Does this mean what I think it does? He curbed his expectations and smiled at Ayesha as she was hi-fiving Anusha.

"This is a pleasant surprise. And where is my little brother?" he said while giving her a side hug.

"Preparing for interviews and GRE," Ayesha said, rolling her eyes.

"Of course," he chuckled as they broke the hug.

There was no more delaying the inevitable after this. He turned to look at the green eyes, which were looking at him curiously.

"Hello, Gayatri. How are you?" The thumping of his heart and the battle raging between his practical and dreamy mind, belied the calm smile on his face. He also hoped the slight tremor in his voice wasn't doubt inducing.

"Umm, hello…"

Was it his imagination or did she look a little disheartened?

"I'm fine." Her voice sounded excited but her smile was a bit constrained.

Anusha and Ayesha were talking animatedly and even exchanged numbers. Apparently, being friends with weird movie buffs had made them instant BFFs.

Gayatri pulled at Ayesha's sleeve, indicating they should get moving.

As the girls waved a quick goodbye and moved toward the movie hall, Varun heard her whisper, "I don't want to miss the beginning."

"Oi, lover boy. Shall we also go or do you want to stand here admiring your could-have-been Simran?" Anusha's question made him avert his gaze from the retreating figures of Ayesha and Gayatri.

Varun draped his hand over Anusha's shoulder as they made their way into the hall. The lights were already off and a commercial was playing on the screen. They hunted for their seats for a few minutes and settled down once the Yash Raj film's music came on.

Once the movie started, what Varun had anticipated and hoped for soon came true. The theatre was fairly full and he had tried searching for Gayatri and Ayesha before taking his seat. Of course, that had been futile in the semi-dark hall. A few minutes into the movie though, he heard the excited voice he had been hoping to fall on his ears; not just today. But for years.

Apna hai ya begaana hai wo

Sach hai ya koi afasaana hai wo

Dekhe ghur ghur ke, yun hi dur dur se

Us se kaho meri neend na churaaye

She was singing along to the lyrics of the actress's entry song while bouncing in her seat. He knew the voice well. Sure, it didn't sound childish anymore. But there was no mistaking the similarity it held to the one in his memory, from years ago.

Tera deewaana hun kehta hai wo

Chhup chhup ke fir kyo rahata hai wo

Kar baithha bhul wo, le aya ful wo

Us se kaho jaye chaand le ke ae

Her singing continued and Varun was left feeling climactic.

All of it; his repeat visits to Maratha Mandir since that year, his diminishing hope every year when he failed to find the girl he'd come hoping to run into again, his growing infatuation towards Avni ever since her increased melodrama and love for everything filmy. It was never about Gayatri replacing Avni.

He sat through the rest of the first half of the movie, planning his next move. The smile on his face never left, earning him curious glances from Anusha.

Once the scene before the intermission came on, he quickly typed in a message to Ayesha.

"Meet me at the food counter outside. Alone. I'll ask Anusha to give Gayatri company."

"Oooh, interesting. I hope this doesn't involve me getting abducted… or anyone getting abducted.. wait, maybe we can abduct Gayatri together? She deserves it for making me watch this movie!"

"Nobody is getting abducted.. well, depends on how you define 'abduction'. Hurry! The intermission has started. See you."

He didn't wait to see her reply and pocketed his phone. Asking Anusha to stay with Gayatri and earning a cynical look in response, he moved out of the hall, almost sprinting to the food counter.

Thankfully, Ayesha was already there, saving him precious time. He told her what he had in mind as they ordered popcorn and samosas. Of course, she had a tongue-in-cheek response to the whole thing.

"Man, you two deserve each other. So corny this is."

"Right, and kissing in college in front of hundreds of students including a professor is regular I guess?"

That earned him a punch on the shoulder, but they both laughed at the memory of how Ayesha and Abhi had got together.

"Must be an Agarwal thing," Ayesha said. Her response made him remember something important. Though he had an idea, he had to confirm his doubts.

"Her and Kartik though…"

"Oh that's history. It lasted only a few dates." They moved towards the hall and she made to walk towards her seat. "Anyway, all the best."

He smiled and mouthed a thank you, while sauntering towards his own seat. Anusha looked ready to bombard him with questions as she walked back towards their seats. But he was saved from the accusation and inquiries because the movie restarted even before she sat down.

The rest of the movie passed in eager anticipation. If ever there was a time when he wanted the moments to glide by quickly, this would top the list. The only thing that kept his impatience in check was Gayatri's bursts of whoop, whistles and laughter during her favourite scenes and songs. It was like watching a movie within a movie.

They were soon at the iconic climax scene of the film.

"Jaa Simran Jaa....Jee le apni zindagi..."

Gayatri's enactment of the actor's words could be heard loud and clear now. He smiled remembering how the emotion that voice carried had instantly endeared him back in 2014.

"C'mon Simran, run faster. Yes, girl. You can do this."

She was now bouncing in her seat, cheering for the female actor. Varun's heart grew warmer with increasing affection. It was as if he had been transported back in time.

Pheweep!

Pheweep!

Pheweep!

There were three cheerful and loud whistles, followed by claps and whooping. Varun quickly got up from his seat. This was his cue. As expected, he heard Gayatri say,

"Quick, Ayu. Go to the other end of the hall."

Ayesha passed him an imperceptible sly smile as she moved towards where Gayatri had directed. Once there, she stood at the spot for a few seconds till Gayatri began running towards her from the other end of the hall. She moved away as Gayatri drew closer. There was a thundering look on Gayatri's face for a second; one of anger and betrayal. This was soon replaced by shock as Ayesha's place was taken by somebody else; a towering figure with raging fire eyes. Varun knew she was too deep into her running stride to be able to stop now. He spread his arms out wide, inviting her to him.

As the distance between the actors on the screen closed, the ones off screen held their breath, keeping their eyes locked on each other. He was all ready to lose himself in the pasture fields and when she fell into his embrace, it was like he'd found his home. He enveloped her tightly, sniffing in the familiar scent of her hair.

"Bade bade deshon mein aisi choti choti baatein hoti rehti hai, Senorita," he mumbled and instantly felt her grip around him reinforce. There was no hesitance in the way her hands clutched the circumference of his chest. He picked her up and swirled her in his arms as she let out a surprised yet delighted squeal.

"I knew it! I knew there had to be a bigger, deeper reason for you to keep doing this every year," Anusha said while landing a thump on his back.

Reluctantly, he put Gayatri down as the two broke apart and exited the hall with Ayesha and Anusha in tow. Gayatri's gaze as she looked up at him was full of curiosity, hopes and promises.

Varun landed a kiss on her forehead, while smiling and said teasingly, "Koi bhi ullu ka patha sirf kuch dates pe leja kar tumko mujhse nahi cheen sakta ... tum meri ho, sirf meri."[43]

She laughed but the questions were still on the tip of her tongue. She was about to open her mouth to blurt them out but he shut her with a quick peck while winking mischievously.

There was time to answer all her questions and curb her inquisitiveness. Right now though, he wanted to relish the joy of finding their way to each other. Again. Finally.

---

[43] *Replica of a similar dialogue from the movie Dilwale Dulhaniya Le Jayenge. It roughly translates to, "No idiot can snatch you from me by taking you on a few dates.. you're mine, only mine"*

He Said, She Said

"There are so many ifs, buts and conditions attached to relationships. Why don't people make a disclaimer, an agreement or contract of sorts, for that?"

- Gayatri Kulkarni

November 2019

"Trouble in paradise?" Gayatri asked, observing the deepening frown on Ayesha's face, as the latter read a text on her phone.

"You can say that," Ayesha answered, pocketing her phone while sighing deeply. "This long distance thing is making things really frustrating. We keep arguing almost all the time."

Gayatri put a consoling hand across Ayesha's shoulder.

"I mean Abhi and I always had our differences but it was so much easier when we could talk it out face to face."

Gayatri could only nod her head sympathetically. They were in the college canteen discussing their final year thesis. Neither of the girls could believe the course was almost over and that they would be graduating in just over a couple of months. Despite Gayatri's initial reluctance, she had quite enjoyed the three years. Besides the course subject and materials, which she found deeply engaging, she owed a lot of her liking to the course, to the girl currently giving her company. The two had developed an unbreakable bond and Ayesha was one of the handful people Gayatri could trust with her eyes closed.

"Leave that. Tell me, what are you planning to do after we pass out?," Gayatri probed Ayesha in a bid to change her mood.

A 'tch' escaped Ayesha's mouth and instantly Gayatri regretted her question. It probably showed on her face, because Ayesha gave her hand a reassuring press and answered, "It's not your fault. Your question only pointed towards another problem where Abhi and I seem to be at an impasse. I want to go to Delhi University for my Master's and he insists I should at least try for Columbia. But, why should I? I mean I have always wanted to go to DU and education abroad has never been my goal."

"Babe, if your priorities are clear then he has to understand," Gayatri opined.

"That's what I've been trying to explain to him. I was hoping we would be able to clear out some things if he came to India during the Christmas break. But it seems he won't be able to make it after all."

"Oh", was all Gayatri could manage as a response to that.

"Anyway, enough about me. Tell me about you. How are things between you and Varun? What have *you* thought about doing after the course?", Ayesha asked, changing the topic while braving a smile.

Gayatri hesitated. She did not want to make her best friend feel jealous. Without delving into too much detail, she replied.

"Things are good," she smiled and added as a sudden realisation hit her, "I can't believe it's been more than a year without any more drama between us."

Ayesha's beaming face put Gayatri's worries to rest. How could she have thought her best friend would be jealous of her love life?

"I'm so happy for you, Gayu. Varun seems to be understanding about your ambitions too," Ayesha said observantly.

Gayatri was about to agree when the ringing of her phone interrupted their talk.

Talk of the devil she smiled and answered the call, putting an end to the *DDLJ* theme ringtone song which reverberated through the canteen.

"Hi," she answered, unable to stop the blush spreading across her cheeks.

"Kullu, are we meeting today? I'll drop by your college if you're still there."

She found his calling her 'Kullu' so endearing. It did things to her heart she couldn't put in words. His justification had been, "Gayu is so everyone! And I can't or won't call you what everyone does. I think I'll call you 'Kullu'. You know short for Kulkarni." And that was it.

Shaking herself out of her thoughts, she replied, "Yes, I'm still at Mithibai. Ayesha and I are in the canteen."

"Great, I'll pick you guys up in some time. Can you wait outside the canteen? I'll be there in 10 minutes as per Google aunty."

She chuckled, "Sure. See you," and ended the call.

"Gayu, you guys carry on. I think I'll just head home," Ayesha looked harried.

Gayatri was quick to decipher that Ayesha didn't want to be with Varun. Probably because he reminded her of Abhi and it would only add to her anxieties.

"Hey, no worries. I understand," Gayatri said emphatically while the two of them moved out of the canteen.

As she saw Ayesha's retrieving figure after they bid each other goodbye, Gayatri's heart reached out to her friend. Alongside it though, she couldn't help feeling a bit relieved about her own smooth-flowing relationship.

Agreed that she and Varun had their own bit of drama. But they were together now and more importantly, they were happy.

Right on cue, a horn honked to her left. The black Honda Amaze and the smiling face beckoning her from behind its steering wheel, were a sight for her sore eyes. The fact that Mithibai became a detour for Varun enroute Ogilvy in Andheri to his residence in Dadar didn't bother him from picking her up from college almost every alternate day. They ended up meeting each other after his office timings and he generally dropped her off at Andheri station before continuing on his way home. Sometimes they would also have dinner together before taking their separate routes home. Today was just another one of those days.

Quickly, Gayatri opened the passenger door and settled in, drinking in his debonair office look. He soon changed the gears and put the car in motion, driving away from Mithibai College. The cinching up of his left brow and the curling of his lips were a predictable reaction as he gazed at her inquiringly.

"Yes, yes. You look great," she relented with a chuckle. To be fair, it wasn't a lie either. The grey shirt and dark blue trousers suited him just fine, complementing his fair skin and jet-black hair.

He chortled while giving her a look over when they were at a traffic signal. Then bent towards her over the console and landed a kiss on her lips. It was so unexpected that her responding huff got lost in his mouth and quickly turned into a moan.

"You don't look so bad yourself, Kullu, " he whispered in between mouthfuls of devouring her lips with his own lips and tongue.

A blush crept up her face as she half-heartedly tried to push him away while blurting out in mock hurt, "I don't need your *bheekh mein diye hue* [44] compliments. I know I look amazing."

After a second, while taking in heavy breaths, she added to drive home her point home, "As always."

She felt his answering smile on her lips and it was all she needed to give in with equal fervour. One of her hands automatically reached out to caress the exposed skin on top of his shirt while the other wound its way into his hair. Her lips parted hungrily to give him better access while her tongue entwined with his, wanting to explore every bit of his mouth. Even after doing this multiple times over the past year, she was amazed by the response his touch had on her body. Her level of arousal was frankly embarrassing in the beginning, but he soon made her feel comfortable enough. With his own desire writ large in the manner his hand moved over her neck and thighs, as it currently did, she knew their passions matched.

An incessant honking brought Gayatri to the present, reminding her of their whereabouts. With a quick peck, she gently pushed him away saying, "The car signal is green, so the love signal has to be red."

Settling back in her seat, she gave him a sideways look while winking mischievously, and added, "For now."

Varun's answering snigger as he put the car in motion again, was cut off by two simultaneous noises; one from his phone's incoming call ringtone, which sounded doubly loud because it was connected to the car's stereo. And the second from Gayatri's phone, which had pinged her a new email notification.

Gayatri checked the home screen of her cell phone with trepidation. Before opening the full mail, she wanted to ensure it was the one she'd been anticipating for the past few days.

"Hi dear, where are you? When will you be reaching home?"

Radha's voice on the car speaker broke Gayatri's concentration. Varun mouthed her to keep quiet as he answered, "I'm on my way home, maa. What happened?"

---

[44] *Hindi words which roughly translate to, "Given in alms"*

Gayatri's hand hovered over the mail in anxiety. Yes, it was the mail she had been looking forward to. Suddenly though, she was filled with uncertainty on whether to open it or not.

The subject line said ***Re: Status of Your Application.*** Who keeps it like that? Why can't they have subject lines with a yes or no? She mulled as Radha spoke, "Nothing urgent. We had some news to share and your father was hoping to do it in person."

"Maa, stop with the suspense. What is it? Tell me." Varun sounded exasperated. Gayatri gave him a disapproving look and he pointed towards the phone in her hand inquiringly.

She shrugged, her fingers still hanging over the notification. Varun snatched the phone from her impatiently and opened the mail, scrolling through the contents quickly.

"Hello? Are you there?" Radha's question made Varun hand back the phone to Gayatri hastily as he replied, "I'm here, maa. You had some news to share. I am waiting for you to continue."

"We received a wedding invitation from the Mehtas. Did you know Avni is getting married?"

Varun let out an agitated 'tch'. Gayatri tried to look distracted while reading the contents of the mail that Varun had opened. The words were a blur to her because of her rapidly racing heart. Was it because of the mail or because of what Radha had said? She couldn't quite put her finger on the cause anymore.

Gayatri was jerked forward by a sudden jolt resulting from Varun's unanticipated hitting on the car's brakes. This was followed by a few honks as Varun tried to overtake the vehicle blocking their way. A few choice words Gayatri had rarely heard from his mouth before flew out as Varun succeeded in swiftly swerving the car right and then left before overtaking the vehicle in front of their car.

"No, maa. We're not in touch so how would I know?", Varun replied tersely. Was the bitterness in his voice an indication of jealousy? Gayatri took a deep sigh and commanded her mind to focus on what the mail said.

Dear Miss Kulkarni,

Thank you for your application.

After a thorough look at your resume and accomplishments, we are pleased to inform you of our decision to take things ahead.

However, we'd like for you to come down to our Pune office for further discussions to decide on a probable profile that fits your skill set. The location for the job will also be determined during this meeting. However, we'd like to intimate you that there are high chances of the job being based out of Pune.

Looking forward to hearing from you.

We need someone like you on the team and would be delighted if you reply in the affirmative.

Regards,
Minal Haldwani

Jr. HR Manager (Recruitment & Training)

Adfactors

"But I was under the impression that Avni and Varun like each other…", Shyam Agarwal's voice came through as Radha interrupted and said, "Varun, please talk to your father."

"Avni and I are just friends, papa. We don't even talk anymore." Varun was curt but Gayatri didn't miss the edge in his voice.

"Fine, come home first. Your mother and I would like to talk to you about your future, specifically your marriage. This discussion isn't over," Shyam said gruffly and hung up.

The elation that had ballooned up her heart on reading the mail got pricked inch by inch, as the discussion between the Agarwals had gone by. As she looked at Varun now, his expression was inscrutable. It was the first time in the past year that she was unable to gauge what was going through his mind.

She had questions and thoughts of her own racing through her scattered brain.

If Varun's parents were thinking about Avni in that manner, maybe he still has feelings for her. They can't be having such doubts without reason.

If they're already thinking about his marriage, does he want to get married too? But I haven't begun my career yet and I'm really not willing to get into matrimony at 20.

What about this job opportunity in Pune?

"This long distance thing is making things really frustrating. We keep arguing almost all the time."

Ayesha's words from a while ago ran through her mind.

"If your priorities are clear then he has to understand" She recalled her own response to it and cleared her throat.

When Varun looked at her inquiringly, she pointed to her phone and said, "That was Adfactors' mail. They have asked me to come to Pune to discuss my profile and location."

She expected a 'Congratulations' or at least a smile, but Varun continued to look out the windshield, driving with a stoic expression.

It compelled her to add, "They said the job location might be Pune."

He sighed and nodded imperceptibly.

"Can you not look at job options in Mumbai itself?"

"If your priorities are clear then he has to understand"

"Varun seems to be understanding about your ambitions"

She remained silent as they neared Andheri station and he stopped the car for her to get down.

"I can." She replied while getting out. "But not without giving this opportunity a try first."

She turned and walked away without bidding him good night. With a pang, she also noted that he didn't kiss her like he generally did before she got out of the car.

All the way home, on the train, and then in the rickshaw, she kept hoping Ayesha's assumption *"Varun seems to be understanding about your ambitions"* did not prove to be wrong.

If it did, she was clear about what she needed to do.

***

Change(d)

"A sheltered life keeps you safe, protected and maybe even happy. But moving away from it is what enables you to truly find yourself and create your own happiness."

\- Varun Agarwal

February 2020

"Yes, I'm well settled now, maa. You don't need to worry. The food is also good. I mean it's nothing compared to your cooking which I'm used to but it's not terrible at least."

Varun walked into his rented flat in Navratna Apartment and threw his office bag across the sofa while taking his shoes off. Like most evenings since moving to Pune, Radha had called to ask how the new job and city were treating him.

"Why don't you hire a cook instead of opting for tiffin service?" Radha's worries were ceaseless.

Varun chuckled remembering how she had fussed over Abhi when he was moving to the US for further studies. This was a mellowed-down version in comparison.

"That's what I intend to do, maa. I have asked a few neighbours and some colleagues if they know someone. I'm sure I'll find a good cook soon. Till then I'll manage with this tiffin service."

After stacking his shoes on the shoe rack and stuffing his socks inside them, he sauntered to the sofa and plopped down. He was thankful he didn't need to hunt around for basic furniture like a sofa, bed, or even a shoe rack. The apartment was well furnished. The kitchen too had all the basic cutlery like a few dishes, bowls, and some cooking utensils. He purchased the second-hand fridge in the corner of the small kitchen a few days back. It was a quick decision after realising how essential it was to have one when he didn't know what to do with the leftovers from the tiffin. He certainly didn't want to let it go to waste. So a fridge acquisition hunt had begun the next day leading to solving his lunch issues. The tiffin he received every night sufficed for dinner as well as lunch the following day. He only needed to buy a couple of rotis from the food court at his workplace. He preferred eating the leftover sabzi[45] with it over any other fast food available there.

As for the other electronics, he figured he'd be able to buy a washing machine next week. And a microwave, if need be, in the following days. As for the TV, he had the good sense to bring along the one from his bedroom back in Mumbai. Packing it up and driving with it to Pune during his moveout hadn't been much of a hassle. He had already ordered a replacement for the one in Mumbai. One of the best things about working in Mumbai for over a year was that he had saved up a lot and it was all coming to good use now.

Once everything was packed and ready, which was only a few bags and the TV box, he decided to leave Mumbai and stayed with a friend for a week as he hunted for a place of his own. Smartly, he had made the move to Pune before his new job at the Amazon office started. So he had time on hand and luckily, he found a good apartment on his fifth day in the city itself. It was love at first sight when he walked into the flat at Navratna Apartment for the first time. The fact that its location was in same vicinity as his office, only worked as an add-on. The ten minute drive to and from Amazon in Commerzone IT Park, felt like a joke when compared to his daily work commute to Ogilvy in Mumbai.

As he looked around the hall and the kitchen of the sparsely furnished small 1BHK, he felt at home. He was finally satisfied with his decision to make the switch from Ogilvy to Amazon despite the little hesitance he felt about moving out of his home turf. He was finally beginning to understand what Abhi meant when he talked relentlessly about loving the freedom of being on his own. He was settling down in his new job quite well too. The team and his profile were exciting.

Bidding his mother goodnight, he picked up the TV remote and flicked through the apps on the home screen.

He clicked on YouTube and almost did a double flip at one of the videos that showed up on the screen. Since moving to the US, his little brother had taken up vlogging and his recent upload was what had caused Varun's eyes to almost fall out of their sockets.

---

[45] *A Hindi term for a dish. Sabzi, or subji, simply defines a* **"vegetable dish."** *Sabzi comes from the Persian word sabz, which means green, and is similar to the English expression "greens." However, all vegetables can be included in a sabzi, and the preparation can take many forms, such as serving it with or without liquid.*

Intuitively he pressed the play button and the lyrics of *Bang Bang* reverberated through the house. The two figures on the screen swayed and moved to the upbeat music of the song. The girl in particular would be able to hold any viewer's attention with her grace, flexibility, and oomph.

Once the steamy performance ended, Abhi's face showed up on the screen. He was smiling from ear to ear as he said, "The girl you saw in the video with me has started taking online dance classes. You can contact her on her socials under the name *G's Jhankaar,* through the links in the pinned comments. Thank you for watching."

Good for her! Varun thought bitterly. Luckily the bell dinged at that moment forcing him out of the wormhole he was sure to get sucked into.

After collecting the tiffin and settling in front of the TV again, despite his best efforts to distract himself, he found his thoughts straying to the events of the past year.

"We belong to different worlds, Varun."

That was it. That was her justification and explanation for going MIA.

All four years of acquaintance and one year of a steady relationship were summed up in a single sentence. Deep down he knew there was some substance to what she said. But he felt like he deserved some credit for laying his parents off from meddling in his personal choices. Varun had put his foot down saying he'd marry in his time and with a girl he liked when Shyam had suggested a few of his friends' daughters names as an ideal match for Varun. Rather, ideal for their family, matching the grand Agarwal status and reputation. Varun had stood his ground though, saying he will not marry to make them happy because it was about his life and not theirs. His move to Pune a few months after that showdown had been a ripple effect of that. The environment in the Agarwal residence was getting stifling for him. It was especially frustrating because Gayatri had refused to continue their relationship for a long distance. No explanation was given except that she was starting a new phase in her life and did not think they were compatible.

Radha had been understanding about it all; Varun's dissent towards matrimony and then his decision to move out of Mumbai. But there was still some friction between Varun and Shyam.

For whom did he do all of this? Okay, maybe more for himself. But his thoughts and action had been around Gayatri as well. He knew she needed time and he'd bargained for it. In his mind, he already envisioned a future with her, including marriage and kids.

But no, *Miss I-want-to-be-independent* and *what-about-my career* had other plans. He shoved the food down his throat not registering the taste of anything he ate.

He had a fitful night that day, fleeting in and out of sleep, trying to push the anger and regret out of his system.

"*Mr. Mature* and *I-know-better-than-her*, have you forgotten the main reason for moving to Pune?" His inner know-it-all kept chiding him all the while as he tossed and turned in bed.

***

Varun was glad he had his job and work deadlines to keep himself distracted. It kept him occupied over the next couple of weeks and he only fleetingly thought of his, *down in the drains*, personal life, rather his love life.

One evening, he was whistling away, scrolling through his phone, and waiting for the elevator after a particularly productive day. When it dinged, he entered without looking up. The aroma that engulfed him felt oddly familiar but it was the sharp intake of breath that made him look up.

Of course! Given their history, he had been expecting an accidental bump in like this. Even hoping for it on some level. But none of it had prepared him for the rush of feelings to be so overpowering. Why was he angry at her? What had made them fall apart again? All of it seemed inconsequential as his eyes bore into hers. The pasture fields were just as inviting as he remembered. They carried an expression of disbelief, hurt and…was that relief?

Before he could register anything else besides her grey figure-hugging yoga pants and matching sleeveless top, she rushed forth and threw herself on him. The impact of her ambush led to a collision with the elevator's wall and the car shook wildly. His hands were in her hair and he was just soaking in the snug comfort, commanding his body to keep the slowly mounting arousal in check when he felt her shaking against his body. Was she crying?

He got his answer when she let out a sniff a few seconds later. He had never been good at handling emotions, neither his own, nor that of others. Having no idea what else to do, he simply tried consoling her by moving his hand up and down her back. The sniffing and shaking continued, so he added expressions like 'shhhh' and 'it's okay' while patting the top of her head and her back. When the elevator arrived at the ground level, she stayed that way, refusing to let go of her tight clutch on his shirt, while her sobbing continued.

Varun walked out, gently dragging Gayatri along. He led her towards his car with his arms possessively around her waist and shoulder. Her sobbing had subsided, but she held onto his shirt as if holding on for dear life. His own mind was a maze of worries and unpleasant thoughts as he wondered what had led to her breaking down like this. The bigger worry was, what would have happened if they hadn't run into each other like this?

He helped her settle down in the car and they drove in silence. Keeping his gaze on the road, from the corner of his eyes, he noticed her leaning her head against the window and looking listlessly ahead. Silent tears continued to run down her cheeks. He was about to ask where to drop her, when Gayatri's phone rang and she answered it with trembling hands.

There was no response from her besides 'hmm', 'okay', 'yes', 'no' and finally 'bye, good night'. Varun was pretty sure the person on the other end was Sharad and somewhere behind him, Varun also heard a female voice which he figured to be Uma. Gayatri hung up, and with her face turned away as she gazed out the window, requested in a tired and timid voice, "Can I stay with you tonight?"

Varun anyway didn't feel like leaving her alone when she was in such a pensive mood. He cleared his throat and croaked, "Yes, of course."

After a while, she began in a low voice, "Baba is showing symptoms of COVID-19. I kept telling him to avoid meeting people. Aai and bhav also warned him so much. But no." Her voice choked up and she continued after a sniff, "He was all 'My friend is here after so many years. It doesn't look nice'. The guidelines clearly told us to avoid meeting people with a travel history. With his premorbid health, it's no wonder he got affected." Her voice carried such pain and anger, he was surprised she wasn't smashing through the car's window. It took all his self-restraint not to reach out and give her hand a reassuring press or comfort her physically in any manner.

Varun had not met Shishir Kulkarni beyond a couple of social occasions. Even in those instances, they had never exchanged more than a hello. Whatever he knew about the older man, was majorly through Gayatri, and somewhat from Radha and Abhi. His heart reached out to Uma, who he was sure must be torn and fraught with worry.

"I am so sorry to hear that. Can I help in any manner? My parents can reach out."

She merely shook her head, looking at him helplessly and then turned her face to the other side. Her sniffing was the only sound in the car for a while. Once they reached Varun's apartment complex, they got out and walked into his house in silence. Gayatri's eyes moved absently over the flat as she took off her footwear. Then she dragged herself to the sofa and settled down with a thud. Leaning her head against the backrest, she closed her eyes and stayed that way, immobile and silent. Varun walked over to the sofa carrying a glass of water. The movement must have alerted her as she opened her eyes and looked at him with tear-filled eyes.

"He'll be fine, right?" She asked falteringly, then taking the glass from his hand, she gulped the water down in one stroke.

"He has to be fine." She answered her own question, her eyes darting here and there while pushing the glass toward his outstretched hand. Varun settled down next to her, consciously keeping a distance between them.

She kept mumbling, rocking her body back and forth while hugging herself and running her hands through her hair intermittently.

"Hey, it'll be okay. When was the last time you ate? You look tired. Why don't you have something and then lie down for a while?" Varun asked, taking in her drawn face and slouched shoulders.

"I don't remember. I had lunch around 2 p.m. Then a cup of coffee before leaving work and coming to the Amazon office. They wanted to discuss a probable dance class collaboration for the employees. The HR then asked me to check out the studio and use it for a bit to get an overall feel."

This was good. At least she was talking now instead of fretting about Shishir. Varun's ploy to distract her had worked. He got up to get something for her to eat as she continued.

"It's a great studio they have in-house. I changed and danced for a bit before a few people from the HR team came and joined me. It was a fun practice session while it lasted. The call came in right after we finalised my commercials and fixed a date and time for the first session in the coming week. I was so happy…" Her voice broke. "And then… Sharad called and told me baba was unwell… they got the tests done and the doctors were pretty sure it was COVID-19…everything was a haze after I heard those words…Sharad said baba was running a fever and constantly coughing, having difficulty breathing.. he hung up saying he'll update with more details later." Tears were rolling down her cheeks now. "I don't know how and what I told the HR employees as I excused myself and got into the lift…when I saw you, I thought I was imagining it. But you were really there and it was all I needed to lose control and reality to hit me hard."

Varun rushed forth with an apple in his hand. Throwing it aside on the sofa, he enveloped her in a hug and rocked her back and forth. She was bawling loudly while saying "I should have been there" and "I could have stopped him."

Varun pulled her face up to look at him, "Listen to me. Do not feel guilty, okay? You already said he didn't listen to Sharad and your mom. I don't think he would have listened to you either. You hear me? It's not your fault, okay?"

She nodded and buried her face in his chest again. His shirt was soaked with tears that refused to stop. He tried to move away but she held on tight, so he had to chuckle and say, "Not that I mind this" he grabbed her face, holding it between his palms, and tucked her hair behind her ears. "I don't know about you but I'm really hungry."

He grabbed the apple beside him and bit into it, then offered it to her. When she shook her head, he grunted angrily. That brought on a faint smile on her face as she took it and started taking large bites.

"Good girl," He said approvingly and turned on the TV, while leaning back into the sofa and getting comfortable. The news channel came on where Prime Minister Narendra Modi's announcement about the Janta Curfew on the following day was being replayed.

"I want to go home," Gayatri said wistfully, staring at the screen as she took another bite.

Varun looked at her incredulously. The expression on her face stopped him from saying anything. It was a look of defeat; a look similar to that of a soldier who knows he has lost the war but has to continue fighting till his last breath anyway.

"I know how risky that is and how it would be of no use or how it will only add to our worries." She looked away and continued, her voice breaking a bit again. "If something happens…I want to be with him, hold his hand and assure him it's going to be fine…"

Varun reached out and pressed a reassuring hand on her shoulder. He let out an involuntary sigh at his own helpless state in the situation. What more could he do besides telling her it'll be fine or that her father will push through when they both knew that the chances of that were slim? The thought made him feel shallow but he knew from the news channels and a few colleagues that whoever had contracted the virus so far, especially senior citizens and those with already low immunity, had not survived. He could only hope and pray that Shishir's body fought the virus off and that he would be fit and fine soon.

Varun ordered dinner after a while. The tiffin services had been called off indefinitely because one of the delivery men had tested positive. He then ordered some groceries too, figuring they would need them for the coming day and his limited stock wouldn't do for two people. He wasn't sure if food deliveries from restaurants would be open and allowed for long either. It was better to be prepared for the worst so he ordered everything in bulk.

A couple of hours later, Gayatri retired to the bedroom to sleep while he flicked through channels absently. It had taken some convincing but she had finally relented to his pleas. They had dinner a while back and he had to literally order her to sleep while snatching her phone away. He himself rubbed his eyes and switched the TV off, while still wondering how uncomfortable sleeping on the couch would be. Soon enough though, the fatigue took over and he dozed off.

***

When he woke up the next day, he found himself in a sleeping position with a blanket covering his body. The thought of Gayatri's tiny self, adjusting his body in a sleeping position, and then covering it with a blanket, brought on an immediate smile, and a warmth spread through his being.

Most of the morning went by preparing breakfast and then some lunch together while watching TV in between the food preparation and then eating lunch and breakfast. Varun consciously kept away from news channels sensing Gayatri's discomfiture whenever they showed footage or figures related to COVID-19. They ended up watching F.R.I.E.N.D.S. till the afternoon and then switched to another sitcom.

In a particular episode of The Big Bang Theory, the lead female character, Penny, suddenly has a moment of self-realisation and says, "Oh my God, I need help." Immediately, Gayatri looked down at herself, sniffed her clothes and a disgusted look crossed her face.

"I need to bathe and change."

She had borrowed one of his t-shirts yesterday and worn it over her yoga pants, sleeping off in it. The things it did to Varun's body on seeing her in his clothes could only be termed inappropriate, especially in a time as tense as their current one. Varun had woken up earlier than her, freshened up, showered, and was halfway through making an omelette when she joined him in the kitchen. Breakfast turned to lunch and she hadn't moved from the sofa, still in the same clothes since the previous evening. Varun didn't feel like asking her to change or freshen up, sensing she needed distraction in the form of entertainment.

Presently, he suppressed a laugh and jumped off the sofa. Sprinting towards his wardrobe, he came out in a while holding out a towel, a t-shirt and a pair of boxer shorts.

She grabbed, rather snatched the clothes from his outstretched hands, and went straight to the bathroom. When she emerged out after ten minutes, all damp hair, and with the shorts and T-shirt both reaching up to her knees, covering more than half her body, his mouth fell open. Not only was her face all pink and glowing, inviting his lips to smother it with kisses, but probably because she must have had only that one pair she had worn yesterday, it was clear she wasn't wearing any bra. Her nipples were poking through the T-shirt's fabric and as she shook her head, running her hands through her moist hair, her bosom shook freely, stirring his manhood. The fact that the droplets landing on the fabric made the T-shirt see-through, accentuating the roundness of her mounds and hips, not leaving much to the imagination, or rather, drove his imagination further wild, was no help.

Oblivious to her effect on him, she hummed a tune, completely engrossed in untangling her hair with her fingers, and asked, "Do you have a hair dryer by any chance?"

He gulped, with his throat running drier every second, and shook his head. Apparently, he had become incapable of speaking. Not hearing his response and because she wasn't looking at him when he shook his head, she turned her gaze towards him. His breath caught in his throat, but he somehow managed to croak out a hoarse "No".

Turning his face towards the TV, he forced his eyes and mind to concentrate on the screen. She let out an exasperated sigh and walked over to the window, to stand in the sunlight streaming in. Resuming the humming and untangling of her hair, she continued with it for a few minutes while looking out the window. He stole glances at her, taking in her sun kissed face and hair, and couldn't help his mind from mentally playing the song *Maula mere maula*. He hummed *Zulfe teri itni ghani dekh ke inko ye sochta hoon, saaye mein inki mein jiyoon* while taking in the picture-perfect woman in front of him. She appeared nothing less than a heroine, being the centre of attention of the lead guy, in a song or movie. Or in their case, HIM.

When she quirked up an inquiring eyebrow in his direction, her smug smile, though imperceptible, did not miss his eyes. He quickly grabbed a pillow to hide his obvious arousal and looked away.

What kind of a man would he be if he took advantage of their situational proximity at a time she was vulnerable and needed him for emotional support? The word 'tharki'[46] propped up in his head and he pressed his lips together as a bitter taste ran in his mouth. He didn't realise when she walked up to the sofa and settled next to him. How did she smell this good? She'd used his bathroom and his soap and shampoo, yet she smelled better than he had ever done using the same products. His face was resolutely turned toward the TV screen as he pretended not to notice the miniscule distance between them. Laughing lightly, she snatched the pillow from his lap and dropped a kiss on his cheek, trailing her tongue from the right side of his face, down his throat, to the top of his T-shirt. He groaned with pleasure as his hands wound around her hair, pulling her closer, all his self-restraint going out the window. His own lips landed on her collarbone, licking the water droplets, then sucking on the soft skin as

---

[46] *Hindi term which means lustful*

she mewled. The passage of time and the reasons for them falling apart, all melted away as their bodies meshed against each other, with mounting desire.

Ek zindagi meri sau khwahishan

Main jeena, main jeena, main poori tarah

Main jeena, main jeena, main poori tarah

The ringing of Gayatri's phone broke their spell and they drew apart as a mixture of guilt and pleasure overtook Varun. The change in Gayatri's mood and body posture once she answered the call, was instantaneous. She went rigid as the person on the other end, probably Sharad, talked and Gayatri merely responded with 'Okay' before hanging up.

"He's the same. There is no improvement…" She sounded dejected. Before Varun could reach out a comforting hand, she got up and headed to the bathroom, coming out only after he tapped on the door. Her eyes were red and swollen, an obvious indication that she had been crying all the while.

Not wanting to make her feel further uncomfortable and awkward, he only said, "I've made some tea. Let's have it before it gets cold."

The rest of the day was strained and uneventful, followed by a quiet dinner. Before bidding him goodnight, she asked him if he could leave early for work the next day.

"So that I can pick up my moped from Amazon, and go home first before I drop in to work." She kept fidgeting with the hem of the T-shirt and her eyes had a faraway look as she went on.

"I'll be heading to my place after work tomorrow…umm… thanks for letting me stay here."

With that, she walked in, not giving him a chance, yet again, to express his thoughts and feelings.

He let it be, consoling himself, that, at least this time, she deserved her space.

***

Locked Down

"Maybe being confined to your home and having limited human interaction isn't as dreadful as it is made out to be."

- Varun Agarwal

March 2020 - February 2021

The next couple of days were hectic, work and otherwise. Rumours were rampant about an impending lockdown, adding to the already heightened panic around the novel coronavirus. Following anxiety-ridden calls and warnings from Radha, Varun had stocked up on his groceries, just to get her off his back. Now his apartment had supplies that would last him more than a month. A quarter of it was sanitizers in various forms, right from small squeezy ones for rubbing on the palms, to bigger spray bottles for clothes and furniture. About another quarter of the stock were face masks, both cloth ones and surgical ones.

Many times, he thought of calling up or at least dropping in a text to Gayatri to check up on Shishir's health and even hers or to ask her if she needed anything. But he stopped short, thinking it would be intruding. Somewhere he was also hesitant because he didn't want her to feel incapable of taking care of herself.

Added to this was the fact that he was reminded of her constantly. Even when at home. Somehow her aura still lingered in every corner of the house; on the sofa, in the kitchen, in the bathroom, and most agonisingly, on the bed. He knew that talking to her would only make it harder for him to get the salacious thoughts out of his mind.

On the evening of 24th March, Varun was sitting in front of the TV for the PM's public addressal. Listening to the announcement of a 21 day lockdown, he was just feeling thankful to Radha for strong-arming him into buying everything in bulk, when his phone rang. He didn't look at the screen and picked up without checking who it was. Expecting it to be Radha, he immediately went, "Yes yes. You were right, maa. Thank you. And I'll talk to my boss about going to the office."

When no scoff or "Yeah, fine" came from the other side as a standard response, he checked the caller ID. Why was she calling? Did something happen to Shishir? Is she okay? A gamut of unpleasant thoughts came up in his mind and he prepared himself to question her, when he heard a sniff.

"I… want… to.. go home…" Suddenly the sniffing turned into bawling. It broke his heart into tiny pieces as she drew in long breaths in between her howls. He let her take it all out.

When there was a comparative calm, he asked, "Where are you?"

"At my PG…my housemates have gone home…Sharad said the doctors have given up… it's only a matter of time now…the PMs announcement… I should have left when I could…"

"Shh, don't do that to yourself…" He began but was cut off immediately.

"I have to go, sorry." Just like that the line went dead.

"I'll be fine. Sorry to have bothered you." A text message popped up as soon as he took the phone away from his ear and looked at the screen.

He immediately grabbed his car keys, a cloth mask, a small squeezy bottle of sanitizer, and rushed out. There was only one thing he could do to make her feel better and that was to be with her physically. Being alone at her PG was only going to drown her in further worry and guilt.

He knew she stayed as paying guest in one of the houses at Millennium Society in Wadarwadi. As a way of precaution, after driving her to Amazon, he had followed her moped to ensure she reached home safe. He remembered marvelling at her acuity to find an accommodation so close to the Adfactors office located in Shivajinagar. Presently, he drove in a daze, swerving through the roads, all the while hoping and praying she didn't do anything rash.

The streets were crowded as everyone was out buying medicines and groceries. He swore under his breath, trying to keep his patience in check as he had to slow down or stop the car every few metres. When he finally reached his destination and parked the car outside her house, it was quite late. Hoping that no one complained about a boy's presence at a girl's PG, he pressed the doorbell with trepidation. When no one answered even after five minutes, he had to press it a few more times, with mounting concern. He peeked in through the open window and saw the TV running, but could not spot anyone around. As a last resort, he took his phone out and called her. The ring could be heard from the window and he spotted her cell phone lying on the coffee table in front of the TV.

Where was she? He wondered and pressed the doorbell again. In a state of panic by now, he banged on the door and shouted, "Gayatri, open up. Are you okay? Where are you?"

The door of one of the houses on the opposite side opened and a middle-aged woman walked over. Seeing her cover her mouth with a mask, Varun immediately put on his as well.

"Is there a problem?" Her muffled voice came through as she stood at a little distance from him.

"My friend stays here and I'm worried something is wrong because she is not answering the door or her phone."

"Gayatri Kulkarni?" When Varun nodded, she threw a key in his direction.

As he caught it, she explained, "I'm Shilpa Kelkar, the owner of the house. You can go in and check. Please update me. I'm waiting here."

Varun unlocked the door and rushed in, shouting out, "Gayatri, are you there?"

He walked into the hall, where news headlines from the TV blared out. There was no one on the sofa, on the dining table, or in the kitchen. He rushed into the nearest bedroom, but that was empty too. Then he opened the bathroom and his breath caught in his throat.

There, sprawled out on the floor, with her pyjamas riding up her knees and her hair spread out wildly, lay Gayatri. He went down on his knees and shook her, crying out, "Gayatri, Gayatri. Can you hear me?" When she remained unconscious, he took some water from the basin and threw it on her face.

Her eyes opened and she began coughing incessantly. Hugging her to his chest, he heaved a sigh of relief even as her eyes began to close again. She limped when he tried to help her up. Seeing no other way out, he carried her in his arms and took her out of the house, placing her in the backseat of his car.

"Ma'am, can you tell me which room is hers?" He asked Shilpa, who was witnessing the whole scene with worry and suspicion.

She didn't answer and inquired about who he was and how he was related to Gayatri.

"I'm Varun, an old friend of Gayatri's and I'm taking her with me, ma'am." He answered while repeating his question about Gayatri's room.

"The one on the right-hand side, next to the kitchen is hers," Shilpa informed him, still clearly apprehensive. Varun didn't care about winning her trust at the moment and ran into the house again. Packing up as many clothes as he could in a bag he found in the only wardrobe inside the room, he was out in minutes. He found Shilpa near his car, observing Gayatri's unconscious figure and talking to someone over the phone, "He says his name is Tarun. Can you talk to him please?"

"Varun? Is that you?" Varun heard Sharad's voice as the woman put the phone on speaker.

"Hi, Sharad. Yes, I'm taking Gayatri with me. I guess she must not have had anything to eat and fainted because of weakness and dehydration."

"Okay. Please make her eat something.. and…" His voice broke before he continued, "Baba is…I.. we…"

"Hey, she's fine. I'll take care of her. You and aunty take care of Uncle." Varun said in a consoling tone.

He handed the key to Shilpa and drove back to his apartment. Gayatri lay immobile in the backseat, grunting out broken words and sentences like "I'm coming baba", "I'm here baba" and "Gayu will take care of you baba". When they reached home, he carried her up, not trusting her to stay stable on her feet.

He laid her down on the sofa, covering her up with a blanket. Then he got busy in the kitchen, putting together a quick meal of rice and dal.

Her phone rang when he was serving the dal-rice into two bowls. When she didn't stir, he went forward to answer it and wasn't surprised when he saw Sharad's name on the screen.

"Hello, Sharad. It's Varun." He answered before Sharad assumed it was Gayatri who had answered the call.

"Is she okay? How is she? Can I talk to her?" Sharad blurted out in a single breath.

"She is sleeping. I'll feed her the dal-rice I have just prepared and have her call you back."

Sharad hung up asking him to call without fail once Gayatri was better.

"It's urgent, please," He added before hanging up.

Because the desperation in Sharad's voice lingered on, Varun shook Gayatri awake right away.

"You're at my place. It's okay, you're good." He responded to the look of panic spreading on her face.

She sat up, keeping the blanket curled around her feet and covering her knees.

"Here, please have this first." He held the bowl of dal-rice in front of her and she accepted it with a weak smile. Her hands trembled a bit and he kept his own bowl aside, grabbing hers and feeding her himself. With each spoon that he fed into her mouth, he was glad to see some colour coming back to her face.

It was only after she had some spoonful's and the bowl was almost empty that he said, "Sharad has asked you to call him. He said it's urgent."

She racked her hands through her hair and hugging her knees tight, began to mumble while moving, shaking her head, "No... I can't... I don't want to know... it's bad news.. I know it..."

He kept the bowl aside and rushed to embrace her.

"Hey.. hey.. It's okay. You don't have to if you don't want to."

She hid her face in his chest, clinging to his shirt. It was only when he felt a wetness on the fabric that he realised she was weeping. He drew in a deep breath. Not knowing the right words to make her feel better, he merely comforted her by rubbing and patting her back.

"You know it was baba who told me I could do it. I didn't know if I had it in me to stay away from my family and manage to live by myself. He was all 'Of course you can, thoda vishwas thev[47]'. That was his go-to advice whenever I lost confidence in myself..." She stopped short, looked up into his eyes while drawing in a deep breath with tears streaming down her cheeks. He held her face in his palms, kissing away the tears, and nodding encouragingly.

She heaved heavily as the tears wreaked her body and she continued in a broken voice, "I'm already saying 'was'... I hate myself for accepting that his passing is inevitable...I hate myself for choosing to be away..." A

---

[47] *Marathi words translate to "Have a little faith in yourself"*

huge sob escaped her, and she covered her face with shaking hands. Varun's hands wound around her again as he consoled her and said, 'Shh, it's okay'.

The sounds of his cooing and her weeping were broken by the ringing of her phone. She moved away, wiping the tears rapidly from her face and answered the phone with a tremor in her voice, "He's gone isn't he?" She croaked out.

A howl escaped her mouth and the phone fell from her hands. Varun held it to her ear again but she pushed it away, her chin and lips trembling as her eyes pooled up again. Varun put the phone on speaker. Jumbled noises of choking and sniffling could be heard, then Sharad's voice came through, "They're wrapping up the body. We won't be able to do the last rites either…"

"Gayu, Gayu.. he kept saying he was so proud of you.. and that he only wished to see you one more time but he understood." It was Uma's voice now. "He asked me to keep reminding you *thoda vishwas thev*…"

There was silence on both ends as all the Kulkarnis mourned collectively. The only sounds for a while were of wails, whimpers, sniffs and heaves. Gayatri held on to Varun's palm with her eyes closed, as silent tears rolled down her cheeks. After a while, Sharad spoke, "Aai is a little away. I haven't told her about your fainting and that Varun and you are together. Let's keep it that way for now. Why add to her worries, right? But.. I think… it's better you stay with Varun.. I mean… it will be…" an audible sigh escaped him, "Will you be fine Gayu?"

Gayatri's clutch on Varun's palm tightened and he gave it a reassuring press.

"I don't know," Gayatri croaked out.

"Sharad, I'm so sorry for your loss. I'll look after Gayatri. You're right. She should stay here." Varun intervened.

Another sigh and then, "Thanks, Varun. I have to go now. Gayu, don't blame yourself, okay? There was nothing you or any of us could have done differently. Baba had accepted it towards the end too."

A moan escaped Gayatri's mouth before she spoke, "You take care of aai, okay? I promise I'll be back as soon as things are better. And bhav… you don't blame yourself either. We know how stubborn he was and…" She paused to sniff and wiped her nose with her sleeve. "Try to get some sleep."

They bid each other good night, promising to eat and get some rest, before hanging up.

Gayatri stayed that way, holding Varun's hand, gazing out the window, for a long time. When she turned her face, her eyes fell on the bowl on the coffee table.

"You haven't eaten yet?" She asked with a slight tremor, trying to sound casual but failing.

Varun shook his head and grabbed his bowl of rice before she could reprimand him. Grinning sheepishly, he began to eat while she gave a faltering smile in response and leaned back into the sofa.

Later, despite her resistance, he cajoled her into sleeping, or at least lying down in the bed instead of sitting on the sofa. He stood leaning against the door frame to ensure she was comfortable, and more importantly, not crying anymore. Then gently shutting the door behind him, he settled down in the hall.

Dropping a quick message to Abhi about the tragedy, he called up Radha. The whole episode had made Varun confront his own feelings of animosity towards his father. It felt so inconsequential, that as soon as Radha picked up, he felt his own eyes going moist.

"Is everything okay? What's wrong, Varun?" Radha sounded worried.

"Is Papa there?" Radha nodded and turned the phone screen towards Shyam who was watching TV. The predictable scene brought a smile to his face.

"Take care of yourselves okay? There's no need to go out for anything. I'll order the groceries for you. Give me a list."

"We already got everything dear. The committee at Pashmina has allowed delivery of essentials for a couple of hours every day. We've both learned how to use the delivery apps like BigBasket and others, so there'll be no need for us to go out to buy anything anyway." Radha informed him, while Shyam grunted. Clearly, Radha was exaggerating her technological knowhow and it made Varun chuckle.

He hesitated but before he could say anything, Radha continued, "Shishir Kulkarni passed away today."

"Yes, I heard."

"It's so heart-breaking. Your father and I spoke to Uma and Sharad a while back."

"Are you okay, son?" Shyam's question surprised Varun. Maybe his father had realised the triviality of their differences too. Varun nodded and turned his face away to hide the tears that suddenly welled up in his eyes.

They talked a bit more before hanging up and after Varun made them swear they'll not go out for absolutely anything at all. A sudden tiredness took over as he placed his phone on the table and stretched his arms out. Not wanting to disturb Gayatri, he pushed aside the thought of watching TV and snuggled up inside the blanket. Sighing, he closed his eyes thinking about the days ahead and how he would handle an emotional Gayatri, not realising when sleep took over.

A sudden shriek made him jerk up from the sofa. Had he imagined it? He checked the time on the phone. 4 a.m. Thinking it was just a bad dream, he was about to lie down again when he heard it for the second time. There was no mistaking the sound that had come from the bedroom. He pulled the blanket off himself and sprinted in, not bothering to knock on the door as he barged in.

Gayatri was rocking back and forth in bed, with her hands covering her face as she cried out, "No, baba... no, I'm here... please, look at me... turn around, baba... I'm here... don't leave me, please...." She let out a shriek and one of her hands reached out toward something in front of her, before falling limp. She then began to tremble convulsively and fell on one side in the bed, bumping her head into the mattress while continuing to shiver.

Varun rushed forth, settling in next to her and gently placed her head in his lap. Running his hands through her hair and caressing her forehead, he said, "It's okay, I'm here. You're fine."

Her body relaxed after a while and he put her in a sleeping position again. When he made to get up, he found his hand in a tight clutch, pinning him in place. He tried to let it free, but Gayatri mumbled in her sleep and tucked his palm beneath her face, locking him in place. He chuckled, causing her to stir while he adjusted himself next to her, trying his best not to disrupt her sleep.

Incomprehensible words kept tumbling out of Gayatri's mouth every few minutes and Varun placated her by moving his hands across her back and on her forehead. His own head kept lolling back and forth as he tried to keep himself awake.

"Varun, don't leave me. I love you. I need you, please. If you also leave, what will I do?" Gayatri's words jerked him awake.

She was talking in her sleep again, her hands gesticulating over the mattress aggressively, trying to reach out, as if to grab someone. Suddenly she wailed out, and her eyes flew open as tears started running down her face.

Did she just say I love you? He shoved the thought aside and stretched his arms across her shoulder. She pulled herself up and embraced him tight, still weeping profusely.

"Shh, I'm here. It was just a nightmare. I'm not going anywhere."

She shoved her face deeper into his chest and clung to him, shaking and weeping. He pulled her face away, titling it upwards with his hand on her chin. Her face was streaked with hair and teardrops. He tucked the hair behind her ears and wiped away the tears, burying her face in his chest again while saying, "I'm not leaving, okay? You can trust me on that."

He felt her nod as she heaved a sigh. They stayed that way, her breasts crushing against his chest and their breaths mingling over each other's bodies. Slowly, she pulled up her face to look into his eyes, her expression a mixture of heartbreak and gratitude. In the semi-darkness of the room, the pasture fields of her irises looked like an abandoned dark green forest, but just as inviting. Her lips trembled as her eyes roved over his forehead, his orbs, his nose, finally landing on his lips. Her breath hitched and she bit her lower lip, running her tongue over it while her gaze stayed put on his mouth.

His own chest rose and fell with rapid breaths. When her hand moved across his face, caressing his left cheek and tracing its path towards his lips, he groaned and reached out to grab her hair with one hand. She mewled lightly and moved her fingers over his lips, while her other hand roved over the exposed skin of his neck and collarbone.

As she leaned in towards him, closing the gap between their lips, he put a hand on her shoulder to stop her. Looking into her eyes, which held so many wishes and promises, he asked, "Are you sure?"

A fierce look came over her eyes and she closed the already miniscule distance between their bodies, yanking him towards her in one aggressive pull as she landed her lips over his. A swimming giddiness took over his senses as everything around them blurred to nothingness. Her answering moan was all the permission he needed to explore her lips. He stuck his tongue out moving it first over her upper lip, then the lower one, biting, nibbling and sucking on them, as if they were the only source to quench his thirst.

She tasted sweet and chocolatey, the taste of Cadbury Silk they had shared after dinner, driving him crazy. Never before had it felt more delicious, and he found himself licking off its remnants hungrily as his tongue rolled over the pout of her lower lip, forcing her mouth open. His right hand gripped her hair tightly, the other one exploring her neck, moving slowly towards her cleavage, while his tongue found its way into her mouth, rolling around, tangling itself with her own hungry, curious and eager to please tongue. She let out a groan when his hand pressed her right breast and she moved in closer, helping him explore it further. When she guided his hand inside her shirt, he knew they had to stop.

He pulled apart, touching his forehead to hers, "Kullu, this is not a good time. I don't want to take advantage of your vulnerability."

She yanked off her top in response, grabbed his hands and placed them on both her breasts. God! She was perfect. Her petite waist, the flat abs, and the perfectly rounded mounds covered by her lacy bra; it was all way better than he'd imagined in his countless lascivious dreams. He exhaled sharply, turning away while pulling his hands off her body and getting off the bed.

He felt her body hurled on his back as he moved towards the door. He held her wrists and dragged her to the bed, helping her sit down. Then turning to face her, he went on his knees bringing his face below hers. The anguish in her eyes made him clutch her face and bury in his chest.

"Kullu, please." He pulled her face up again and planted a kiss on her temple. He got up and made to move away but she held his wrist tightly.

"I need this. I need you."

His conflicted feelings were beaten to the ground when she pulled herself up to his height and kissed his cheek, one after the other. Then she rolled her tongue over his lips, trailing it down to his neck, his collarbone, and the top of his chest. Her fingers moved beneath his shirt, moving in circles as they held its edges and pulled it over his shoulder. Both their upper bodies were now touching, bare skin to skin, with only the thin lace material of her bra as a barrier. Her lips had now moved down from his collarbone to his chest. She kissed, sucked, and bit on his skin, leaving behind moans and hot trails in its wake. Her hand now worked on his boxers, moving on the rim, teasing, tickling, and titillating his skin.

With her other hand, she guided his right hand to her back, towards the hooks of her bra. She looked up at him once and winked mischievously, "You want this as much as I do." Her hand was inside his boxers now, touching his arousal. He felt his restraint fading away and yanked the bra off her chest as her hand moved over his erect shaft in an up-and-down stroke.

He groaned, taking in the sight of her beautiful bosom, hanging free. Oh! To hell with chivalry, he thought and grabbed the right one while bending down to put the left one in his mouth. She melted in his arms, mewling in pleasure, gripping his left buttcheek in her left palm while her right palm moved up and down his bare back, sending goosebumps to the tips of his toes, while the bulge in his shorts grew larger.

"My my, and you said you didn't want it." She whispered against his ear while her hand moved over his boner.

He gasped at the hedonism that took over him at her touch. Chuckling slightly at her eagerness, he moved his lips over her nipple, licking over the mound, while his hand pressed over the other one. He moved his tongue trailing along the width of her chest, covering the distance from one nipple to the other, while his hand moved to the rim of her pyjamas.

It was as if she had been waiting for that move, and she yanked them off her feet in a single stroke. Taking in the sight of her, standing in front of him in just her lace undies, he felt the last of his sanity leave him. He pulled her towards him, forcing his lips upon hers, exploring it with renewed arousal while guiding her hand towards his arousal which was out in full-throttle now.

A gasp escaped her mouth as her hand explored the size and her eyes turned a mix of fear and hunger. He laughed into her mouth and said, "You woke the beast, now bear its wrath."

There was a *challenge accepted* look in her gaze as she tugged at the strings of his boxers and said, "Not fair. Off with those, mister." She landed a spank on his butt and winked while sticking her tongue out.

He willingly took them off, his eyes never leaving her gaze, as his other hand moved over her core through the thin material of her panties. He then took off his briefs, earning a gulp from Gayatri.

He moved closer, touching his manhood to her panties. She moaned, and pulled him closer, landing an aggressive kiss on his lips, then moving to his neck. Her hand trailed down his torso, inching towards his shaft, gripping it with both palms and moving her hands up and down its length.

"Oh my fucking God... Gayatri..." He whimpered like a dog and picking her up in a fireman lift, threw her over the bed. As he moved to get on top of her, his one hand caressed both her breasts, one after the other, while the fingers of his other hand moved over her core. She whimpered in response to his touch and he moved the thin fabric of her panties aside, gaining full access to her crux.

"Look at you already wet and inviting."

"Don't tease me, Varun."

He smiled smugly and slid one finger in, moving it around, opening her up to him like a spring flower, as she cried out his name. Moving further closer, he let his manhood touch her core. The purr he received in response made him tear the panties off, leaving her completely naked.

She shrieked, in shock as much as in pleasure, as he inserted two fingers in, preparing her for the full ride. Her hands moved over his chest and in his hair, pulling his face closer, kissing him fiercely, begging for more.

"Varun... please..." She pleaded and wound her hand around his erection, pulling it towards her opening.

"This will hurt baby." He warned her, before sliding into her and kissing her while slowly fitting his manhood into her clit. She cried out in pain, but her core opened up as if welcoming his entry. He began to push in while she held on to him, her nails digging into his back. Once he was snugly fit, they began to move together, rocking back and forth in a unanimous rhythm, crying out and moaning, before coming together and falling apart in each other's arms.

Varun gently got off her and kissing her temple, excused himself to clean up.

He smiled and snuggled next to her as he settled into the bed again, hugging her curled-up figure as he took in her scent.

"That was magical, Kullu."

He received a snore in response. Chuckling lightly, he spread the duvet over their bodies, cuddling her warm body.

Planting a kiss on her shoulder, he whispered, "I love you too, Kullu." She murmured something which seemed very much like, "Get off me." He rolled over to the other side with a smile. She reached out and grabbed his palm, placing it on her chest. The feel of her even breaths against his hand, soothed him and a sense of peace pervaded his being.

He was soon enveloped by a tranquil sleep himself. His last lucid thought was, "If this is what the first day of being locked down with her was like, I wonder what the remaining 20 days will bring!"

***

Over the next few months, they, slowly and grudgingly at first, then having no way out, adjusted to each other's routines and habits. Sure, both had their quirks and peculiarities, which either made the other person scoff in disbelief or grunt in annoyance.

For instance, Varun's habit of having his coffee black was met with a gasp. When he offered it to her, he received a tongue-in-cheek remark, "No, thank you. Unlike you, I love myself and would like to die with the knowledge that I gave my body what it craved."

Gayatri's habit of listening to music while working had led to multiple arguments.

"But what is the problem with plugging in earphones? Why must I endure it when I don't want to?"

"Fine! You better remember that I made an adjustment and you could just as easily plug in noise-cancelling earplugs too. Your work calls disturb me too. Do you see me complaining?"

The conflicts added on, right from what to cook, who will cook, who will do the laundry, who will order the groceries, who will take out the trash, and everything that came with being cohabitants.

"Oh, so I'm expected to cook because I'm a woman?" Gayatri scoffed when Varun suggested they divide the house chores. He opined that she could do the cooking whereas he'll do the miscellaneous household tasks. Of course, he should have expected her to resist.

"Hey, don't play that gender card with me. Fine, I'll cook and you clean."

After a couple of days though, Gayatri burst out while clanging the used utensils in the kitchen sink, "This is endless. I can't sweep, mop, and do the dishes, alongside two jobs."

Varun sighed and took over the pending task without comment. He had learned out of experience that saying *I told you so* would only make things worse. This was exactly why he had suggested she do the cooking. He figured that the household chores, coupled with her Adfactors job and her choreography classes, would tire her out physically. He, on the other hand, was comparatively free, at least in the evenings.

Despite it being a bit of hustle, it was a good thing that Gayatri had kept her online dance classes running. That and a job she really seemed to like, kept her engaged most hours of the day. The remaining time was spent in cooking and watching some TV, hardly giving her mind any space to think beyond work and personal life. But she did have episodes when she broke down or got lost in thoughts while working, cooking, or even watching TV, without a preamble sometimes. The frequency of these bouts however, decreased over passage of time. She had more or less accepted the grief and what came with the passing of her father.

At the end of their first month together, she moved in with him. It didn't make sense to continue paying rent at her PG and they didn't even need to talk about it. One day she just said, "I should get my remaining stuff" and that was it. They packed all her belongings under the very disbelieving gaze of Sonali, and were out in less than half an hour.

What the future held seemed so immaterial at the moment. The lockdown and life in COVID-19 had made everything so hazy that they were taking the relationship as it went, one day at a time.

They had gotten comfortable sleeping together, cuddling, or holding hands. They kissed frequently too, and the spark was definitely there. But there was a hesitance on both their parts to repeat what happened that first night.

She woke up screaming and calling out for Shishir almost every day. It took a while but Varun had managed to convince her into taking therapy. As a result, the frequency of her ephialtes went down too.

All in all, life was on the upward curve.

Did he love her? Varun was sure he did.

Did she love him? Varun wasn't sure. Especially since she seemed to have forgotten that she'd blurted it out during their *'night of passion'* as Varun had come to refer to it.

All he knew for sure was that he didn't regret any of it. Neither their lovemaking, nor the way things stood between them at the moment.

***

Back to Square One

"What is 'taking things to the next level'? It's a relationship, not an apartment complex we're climbing up."

- Gayatri Kulkarni

March 2022 - October 2023

"Hello, bhabhs. Still keeping my brother hanging?"

"Firstly, please stop calling me that. And secondly, your brother wants to do this for reasons that are beyond my understanding."

Gayatri was talking to Abhi as she caught a rickshaw from *G's Jhankaar*, her dance studio. In the post-COVID-19 times, once things had gone back to normal, Gayatri moved back to Mumbai. Her request to get transferred to Adfactors Mumbai branch was approved without resistance. She was anyway working from home even while in Pune and they knew about Shishir's passing. That, coupled with her consistently good performance as a Digital Content Strategist, ensured that her manager expedited her application to the Mumbai office within a month of her expressing the desire. She had also been promoted from associate to junior level and was now dealing directly with the political team of some of Adfactors leading political clientele.

Gayatri had her own reasons for wanting to stay with her family. Things were better with Uma and Sharad, and when Gayatri vocalised her desire to move back to Mumbai, neither of the Kulkarnis objected. Despite showing a resilience that had shocked her kids, a tear escaped Uma's eyes when Gayatri said, "I couldn't be there with baba. I don't want to lose out on precious time with you too, aai."

Come March 2022, exactly two years after losing Shishir, Gayatri was beside Uma, hugging, crying, and consoling her mother, just as much as she needed it all herself. The two women mourned collectively as if they had lost the most important man in their life, all over again.

Varun, despite resisting Gayatri's move, had come to accept it over time. Gayatri understood his insecurities, what with their own history and Varun's permanent aversion to long-distance relationships. She, however, could not bring herself to ask him to consider moving back to their home city along with her. It would not only be unfair but also highly selfish of her to expect that kind of compromise from him. Not when she knew how much the whole *staying away from the family* phase had helped him grow. Then there was the other itch too.

She knew from his conversations with Radha and sometimes with Shyam that his parents expected him to marry soon. On their last day in the apartment, they'd come to refer to as *Prem Nivas (aka Love Nest)*, he threw her a surprise, which was not so pleasant.

She returned after a farewell lunch with her Adfactors colleagues, which was followed by a get-together cum goodbye party from some of her local dance students. It had been a fun but exhausting day and she was ready to put her feet up in bed and just read and call it a night before catching her early morning train. Laden with bags of over a dozen gifts, she opened the door of *Prem Nivas* and called out to Varun for help, "Aru, can you give me a hand please?" She didn't remember when she started calling him *Aru* but one day it just happened and then it stuck.

She registered soft music and dim lights when she opened her mouth to call for him again. The theme music of DDLJ hit her ears and she gasped, taking in the tealight candles across the perimeter of the entryway, strewn with rose petals in the center. She entered, and putting the bags on one side, made her way, walking over the petals, choking up, as she took in the decor. The tealight candles were around the border of the entire house, casting soft shadows from the furniture on the walls, giving it an alluring aura.

In the middle of the hall, Varun was down on his knees. A heart-shaped border made from rose petals surrounded him. With his right hand stretched out, he said, "Kullu, from the moment I first saw you, I knew you were special. Your melodrama is the perfect antithesis to my calm. Together, though chalk and cheese, we fit like a glove to a hand." He chuckled.

"Though you might say the glove isn't glam enough for your tastes, or that your hand is too small for a glove of mine, all I can say is we can still make it work. It took me, and us together, a long time to realize that we were meant to be."

He paused, gulping, his eyes glistening with tears that threatened to tumble out any second. "I love you. I've loved you from that first time when you shouted out *Jaa Simran Jaa* in a hall full of strangers without a care about who was watching you. I want that Gayatri and the Gayatri you've grown into, by my side, not just as a friend or a live-in partner. But as my companion for life. So, will you do me the honor of being my wife?"

Gayatri's eyes were moist and she settled on her knees in front of the man who had taught her everything she knew about love. It broke her heart, and she knew it would break his too, but she had to ask the inevitable, "Aru, are you doing this for the right reasons?"

A guilty look crossed his face encouraging her to go on, "I love you too and I want you in my life." She held up her hand when he tried to interrupt, his eyes a pool of unshed tears with the impending loss. "But let's do this for the right reasons and when we're both ready. I'm sorry to leave you behind. I'm sorry that I..."

Gayatri had to stop to gulp in some air, as tears rolled down her eyes. She took his hands in her palms and pressed them with as much feeling as she could convey through that simple gesture.

"Kullu, the only thing that will motivate me to stay under the same roof or even the same city as my parents.." he paused to take a deep breath, "is to get married and have my own family. I'll be suffocated with their reminders and the constant suggestions of suitable partners."

Gayatri shook her head and continued, "I understand your position. But please try to understand mine too. I can't say yes when I'm not ready, knowing that somewhere deep down, even you aren't."

She hugged him then, both of them staying enveloped in each other's arms till the candles burned out. A few hours of fitful sleep later, he dropped her off at the station. His parting words were, "I believe it's about time we make this official and take the relationship to the next level. Please think about this again."

She simply responded, "Bye. I will see you soon." Then turning around walked into the station.

It had now been over three months since that day but his words *It's time to take the relationship to the next level* hovered around. In every call and every meeting when either of them visited Pune or Mumbai, Varun was sure to drop in subtle hints with statements like, "Maa was saying today that she spoke to Abhi about marriage. Her justification is that if the elder one isn't ready, maybe the younger one can fulfil her desire." or "I attended a friend's wedding. They were saying *you're next*. Of course, I told them that's not happening."

It was cute, the way he tried to gauge her thoughts on the topic but she'd learned to remain impassive.

Presently, as she waited at Lower Parel station for the local train to head towards Kandivali, she received a call from Abhi.

"Hey, can I call you back in a few hours? I'll be done with the dance classes by then."

She had managed to rent out a small shop in Mahavir Nagar itself for conducting classes. With Navratri right around the corner, her batches were going at full capacity. On the weekdays, she could squeeze in only two evening batches and over the weekends she conducted either four or six batches, depending on her plans with Varun. They took turns visiting Mumbai or Pune. Over the past couple of months though, owing to her Navratri batches which had her working round the clock, she couldn't think of keeping the studio closed for even one day. Hence, Varun had been coming over almost every week or once every fortnight.

About three hours later, once she got done with both batches, and was headed out of the dance studio, she called Abhi. Of course, since his favorite hobby was *let's make Gayatri feel guilty* he had to begin by asking the very question she had been avoiding confronting, even to herself.

"Do the reasons really matter, Gayu?" Abhi asked, responding to her statement on Varun's intentions.

"Anyway, I have to log in to work now. I'll catch up with you later. But think about what I said, okay? Bye, take care."

Bidding Abhi goodbye, Gayatri sighed and got down from the rickshaw as she reached her destination.

A familiar voice chirped from behind while she made her way into Magari, a cozy cafe in Kandivali.

"Hey, Gayu. You're right on time."

She turned around just in time to envelop the rushing figure in a hug.

"Ah, that smiling face is a soothing balm after a tiring day. I had forgotten what life in Mumbai is like."

Ayesha took in Gayatri's body, scanning her from top to bottom.

Gayatri did a twirl to help her in the process.

"So, do I get the Banerjee pass?" She asked, chuckling at Ayesha's cocked eyebrow and smug face.

"A definite improvement from the last time. Damn, those hips girl. You've got them in shape and how! But I'd like a bit more colour on your cheeks. You still look pale."

Gayatri huffed and was about to retort when another figure joined them from behind Ayesha.

Her frown immediately transformed into a huge smile as she was enveloped in another hug.

"The best matchmaker and friend finder awards goes to…" Ayesha pointed a finger toward herself and joined the hug, as the three girls broke into unanimous laughter.

"It'd be nice if you three can join me at the table. I've been sitting here for the past half an hour, looking like a desperate guy whose Tinder date stood him up." A drawl reached across the trio from the door of the cafe.

Sharad threw his hands open when one of the girls broke free from the group hug and rushed towards him.

"Well, there you go. You're welcome."

Sharad quickly landed a kiss on her cheek, making Gayatri and Ayesha go 'awww' as Nalini blushed and hid her face in his chest.

The four of them settled on a table inside Magari. Although a bit smaller than most cafes, Magari had a charm of its own and ran two story's. Their choice of fast food, milkshakes and beverages, which were not only continental and varied, not to mention delectable, made it a top choice among the young crowds. The aesthetic setting and the warmth exuding from the interiors and the staff only added to people dropping by more than once.

Since Gayatri and Sharad were almost regulars, they placed the order on behalf of everyone, and the banter of catching up followed.

After their meeting at the Holi celebration of Pashmina, Sharad and Nalini quickly got close and were now in a relationship. It came as a surprise for no one, except maybe the two people involved in the actual relationship. Ayesha of course had played cupid one more time and Gayatri often teased her that matchmaking could be her side hustle. She was currently pursuing her master's in Delhi University and was in town only for a few days.

"How did the meeting with Professor Das go?" Gayatri asked Ayesha. Mr. Das had been their professor at Mithibai. Ayesha needed his guidance on her current final semester thesis and also her Ph.D. thesis which she was hoping to start right after completing her master's.

"There's nothing concrete yet but he says he'll be happy to write me a recommendation when the time comes. In typical *Mr. Das* fashion, he told me to concentrate on my current thesis first and get through DU before deciding on my next course of action."

"So when are you headed back to Delhi?" Sharad asked while eyeing Nalini who was poring over the menu again. Rolling his eyes, he signalled the waiter and ordered a large iced coffee.

"Why even bother looking at it? I know you'd have ordered iced coffee after wasting twenty minutes scanning every item like you're gonna try something new."

Ayesha chuckled as Nalini stuck her tongue out. Then looking a bit miffed, she gathered herself and answered, "I leave the day after tomorrow. I had to get this thing sorted and meeting professor Das in person was essential. I also had to get his signatures on a few research-related documents."

Sharad nodded as he took the glass of iced tea from the waiter's tray. Ayesha sighed and turned her face away when Nalini reached out to feed the last piece of her cheese sandwich to Sharad. Gayatri looked at her inquiringly asking *What's up with you,* but Ayesha merely shrugged and shook her head.

"Anyway, enough about me. Tell me about you guys. What's happening with you and Varun?"

She had deliberately kept her voice low so as not to involve Sharad and Nalini in the conversation. Gayatri told her about how Varun expected an answer to his proposal and what her views on the whole thing were. Ayesha reached out and pressed Gayatri's shoulder consolingly. Then throwing a rueful look at Nalini and Sharad, who were whispering sweet nothings into each other's ears, she said, "Gayu, I don't know what's stopping you when you're sure about him. You know about me and Abhi. All I can say is, after being together for more than a couple of years, the relationship needs concrete answers." She paused and turned her face towards Gayatri again, looking straight into her eyes. "My understanding is that after some years if you're not sure of the future, let the person go. And if you're sure, what's wrong with taking that monumental step together with them? In your case, the career factor isn't that much of an impediment either. The other factors like age and families are secondary."

Gayatri nodded, suddenly looking at her position in a new light. She'd herself wondered on a few occasions whether her stance was more out of practicality or stubbornness. All through the rest of the night, and while she lay in bed before sleep enveloped her, she kept wondering what was holding her back.

If you're sure, what's wrong with taking that monumental step together with them?

***

"Welcome, my dear."

Gayatri stepped into the Agarwal residence as Radha opened the door for her.

"Come. We've been expecting you." Radha put a hand on Gayatri's right shoulder, guiding her into the living room.

Shyam Agarwal was seated on the sofa with a gruff expression on his face.

"Would you like something to eat or drink?"

"Let's get this over with."

The crudeness in Shyam's tone shocked Gayatri. She knew there would be some hostility but now that she was here, all she could think of was running out the door and declaring, "I quit. Game over". The words from a reality show she watched as a child reverberated through her mind. The host used to say *Aap jaa sakte hai namaste*[48] to the contestants who failed to answer their questions correctly. Even the title of the show *Kamzor Kadii Kaun* seemed to fit her current situation, in which she was aptly the weakest link.

"Shyam, you promised you would be polite!" Radha's tone was disapproving and carried a bitterness Gayatri had never heard before.

"You said you would need a computer? I have dug up one of Abhi's old laptops. You can use that dear. Although, I'm afraid if it has any lock

---

[48] *Hindi words which roughly translate, "Thank you, you may leave now."*

codes, I wouldn't know of it." Radha pointed towards the laptop on the coffee table and looked expectantly at Gayatri. She smiled gratefully and got around to connecting the laptop to the television. Knowing the Agarwal children a tad better than the Agarwal parents, she was able to guess the passcode without resorting to calling up Abhi and asking him. That would have surely led to another awkward conversation that Gayatri didn't need adding on to her plate. Her life was already Indian soap opera worthy without adding an episode (yet another!) of devar ji-bhabhi ji[49] bonding in it. Thank you very much. No one was waiting for her with a pooja thali at the end of that conversation. The way Shyam's gaze was throwing daggers in her direction, there were chances of that thali setting the house on fire, quite literally.

The coldness in the room didn't miss Gayatri's radar as she went about the setup. Once done, she looked over unsurely at Radha, wondering how to begin. She cleared her throat to catch her audience's attention and switching on the slideshow, began nervously.

A screen titled *Why Gayatri is Varun's Best Option* showed up on the TV screen. Shyam's eyebrows quirked up and Radha hid her chuckle by covering her mouth with her right hand.

"As I'm sure Radha aunty has already told you, I intend to get married to your son." Gayatri began, somewhat nervously.

Shyam coughed, leading Gayatri to clarify, "Your elder son, Varun Agarwal. Just to be clear."

Shyam's lips twitched just a bit and it was enough to give Gayatri the confidence to go on.

"Not that there's anything wrong with Abhi." She hastened and went on when Shyam let out an audible sigh. "Anyway, through my sources I have gathered that you're a man who understands logic more than emotion." Both Shyam and Gayatri threw furtive glances in Radha's direction who feigned ignorance.

Pressing her bottom lip to control her laughter, Gayatri went on, "To show you how and why my intentions are well-backed, I have prepared a list of ten reasons to prove why I'm best suited to be Varun's wife."

---

[49] *Hindi terms for (younger) brother-in-law (husband's brother) and sister-in-law (brother's wife)*

Radha tilted her head slightly and discreetly pointed a finger in Shyam's direction, making Gayatri add quickly. "And also why I would make a good daughter-in-law for the Agarwal family."

Radha gave a thumbs-up using both her palms, while Shyam merely grunted. Taking that as her cue, Gayatri went from one slide to the next. Her reasons included points like how she was a self-made person just like Shyam and her sons, how their families were already well-acquainted with each other, and also how close Abhi was with herself and Sharad. Shyam remained impassive through most of the presentation, showing hardly any signs of approval. But he hadn't shown any disapproval or worse, said *Aap jaa sakte hai namaste*[50], which Gayatri took as a good sign.

In the last slide, Gayatri pointed out, "Because Agarwal women won't be able to tolerate Varun's non-agarwalness". This had Shyam in splits for at least ten minutes. After getting his bearings back, he simply said, while looking pointedly at Gayatri, "I only have one condition. Get him back to Mumbai and close to us."

Radha jumped out of the sofa and rushed to hug Gayatri as both the women thanked Shyam profusely. For the next couple of days, Gayatri constantly heaved a sigh of relief. Now that the toughest Shark from the tank was already in, only one, and in Gayatri's opinion, the least vicious one, remained. She wanted to handle it herself, but just in case things went south, she had a backup plan. If Uma showed resistance, she would ask Radha to intervene and help her in convincing the matriarch. She would also work as a safety net in case the *Maa kali*[51] avatar that had been lying dormant for a few years decided to show up again.

On a Sunday evening when all three Kulkarnis were at home, Gayatri opened the door of the Kulkarni residence, letting an excited-looking Radha in, greeted by one nervous and two confused-looking Kulkarnis.

"Hello, Radha aunty. Welcome to our house," Gayatri said leading Radha toward the couch in the hall.

---

[50] *Hindi words which roughly translate, "Thank you, you may leave now."*
[51] *Kali is a Hindu goddess, considered to be the goddess of ultimate power, time, destruction and change. She is considered as a ferocious being whose anger is often associated with people having high temper.*

"Pfft! Please, what's with the aunty? Start calling me maa or mummy ji[52] now, dear." Radha declared, leading to a gasp from Uma and a shriek from Gayatri as well as Sharad.

"Okay, aai. Don't freak out, please? That's what I wanted to talk to you and Sharad about."

Uma was still gaping. Suddenly remembering her manners, she asked Radha, "Would you like something? Tea, coffee, water? Sharad go fetch a glass of water."

Sharad gave Gayatri a terse look and scattered into the kitchen. Gayatri looked from Radha to Uma, and clutching Uma's arm, made her sit next to Radha on the sofa.

Taking both her palms in her own hands, she began, "Aai, I have been in a relationship for a while now. In fact he was the one who took care of me when baba…" her breath hitched a bit but she went on, "We were staying together all this time, since baba's passing till the time I moved back to Mumbai from Pune."

A thunderous look crossed Uma's face, but she kept her words to herself. Then she turned to Radha and said in an apologetic tone, " Radha ji, I had no idea about this. I am so sorry for her behaviour."

Radha reached out and pressed a hand on Uma's arm.

"Uma, what's there to apologize in this? Times have changed now. I trust the kids and I'm actually glad Varun was there with Gayatri at such a difficult time. If anything, I should be thanking Gayatri and of course you too. I see how much my son has changed for the better in the past two years."

Gayatri turned to look at Radha gratefully before continuing, "Aai, I want to get married to him and I don't want to do it without your blessing."

Uma jerked her hands out of Gayatri's grip, shaking her head while muttering, "Wants to get married… not even 24 yet.. have you thought how different…?" She stopped short looking at Radha.

Radha chuckled, and moving closer, took Uma's hand in hers.

"Uma, when the kids are happy, do these differences matter? I have always liked Gayatri and I'll be lucky to have her as a daughter-in-law. As

---

[52] *A term used by Indian women (Hindu women, especially North Indians) to refer to their mother-in-law*

for my son, I can't guarantee your fortune or misfortune for landing him as your son-in-law."

Uma chuckled as tears pooled in her eyes and the two women hugged.

Gayatri sighed in relief, not sure if Uma was actually convinced or had simply caved in to the pressure. Her doubts were cleared later in the day once Radha left.

Gayatri was on call with Ayesha, sharing the latest update and planning her next move.

"The parents are in, Ayu. I can't believe I managed to pull that off. Anyway, I now need to keep scouring for job opportunities to get Varun back in town. We need to talk to…"

"Ahem."

She turned around to see Uma who was standing at the door of the bedroom. When she saw she had Gayatri's attention, she walked inside and made herself comfortable on the bed. Gayatri quirked her eyebrows inquiringly to which Uma simply responded by jutting her chin out and pursing her lips.

"Ayu, I'll call you back later. I have to go. Bye." She hung up and sat down next to Uma.

Clearing her throat, Uma said, "That was unexpected Gayu. Anyway…I…" She stopped midway, fiddling with the pallu of her saree, giving Gayatri a look of uncertainty.

Gayatri had never seen her mother so hesitant and reached out a hand to her shoulder.

"What is it aai? I am sorry for throwing this at you suddenly. Do you not like Varun? What's the problem?"

"No no no.. not at all." Uma quickly added. "I have always liked both the Agarwal sons.

She gulped, visibly anxious.

Gayatri moved closer, putting a hand across Uma's shoulder in a half-embrace.

"Aai, you can tell me. C'mon."

Heaving a deep sigh, Uma removed something she had been hiding inside the pallu of her saree. It was an envelope with something scrawled across the cover.

With slightly trembling hands, Uma handed it to Gayatri. Her eyes darted back and forth, and when her gaze landed on Gayatri, her eyes were damp.

Giving her palm a reassuring press, Gayatri read the words on the envelope.

For my princess about to become a queen

Gayatri's own eyes turned soggy and she looked up questioningly at her mother. She already kind of had an inkling about this.

"Baba wrote this before we moved him to the hospital. He kind of knew that he wouldn't make it back. He handed it to me and said, 'Give this to our princess when she's about to make her own kingdom and become a queen of her world'. He…" She couldn't go on and pressed her palm to her mouth, biting on her index and middle finger.

Gayatri gulped and opened the envelope, slowly taking in her father's last message to her.

My dear princess,

Congratulations on finding your Mr. Right.

If you're reading this without me by your side, it only means I won't be with you on this journey as you become somebody's wife. My dear daughter becoming a queen! How fast you grew up and we didn't even realize it. It feels like just yesterday when you asked for dancing shoes instead of dolls unlike most girls your age. How hard your mother and I laughed when you threw the many dolls people gifted you year after year on your birthdays. Ask your mother for the photos. I'm sure she'll be able to dig them up.

Your mother and I didn't quite see eye to eye with you on a few things, especially your passion for dance. Forgive me, and both of us, for not being the parents you wanted or expected. Forgive me, for not providing enough, to be able to afford your dreams. The day I had to walk out of the Dance Beat studio, I didn't show, but I cried myself to sleep, and cursed my luck, for not letting you follow your passion and for not being capable enough to back your dreams. Believe me, my princess, I have spent every day after that, wondering about the **What Ifs** *and* **If Only,** *wishing I could have been a better father. Believe me, my princess, my only intention, has always been for you to struggle a little lesser, than me, or your mother.*

If you've ever felt like we clipped your wings in the process of doing so, I apologize for it.

I see you today and only have pride in my heart. For achieving your goals and going above and beyond our expectations in every aspect.

Much more and many great things await you in the future, my princess. For you, even the sky is not the limit. And whenever in doubt, always remember, **thoda vishwas thev.**

I hope you find it in your heart to let go of the grudges, including the last action of mine which might lead to our final communication via this letter.

I hope you will not live with regret and guilt for the rest of your life, wondering about the **What Ifs** *and* **If Only.** *I have led a very fulfilling life, mostly thanks to your aai, Sharad, and yourself. Both of you have turned out to be the kind of children any parent would be proud of.*

Your aai and I haven't always had a happily married life. But we have stood by each other, and have taken every action and decision, keeping you two as our priority. I hope whoever your life partner is, turns out the same, or even better than the kind of partners Uma and I have been for each other.

One last time, I also apologize for not being there, walking you down the aisle, and giving your hand to the man of your dreams.

Knowing you, I'm sure he's someone you have chosen yourself. Knowing you, I'm also sure he's somebody your aai and I already like and will approve of.

I hope he's everything you're looking for in a life partner. I hope he turns out better than you expected. I hope he treats you like the queen you deserve to be in the kingdom you create together.

Love Always,

Baba

Gayatri hugged the letter to her bosom, crying profusely. As she lamented the loss of the man she had lost, she was also filled with the hope of a future, she was now surer of than ever before.

***

"Okay, okay. He's coming." Nalini waved her hand towards someone and sneaked out, whispering a quick "All the best" to Gayatri.

"Oh hi, Varun. I was just getting popcorn." Gayatri heard Nalini say. This was her cue and she quickly ran to her designated spot. Varun's response was muffled and she didn't even register it what with the butterflies playing havoc in her stomach, as she looked around one more time to ensure everything was in place,

"Not now." She commanded, getting her jitters in control, and took a deep breath as the approaching footsteps inched closer. The door opened and the first thing she registered was his tall frame in a jeans and shirt. The dim lights didn't allow her to catch the colour of his clothes but she didn't miss the look of incredulousness crossing his face as he looked around the hall. He was probably still wondering why it was empty when the screen started playing something. Not understanding what was happening, he fumbled in the semi-darkness for a bit and settled in the nearest seat.

Gayatri could now see his expressions clearly, ranging from shock to disbelief and finally enraptured, as the screen played moments from their relationship with photos and videos of the memories they had created together. When the last slide showed up and Gayatri's face came up on the screen, she took her phone and began typing a message.

The Gayatri on the screen said, "Hey there. I know you were expecting our favorite movie's show today. But I did one better, didn't I? What was all that about?" There was a pause in which the on-screen Gayatri scratched her head with one hand and tapped the index finger of her other hand on her cheek.

"Now if you will turn to your left, you will see my sexy, amazing, *too good for you*, friend, asking you a question." With that, the screen went blank.

"Do it NOW." Gayatri sent the message.

The theme music of *Dilwale Dulhaniya Le Jaayenge* reverberated around the hall and the whole place lit up. The entire space was illuminated with tealights placed on the ground and string lights hung across the walls' edges.

Varun's eyes moved around, taking it all in with an awestruck look before landing on Gayatri. An audible gasp escaped his mouth which remained open as he made his way toward her. Tears glistened in his eyes and there was an astonished look about him, as he observed Gayatri who was down on her knees with her right hand outstretched.

"Mr. Varun Agarwal. From the moment you said *Bade bade deshon mein aisi chhoti chhoti baatein hoti rehti hai* to my *Jaa Simran Jaa*, I knew I had found someone who understood my melodrama. Then you became my *Dilwala Dost* who slowly captured my heart. But very quickly you broke it too, not once, but twice, in quick succession."

Varun opened his mouth to counter her, but she held up her hand and went on, "I know I know, that was all more in my head than your doing. But, then I lost baba and I thought no other man could ever fill his place or love me the way he did. That's when you walked in and taught me how wrong I was. Not only about you, but also about myself, about us, and most importantly, about all my ideas around love."

She paused, gulping in some air, and brushed away the tears from her face. Sniffing, she went on, "You said you want to take the relationship to the next level and I said I'm not ready. But now I am. So, Mr. Agarwal, my dear Aru, will you do yourself the honour of being my husband?"

Varun chuckled, and Gayatri went on, "Everything has already been taken care of. There are only three things you need to do." She counted them off by popping up the fingers of her left hand, "Say yes to me, say yes to the job offer you've received from Ogilvy, and pick your outfits for all the functions." She paused as if to recall if she had forgotten something. "You know that's going to hold true for all your coming days and the rest of our lives together. That should be your mantra: Say yes to Gayatri."

With that, she quirked up an eyebrow and opened the lid of the box she had been holding in her left hand. Taking the ring out, she held it out towards him, awaiting his response.

"Oh, what the hell! Yes. A million times. OF COURSE YES!" Varun shouted out in jubilation, and covering the distance between them, held out his ring finger toward her. Once she slid it on, he picked her up and twirled her around before hugging her.

The door of the halls flew open and they were drowned amidst whoops, whistles, and cheers as Sharad, Nalini, Ayesha, and Anusha filed in. The whole lot of them rushed forth, shrieking loudly, and engulfed them in a group hug.

It's just the beginning Gayatri's inner self chided her as she wondered whether there would be any end to the drama around their story.

***

Before & After (The Happily Ever After)

"Happily Ever After isn't a myth. It is a reality; albeit a bittersweet one and something you need to find, create and sustain yourself."

- Varun Agarwal

December 2023 - December 2025

"It's been nice catching up with you and reminiscing our school days." Varun typed in and sent the message. He was aware of Gayatri's watchful eyes on him.

His phone beeped with a response right away. "Same here. It's a small world after all."

"Hey, by the way, Viren. Since Nalini is already attending the wedding, why don't you join the celebrations as her +1 too? I could do with some friends from my side. My soon-to-be-wife seems to be winning in that department. Come and attend one function at least?"

"Lol, don't give up so soon. I think I'll be in Mumbai at that time. I'll come for the main event. I mean the wedding. Let me know if I can be useful in any other way. Anything to help a brother win."

"Thanks, bro. This means a lot. I'll let you know. See you soon. Take care." He tucked the phone away in his pocket again.

"It's done. Are you happy now? I thought you said the only things I need to do are say yes and pick out my outfits. There are ten other things you've made me do so far, including inviting people, picking your outfits and literally dancing to your tunes."

Gayatri shrugged her shoulders and giving a slight chuckle, came forward to give him a hug. Landing a peck on his cheek, she returned to her position in front of the mirror.

"You're the best, Aru. Also, dancing to my tunes is something you've been doing for a while now and it's good net practice for what's to come, don't you think?" She winked at him through the reflection in the mirror. "Anyway, what do you think?" She asked while checking the outfit she'd put on. Honestly, Varun couldn't tell the difference between this and the previous one she'd put on, or the dozen others she had tried so far. Of course, he couldn't say that. So he put on a careful smile and said, "You'd look beautiful in anything babe. Just pick any of the ones you've tried so far."

They were only two weeks away from their wedding and where Varun had been done with picking all his outfits in a single day, mademoiselle's hunt was still on. As far as Varun could recall, they had both covered the outfits for all the main events, including sangeet, haldi, grah shanti, and of course the main event aka the *pheras*. God only knows which event outfit they were choosing currently and he didn't dare ask. From what he could understand, she was now shopping for Indian outfits for events after the wedding where they would be meeting the extended families.

"I want to be prepared for lunch and dinner invitations to people's places or going out somewhere for family get-togethers." She explained, justifying the incredulous look on his face.

True to her promise though, she had indeed taken care of most of the planning. Varun was sure Gayatri had hoodwinked or spiked their drinks with some magic potion to get Radha and Shyam's approval. As their son, it still felt unbelievable that they were Gung ho for the *Kuarwal* wedding; a term coined together for their intercaste marriage by the two mothers.

Right after he had said yes to her proposal, when he had dropped in at Pashmina, Radha asked, "So, did you like my daughter-in-law's proposal? Did you say yes?"

When he nodded, she clapped gleefully and danced around the living room, yelling excitedly, "Shaadi Mubarak."

Apparently, there was no resistance from Radha and despite some initial hesitance, Shyam had caved in too. It had taken three people, Radha, Abhi, and sometimes Gayatri herself, to help him see why Varun and she were suited together. Ultimately, it was Gayatri's presentation that did the trick.

Gayatri became a woman on a mission after that. Pulling some strings here and there, she managed to get him an offer from his old firm *Ogilvy*. An offer so lucrative that he obviously couldn't turn it down. Of course, with the problem of family pressure about his marriage already gone now, Varun was only happy for the chance to move back to the city of dreams, his home turf. In less than a month after Gayatri's grand proposal, he was back at Pashmina to a rather teary-eyed welcome from both his parents.

Long before that, the families had already joined forces to block the dates for all wedding-related events, like booking the venue, and getting the decor and catering in place.

The friends, including Anusha, who was somehow team Gayatri now, assisted her in convincing the owners and getting Maratha Mandir booked on a day around the anniversary of *Dilwale Dulhaniya Le Jaayenge*. A weekday when they were expecting minimal footfall was chosen. To ensure Varun was in town, they picked a day around his interview date at Ogilvy.

Everyone pitched in to help Gayatri plan and execute the details to the T.

Just like that, things fell into place, and they were now soon going to be Mr. and Mrs. Agarwal. The countdown had already begun and in no time they were facing D-day.

***

The *Kuarwal* wedding festivities were kicked off by the sangeet ceremony. And with quite a bang.

Given Gayatri's background, everyone had their money on this one to be the highlight of the three-day galore, with Miss Kulkarni being the star of the show. Her solo performance was a big hit. She had kept it a secret from everyone and even Varun only knew bits and parts she'd let slip accidentally in between the chaos of the shopping and other miscellaneous preps.

The performances started with Varun's solo performance. Despite Gayatri leading it all from the front, he had managed to keep a few elements from his own performance a surprise as well.

It was hardly alarming that Gayatri's shriek of delight was the loudest when the monologue *Ek ladki thi deewani si* played while Varun's back was turned towards the spectators. The following two songs *Sajanji ghar aaye* and *Mujhse shaadi karogi* were choreographed by Gayatri herself. Her initial reaction to his well-thought-out surprise pumped him up, and throughout the rest of it, Varun couldn't help but smile widely and blow kisses to his to-be-wife. She was equally if not more enthusiastic as she clapped, whistled, and returned his kisses while jumping up and down in her seat.

After this, the bridesmaids, along with Abhi, did a medley of songs to introduce Gayatri to the audience. It was a mashup of the songs *Pretty Woman, Desi Girl,* and *Drama Queen.*

Post this, Ayesha and Nalini happily took over as emcees of the event.

"Ladies and gentlemen. Now that you know what our bride's personality is like. Would you also like to see what she looks like?" Ayesha asked to a clapping and cheering audience.

"Wait, wait, wait. This is Gayatri we're talking about. So it can't be a *rukha shuka* entry, right? I'm sure she has something up her sleeve and even we don't know what it is. Our instructions are only to step off the stage and switch off all the lights."

Both the girls bowed to the cheering audience and stepped down. At the same moment, all the lights in the huge hall were turned off too. A few scattered whistles later, there was pin-drop silence, with the anticipation mounting every second.

The only source of light was the shimmering and colorfully blinking string lights on the curtains strewn across and forming the backdrop of the stage. After a few seconds, these went off too.

A small girl's voice called out, "Baba, baba" and then her face showed up on the curtains of the stage. She was looking into the camera and bouncing up and down on her feet.

"C'mon Gayu. Show us that step." A male voice said from behind the camera.

The screen went blank and lyrics played out over the loudspeaker.

Be chsey khaanmoj koor

Diy mey rukhsat myaney bhai-jaan'o

Diy mey rukhsat myaney bhai-jaan'o

Be chsey khaanmoj koor....

A shadow dance played out by two palms was projected on the screen. The grace and the poetic fluidity of the fingers, the way they formed waves or did other interpretive movements, earned scattered claps and whistles from the watching crowd.

Amidst heightened curiosity, the next line and lyrics of the song played out.

Ungli pakad ke tune

Chalna sikhaya tha na

Dehleez oonchi hai ye, paar karaa de

At the same moment, a spotlight came up on the stage, putting Gayatri in full focus. Taking a twirl, she stretched her hand out as the next line came up.

Baba main teri mallika

Tukda hoon tere dil ka

Ikk baar phir se dehleez paar karaa de

A collective sigh, followed by a gasp drew up from the spectators. Next to Gayatri was a CGI of Shishir whose hand was now in Gayatri's outstretched one.

Gayatri did another twirl, moving away from Shishir while matching her movements to the song's lyrics. She circled around her father with her ghaghra flowing about her, creating a colourful palette and mesmerizing sight.

When the words *Aisi bidaai ho toh, lambi judaai ho toh, dehleez dard ki bhi paar karaa de* played, she was on the other end of the stage and ran towards Shishir with her hands outstretched. Shishir too spread his arms out and the two figures hugged on stage.

Shishir's figure kissed Gayatri's forehead and cheeks cheeks with the male lyrics alongside.

Mere dilbaro...

Barfein galengi phir se

Mere dilbaro...

Fasalein pakengi phir se

Tere paaon ke tale

Meri dua chalein

Duaa meri chalein...

Then the CGI disappeared as the song faded out and Gayatri remained there with her arms outstretched and bare, reaching out to the father who was no longer in her life.

Tears streamed down the face of every person in the hall, including Gayatri. The somber mood soon turned cheerful though as the beats of *Makhna* reverberated across.

Yeh bhi na jaane

Woh bhi na jaane

Naino ke rang naina jaane

A smile spread across Gayatri's face as she turned to face the audience and pointed towards Varun, her soon-to-be-husband, seated in the front row.

Mila jo sang tera

Uda patang mera

Hawa mein hoke malang

The blush on her face, the ever-present smile, and the twinkle in her eyes, combined with her mesmerizing moves, had everyone spellbound. The song changed from *Makhna* to *Nachde ne saare* but each person's eyes remained glued on the girl on stage.

Of course, after that breathtaking solo performance by Gayatri, it was impossible for anyone else to steal the limelight. But the couple's performance of Gayatri and Varun came quite close. It was another mashup of all the songs that defined their love story starting with *Tujhe Dekha* and ending with a few latest hits like *Rangi Saari* and *Kesariya*.

The spectators clapped, cheered, and whistled to their waltzing, as Varun finished the dance with a flourish by twirling Gayatri in his arms, then picking her up from the waist as she outstretched her hands, swinging and twisting them around herself, while Varun brought her slowly back down and gently placed her on the stage. With one hand around Varun's waist she entwined one leg around his legs and the other stretched out, away from where both of them stood. He landed a peck on her cheek, not breaking eye contact as the beats of *Kesariya* faded. They descended the stage, hand-in-hand amidst tumultuous applause and Varun couldn't remember feeling this giddy with excitement and anticipation ever before.

The next day, arrived and Varun was accompanied by his family and friends as they took the *baarat* from their residence at *Pashmina Serene* in Dadar to *Kino Cottage* in Versova. Once again, Varun had to marvel at the meticulous planning and attention to detail by his fiancée. The venue had been booked keeping its strategic location as well as convenience for the hosts and guests in mind. It was a sea-front venue with jaw-dropping views and stood midway for both the Agarwal and Kulkarni family and guests, who would be commuting from two opposite ends of the city.

If Varun thought the Agarwal quota of dance was done in the sangeet function already, he could not have been more wrong. Before the baarat started, the guests, and more so, the Agarwal parents themselves, danced till Varun had to remind them of the time barrier. Right on the premises of Pashmina, everyone swayed to the tunes and beats of shehnai and dhol nagada for a quarter of an hour. On reaching the venue almost an hour later, the same charade followed at the entry of the Kino Cottage. It would have continued longer if Varun hadn't been quick to notice the increasing crease lines on Uma's forehead who stood at the beautiful makeshift floral entryway with a pooja plate in her hands.

It reminded Varun of the meme that had caught everyone's attention during the lockdown. In it, an Indian woman gives the stink eye to another woman asking *rosode mein kaun tha*. Varun had to press his lips together as he controlled his laughter at the mental image of Uma like that and requested his friends and family to let the Kulkarnis proceed with the rituals.

Sharad had to pull Varun's ear as part of one of the customs. Before he reached his hand out, Uma whispered something in his ear. After a little juggle fight, when Sharad finally caught it, he twisted it a bit too hard. Varun wondered if this was a repercussion of making Uma wait too long and whether she'd somehow sensed his memeful thoughts and instructed her son to not be considerate with his ear.

"That's for delaying your welcome to the family." She said winking and clutching Varun's hand to welcome and take him inside the venue.

From that moment on, Varun assumed his mother-in-law to have magical telepathic powers and swore to never make fun of her, even in his mind, when she was around.

He marched up to the mandap with the Kulkarnis and Agarwals on either side as the song *Mangalayam* played in the background. He only had to wait a few minutes after settling down in his high seat specially picked and designed for the wedding couple.

He was just taking in the sight of the well-decked mandap set against the dusky sky and bouncy waves when Gayatri walked down the aisle with her girlfriends, all smiles and blowing out kisses. Varun took in her bridal attire and marveled at how he got so lucky to find such a beautiful girl as his breath hitched in his throat. A few unshed tears pooled in his eyes which quickly turned into a chuckle when his soon-to-be-wife broke into an impromptu dance matching the lyrics of her entry song *Shumbaarambh*.

When the pandit put her hand in his and as they took circles around the holy fire, Varun looked at Gayatri's blushing, excited face and was reminded of the fifteen-year-old girl he had first seen almost a decade ago. He couldn't believe that girl was his wife now. She had come a long way, but in some ways, she was also the same.

Her passionate streak, the way she reacted to certain things, and above all, her ability to create and attract drama wherever she went – Varun couldn't wait to have it all by his side 24*7, beginning now.

The *Just Married* car whisked them away to their suite amidst tears and cheers. Varun leaned in closer and whispered in Gayatri's ear, "Now it's time for me to prove *Why Varun is Gayatri's Best Option.*"

They chuckled together, and kissed hungrily, till the driver announced their arrival at the hotel. Hand in hand, not leaving each other's gaze even for a second, they walked into their new life.

***

"Play some Bollywood songs, mummy ji. That always works. He'll be distracted for at least another half an hour and won't fuss when you feed him." Gayatri told a harried-looking Radha over the video call.

"Given how filmy his parents are, that's hardly any surprise is it?" Radha was quick to retort.

There was laughter from both ends of the video call.

"Thanks for taking over, Ma. It's been a while since Gayatri and I got away on our own." Varun butted in.

"You kids enjoy. Uma and I will ensure this one stays out of trouble." There was a cooing sound, followed by the noise of thumping, from behind Radha. "Rather we stay out of trouble."

Then she turned the screen towards the toddler messing around with the stuff on the center table. Their eleven-month-old son, Varg, despite being held by Uma, had found his way toward the TV remote control and was banging it on the table while Uma struggled to get the remote out of his clutch.

"Hi, baby." Gayatri and Varun called out in unison.

"Da..da…" Varg babbled out, smiling and pointing towards the phone screen.

"No, say, mama…" a miffed-looking Gayatri cried out.

Varg cackled and said, "Da…da" "Da..da" on loop as if enjoying Gayatri's discontentment.

Gayatri huffed and made a face while all the others guffawed out loud.

They soon hung up after Gayatri apprised both the mothers with some more tips and tricks on how to handle their toddler.

"All you contributed was two drops of your sperm," she began grumbling once the call was cut, "and yet he says 'da..da'. Hmmph! All that carrying him in my womb for nine months and almost dying in labour…what's the point!" She contorted her face and stuck her tongue out, throwing a pillow at him.

"Kullu, let him grow up. I'm sure he'll be mama's boy once he understands things better." He kissed her, drawing her to his chest, and circling his tongue around her pout, which soon resulted in a moan from both ends.

"Besides," he mumbled while sucking on her lower lip, "You'll have your chance with the next one." Chuckling, he bent down to kiss her tummy.

Pushing him off, she got up from the bed and declared, "No time for this now, mister. We have to get ready for the dinner date."

The two of them were in Andaman to celebrate their two-year wedding anniversary. Initially skeptical about taking any trips for the occasion, they decided to go ahead with their long-planned holiday. Varun had specially chosen Andaman because he knew how much Gayatri loved beaches and even after two years she never tired of talking about their honeymoon in Bali. He'd even carefully picked out their stay at Barefoot at Havelock whose rooms, location, and almost every amenity resembled those of the resorts they had stayed in at Bali; their first holiday together as a couple.

Suddenly though, a few weeks before they were to leave, Gayatri began to get cold feet and it intensified with each passing day. According to her, there were too many things to worry about - her job and choreography which she'd just gotten back into after her maternity break. Then the fact that Varg was still too young to be left behind without either of them around. Varun was just wondering why she was suddenly so unsure in life. The spontaneous Gayatri seemed like a ghost of the past compared to this constantly moody and fretful one.

Then it all made sense one day. He walked into the bathroom where she stood in front of the mirror, looking like she had seen a ghost.

"How? This is all your fault." She swung around, an accusatory edge to her tone.

That's when Varun saw the pregnancy test in her hand. The two lines on it meant only one thing. He yelped, and picking her up, twirled her around, not believing that he could feel such joy.

"What are you doing?" She screamed, landing blows on his chest. "I cannot be pregnant again Mr. Agarwal! Varg is only eight months old. Do you realize how difficult this is going to be?"

Varun did realize. And that's why they decided to cancel the Andaman holiday. When they declared the pregnancy, the two families were overjoyed. But Radha also knew how much the young couple, especially Gayatri, needed a break. She'd seen the young girl getting enveloped in family and motherhood, all too soon. With another kid on the way now, Radha only knew their private time together as a couple, and Gayatri's me time individually, would be even more difficult to come by.

So despite Gayatri's resistance, Radha insisted that Varun and Gayatri take the holiday. To make her feel at ease, Radha along with Shyam and Uma offered to take care of Varg for the duration of their week-long sojourn.

Her exact words, which ultimately convinced Gayatri to give in to her request were, "Take it from a mother of two that if you don't grab the time now, you will only end up making this a habit. That's not good for you, dear. Don't make your life all about being a mother. You have to be a wife too. More than that you have to be yourself as well. We're more than just wives and mothers, right?"

Hence, Varun and Gayatri were here now. They had reached in the morning and checked into the Nicobari Cottage. One look at the canopied bed and Gayatri's instant squeal were all the validation Varun needed for having made the right choice. They spent the day lazing on the lounge chairs on the room's sundeck and then walking around the long stretching and beautiful green paths of the resort property. On their return to the room after high tea, they'd received a call from Radha asking Gayatri how to tackle Varg's tantrums.

Currently, they were expected to show up at the lobby of Barefoot at Havelock, in some time. From there, a designated driver was to give them a ride to an undisclosed location. When the hotel staff learned of their anniversary, they'd been generous to provide them with a date package at an unbelievably discounted rate. They'd kept the location and other details a surprise.

Varun was ready in a while donned in a maroon tux and matching pants he had especially saved for this occasion.

In a red one-shouldered full-length gown with a slit in the front, exposing her right leg up to her knees, Gayatri was dressed to kill. A low whistle blew out of Varun's mouth as he her took in his arms.

"Not so bad yourself, Mister Agarwal." She winked and dropped a quick peck on his lips before the two of them made their way arm-in-arm toward the waiting car.

Soon, they reached Lacam Harbour, from where they boarded a private yacht.

"Wow." Exclaimed Gayatri as she took in the decor on board. String lights were hung on its railings and on the floor, in the middle of the yacht, were a small table and two chairs. Tea candles adorned the table, while flower petals were strewn around it.

"Welcome onboard Mr & Mrs. Agarwal." They were greeted by a middle-aged man who helped them to their seats. "I'm Kabir and I will be your server this evening."

Varun shook hands with Kabir while Gayatri nodded.

"Happy Anniversary, sir and madam. Welcome aboard, *Carpe Diem,* your yacht for today's voyage. We will be taking a 4 hour-ride along the Andaman sea as we sail through some lesser-known islands, including South Button, Wilson, Nicholson, John Lawrence, Henry Lawrence, and Peel islands."

Gayatri and Varun nodded and looked around appreciatively as Kabir continued.

"We will be getting off for a bit at Peel Islands, where you can enjoy the sunset. We have also arranged for your dinner at one corner of the unexplored and beautiful island."

Kabir then served them drinks and appetizers as they began their onward sail. While munching on bruschetta and fritters and sipping on mocktails, they devoured the endless sea and the beautiful expanse laid out in front of their eyes. They were lucky to spot a dolphin and some fish bouncing up to their eye level along the ride.

An hour later, just as the sun began its downward sink, they docked off at Peel Islands. Once deboard, both Varun and Gayatri were left speechless as they took in the setting in awe and with opened-mouthed admiration. On a secluded area of the beach, a makeshift gazebo had been set up. There were candles and flowers strewn across its pathway leading up to it. White and blue muslin curtains flew around the gazebo's perimeter. There were string lights spread around as well and the whole aura, coupled with the dim lights and the winds gently blowing the curtains, was a sight straight out of some travel magazine.

A young boy stood in the right corner, playing soft romantic tunes on a violin. With the setting sun and the waves of the sea in the background, they enjoyed a delicious dinner, consisting of the finest wine and mocktails, coupled with some of the best savories and desserts they had ever had.

"We haven't done this in so long. I don't even remember." Varun mused, entwining his hand with Gayatri's.

"I think it was at Bali. Wow! That was our honeymoon. So exactly two years." Gayatri sighed, looking around and taking in the beauty.

The dinner was followed by some slow dancing to the tunes of the violin and before they knew it, the time to return was upon them.

During the ride back, they didn't let go of their entwined hands, neither on the yacht nor in the car. They were both holding on to this moment as if it were a treasure. Truth be told, the days and months following their wedding had felt like they had flown by in a jiffy. Maybe that was because, barely six months into wedlock, Gayatri was expecting. They had no regrets about that and considered becoming parents a blessing. However, lately, especially since Varg was born, the two of them rarely got much time together. Now with a second child on the way, these moments felt even more treasured.

From the intense look her eyes held, Varun knew Gayatri was waiting to rip the clothes off him and make love like never before. To be honest, the twitch in between his own legs hadn't quite settled from the moment he saw her in that red dress.

Suddenly there was a blaring sound followed by a loud honk. A blinding light made it impossible to make out what had happened. Varun reached out to envelop Gayatri in his arms and grabbed one of the car pillows as they were jerked out of their seats and into the windshield.

Varun's last thoughts before he tasted the blood in his mouth were of Varg, and of the safety of their unborn child. Instinctively his palms reached out to cushion Gayatri's womb and he cried out, "Kullu, hold on to me tightly."

The pasture fields bore into his eyes before his vision was blocked out by a blur.

Then he was consumed by blackness.

***

She Rose

"Whatever happens, happens for the best? Maybe those who say and believe that have never really had to face the worst of life yet."

- Gayatri Kulkarni

May 2026

To the grandmother
Who thought **"So what if I don't have a grandson?"**
Instead of, **"We need a boy child to carry forward the family lineage."**
And then made it possible for the women in the family
To feel loved and accepted.

To the mother
Who thought, **"I'll follow the same parenting style for all my children."**
Instead of, **"I must treat my daughter differently than my son."**
And then changed the way children are raised,
Just a little bit.

To the sister
Who said, **"Of course, we can share clothes and shoes."**
Instead of, **"I can carry that off better than you."**
And then made it possible for women under the same roof
To not feel envious of each other

To the teacher
Who thought **"We must let the children mingle."**
Instead of, **"The girls must be taught to stay away from the boys."**
And then made it okay for opposite-gender bondings
To be looked at beyond romantic angles

To the daughter
Who thought, **"If my mother is unhappy and alone, she deserves more from life."**
Instead of, **"Being independent, dating, and finding love after a certain age is unacceptable for women."**

And then made it possible for women
To find and create their identities beyond family ties

To the friend
Who said **"Are you sure about him? Don't settle just because everyone else is getting married. Focus on your career and identity."**
Instead of, **"So, when are you getting married? You're the only one left now! Don't wait too long."**
And taught a woman, then many women
The true meaning of support and empowerment

To the wife
Who demanded, **"But this is your house and family too. Why aren't you contributing beyond the finances?"**
Instead of assuming, **"I'm a woman so it's my duty to take care of the family and kids and his responsibility to earn."**
And changed the course of household dynamics
One person and family at a time

To the mother-in-law
Who said, **"There's no need to give up your job and identity. We are all adults and can all look after ourselves. As for the children, we can all contribute towards their care and upbringing."**
Instead of demanding, **"But how can you be selfish and think only about yourself? What about your husband, his parents, and your children?"**
And then showed by example
What gender equality means

To the colleague
Who said, **"I admire your ability to juggle your personal and professional life."**
Instead of, **"If I had the choice, I'd give up my job to give full attention to my kids."**
And brought somewhat balance
To the male-female sex ratio at workplaces

To all the women
Who disprove the stereotypes
And either break free from it themselves

Or help other women get away
By smashing the patriarchy
By breaking the shackles of misogyny
By disrupting age-old notions of sexism

To us all
Who don't fall victim,
Or accept things lying down
To each woman who cares,
To all those who dare

We're all Sheroes
We're all the She who rose

Together we can, we must and we will
For a better today,
Than yesterday,
For a better tomorrow,
Than today.
For one, for all.

There was deathly silence for a few seconds, and then an applause so loud broke out that the girl who had read out the poem had tears in her eyes. This kind of response to her poetry wasn't new for her, but the inspiration and cause behind this particular one would never stop hurting.

Turning her face the other way to wipe off the tears, she sniffed and looking straight again, addressed the audience.

"The *She Rose* for me, who was one of the biggest inspirations behind this poem is someone I'll never stop admiring." She paused to take a deep breath. "As a mother of two herself, she insisted we do this event today on Mother's day, instead of on Women's Day, as was the initial plan."

Scattered applause broke out allowing the girl to wipe her tears again. She looked at everyone with renewed determination. The packed hall didn't make her nervous as she was used to delivering speeches and poems right from childhood.

"Before we welcome her on stage, let me introduce myself. I'm Ayesha Banerjee, one of the co-founders of the platform we're inaugurating today. What is this platform all about? We, the three founders of **She Rose – For the everyday sheroes,** will be providing girls and women of all ages a platform to tap into their creative sides. These include miscellaneous performing arts and art forms like writing, dancing, spoken word poetry, and painting."

This declaration was received with encouraging applause, giving Ayesha a chance to look at the people in the front row. Varg, who was perched in Radha's lap, pointed towards her and said loudly, "Mau..chiii..."[53]

Ayesha chuckled and blew him a kiss, before continuing, "Please join me in welcoming my co-founder- the brainchild behind it all - Gayatri Kulkarni."

This time, the applause was much more pronounced. Ayesha could see Radha clapping the loudest, as she whispered "See, mumma" into Varg's ears. The elderly woman hid it well, but Ayesha was quick to notice the little movement where she wiped off a stray tear with the pallu of her saree from her cheek.

The lights turned dim as Ayesha went behind the curtains, leaving the stage to the performer-aka her best friend, Gayatri Kulkarni. If there was one place where Ayesha felt Gayatri was her best self it was on stage.

She focused her eyes on the figure making its way to the center with graceful steps, the tinkling sound of anklets that echoed around the large auditorium, adding to the anticipation of her actual performance.

After Gayatri reached the center, she stood with her back towards the audience in a swan pose with the knee cap of her right leg protruding out and its base perched atop the inner thigh of her left leg. Her arms were outstretched like wings, the right one on top of her head and the left one parallel to her hips.

She remained in that position, flapping her arms like a bird, as the beginning tunes of *Aas paas khuda* started playing.

Dhundhla jaayein jo manzilein

Ik pal ko tu nazar jhuka..

A haze of smoke rose around Gayatri's at these lyrics. She half turned her face to the right and then the left, while moving her arms in the air as if trying to find her way in the haziness engulfing her.

Jhuk jaaye sar jahan wahi

---

[53] *Baby talk/babble for the Marathi word Maushi which means maternal aunt*

Milta hai rab ka raasta

She bowed her head before taking a pirouette and turning around to face the audience with her face still downcast.

Teri kismat tu badal de

Rakh himmat bus chal de

Gayatri jerked up her head and took slow, measured, unsure steps towards the edge of the stage. Her left foot hovered in the air once she reached the end, looking in the front as if in a trance. She swayed, trying to balance herself with one foot midair and the other one still on stage. Then she was lifted via aerial support, floating above the stage and audience for a few seconds. Her face carried a faraway look, as if in search of "someone".

Tere saathi mere kadmon ke hain nishan..

Footsteps appeared on stage, one pair on the right and one pair on the left. With echoing sounds that reverberated through the hall, these steps made their way to the center of the stage and **were accompanied by the words, "Thoda vishwas thev, Gayu" which were uttered by a male voice. These were followed by the words, "Kullu, hold to me tightly" spoken by someone else - another younger-sounding man. A collective gasp rose from the audience when the words were cut off by the sound of a loud crash and shattering glass.**

Gayatri let out a shriek struggling to break free of the harness, with her arms stretched towards the footprints. A few people in the audience cried out too as Gayatri flew towards the stage again and was set down in the center, with the footsteps surrounding her. She crouched down, caressing them. For a few seconds, the only sound was that of her sniffling, joined in by each person who was watching her.

Two pairs of shadow hands came up behind Gayatri, hugging her as the song changed and the beginning tunes of *Mein jaahan rahoon* started to play. Gayatri stood up when the lyrics of the song began to play and danced as if letting out all of her pent up anguish. For the first time, her movements weren't mesmerizing but tear-jerking. The pair of shadow hands stayed with her throughout, and her movements circled around them, trying to catch them or calling out to them.

When the song finally ended, Gayatri ended up crumpling on the stage while the audience was on its feet, clapping till their hands hurt. In-between, most of them also brushed away the tears freely flowing down their cheeks.

Ayesha walked onto the stage, gathering Gayatri in her arms and helping her up. When the applause slowed down, and Gayatri had moved backstage, she announced, "Our last presentation for today's launch event will be Nalini Joshi's artwork. You can check them out in the hall located on the right side of the stage. The art pieces are from her recent ***She Rose*** exclusive collection *Relentless*, and they're all up for sale. Please remember that 50% of proceeds will be going to IIMPACT- an NGO that ***She Rose*** will be joining hands with, in their mission to make women creatively independent."

The crowd began to disperse, as Ayesha continued with her final few things to be announced, "Thank you for joining us today. Registration and all other details can be found at the inquiry counter where Nalini Joshi and Sharad Kulkarni will answer all your questions."

Everyone slowly filed out till only a handful people remained in the hall. These included Gayatri, Ayesha, Radha, Uma and Anusha. The latter three were joined by Gayatri and Ayesha who made their way towards the seats from upstage, with Ayesha's hands around Gayatri's shoulder.

Once within arm's reach, Gayatri stretched her hands towards Uma, who immediately handed over the bundle she was holding in her hands.

Gayatri landed kisses on the tiny form of Varya, her one-month-old daughter, wrapping her up in her arms tightly. She clutched Varg's outstretched hand in one palm, and walked out of the hall - a picture of motherhood, while the other women followed behind, in silent admiration.

***

The Daily Wave

Is the myth 'Every day is Women's Day' finally becoming a reality?

11th May, 2026

It's been over two months since we celebrated International Women's Day but attending the inaugural event of **She Rose** felt like the honouring and recognition of women was still ongoing. The purpose of this creative platform seems to be such anyway and *The Daily Wave* team feels more empowered in bringing this story to you today.

If the name of the platform made you wonder, "What's with that name and what's it all about?" you're not alone in that boat because we were right there with you till yesterday evening. More specifically, till the time we attended their launch event and were left, quite literally, spellbound.

She Rose- For the everyday sheroes is a platform started with the purpose of training women of all ages in creative fields like writing, dancing, spoken word poetry and artwork. Their aim is to provide wings to women's creativity which has been limited to households and caretaking of families and kids, since time immemorial.

The twenty-somethings, three-member founding team, consists of *Gayatri Kulkarni*, *Ayesha Banerjee*, and *Nalini Joshi*. Some readers might recall the name *Ayesha Banerjee* whom we featured in our Women's Day exclusive story where we talked about her journey from a YouTuber (*Bandit Banerjee*) to an author (*Angst, Anger & Adulting*).

Nalini Joshi's artworks (most of which can also be found on her socials *Nasty Naari*) have been featured in our *C for Creativity* segment more times than we can recall now. It's safe to assume that most of our current readers have now become regulars to our newspaper probably due to their admiration for her featured works.

Gayatri Kulkarni too, is a known our regular readers might be able to recall. Because just last Friday, in our *Let's Get Mental* weekly special, she talked about how dancing and regular counselling were the only things that kept her mental health in check after losing her father and her husband within a span of five years. A dancepreneur who goes by *G for Jhankaar* on all socials, Gayatri has been in this profession for over a decade now. And anyone who has ever been her student, never tires of singing her praises, or shall we say, never tires of *dancing to her tunes?*

When three such prolific and talented women come together, there's bound to be fireworks. That's just what the audience got to see at the launch event of **She Rose.** Each of them showcased their own creative talent which included, a powerful spoken word poetry from Ayesha Banerjee, an emotional dance performance by Gayatri Kulkarni, and an enthralling artwork display by Nalini Joshi.

The three of them combined, have over 100 million followers across all leading social media platforms. All women have been dabbling in their respective creative fields, right from childhood but could not turn it into a lucrative profession until a few years ago. Their common woe (or foe?) - the society. A society filled with people like you, me and us, who feels that creativity cannot be a profession.

With their platform **She Rose - For the everyday sheroes,** they aim to change this thinking, especially for women. Specifically, those women who had to let go of their passion and creative streak because they were made to feel that there is no money in it.

After watching the performances and looking at the artworks, we were left wondering, "Is the myth 'Every day is Women's Day' finally becoming a reality?" Only time can tell but with platforms like these, we're definitely one step closer.

***

(Not) The End - Epilogue

"Being a wife and a mother isn't everything. But it is definitely an important aspect of being a woman. One that makes your life blissful, if not better."

- Gayatri Kulkarni

December 2026

"Will you stop cribbing, please? My kids do enough of that for everyone."

Gayatri was at the John F. Kennedy International Airport, where they had just walked out of immigration. Varg was walking beside her with his right hand clutched in Gayatri's left palm. She was on a video call with Sharad who sounded agitated because he'd been waiting for almost an hour. When he was finally able to connect with Gayatri, he made the mistake of starting off by the statement, "Any more waiting and I'd have started pulling my hair off. Now come straight out, we're standing at the exit of the arrivals gate."

At that exact moment, Varg dragged Gayatri towards one of the airport shops, exclaiming loudly, "Mumaaa.... chocolates..."

She cut off Sharad's call while trying to stop Varg. He howled and stomped his tiny feet on hearing Gayatri's, "Not now, baby". Somehow though, she managed to veer his protesting body towards the conveyor belt. She ignored the judgmental looks drawn her way because of Varg's shrieks. The way he was crying out, struggling to break free of Gayatri's hold on his palm, any onlooker would think the child was being kidnapped. Gayatri ignored the glances coming their way, suddenly finding her respect for mothers travelling with kids going up ten notches.

Thankfully, Varya was being taken care of by Uma, who was walking a few feet ahead, steering the stroller carrying her peacefully sleeping seven-month-old daughter. The peace lasted only a few seconds though because the minute they reached the conveyor belt, the hubbub of the crowd broke Varya's sleep and she started bawling loudly too.

Uma immediately gathered Varya in her arms, trying to put her back to sleep, while Varg's tantrums were still in full swing. Gayatri felt like crying herself. The exhaustion of the 20-hour journey coupled with her two weeping children was the tipping point of the overwhelmingness to finally catch on.

That's when her phone rang with Sharad's call asking how much longer he would have to wait. Her long pent-up frustration finally burst through and she shouted at Sharad.

Uma took the phone from her. Varya was asleep in the stroller again and Varg had finally stopped howling too. When Uma reached out to grab Varg's hand, he willingly let go of Gayatri's palm and took his grandma's outstretched one.

"Sharad, we'll be out in a bit," Uma told her son while signalling her daughter to collect their luggage.

"Breathe, darling. It's okay. We're here now." She placated Gayatri as the four of them, rather two and two-halves, slowly made their way toward the arrival gate.

Once they were out, Varg rushed towards a figure waiting on the left side, shouting out, "Shru Mamaaaa[54]..."

After many failed attempts, they'd all come to accept that Varg would be calling him Shru instead of Sharad. To be fair, Sharad had never minded it anyway.

He picked up his nephew and perched him on his shoulders after landing kisses on both his cheeks.

"Let me take her." Nalini offered when Varya woke up and started crying again. Uma hugged and thanked her, heaving a sigh of relief.

"Thank God we have others to take over their responsibilities for a while at least," Uma remarked.

A few minutes later, after all the luggage was loaded and the six of them were comfortably settled in the car, they were finally enroute to their destination.

"Abhi is losing his mind worrying about the sangeet," Sharad informed Gayatri.

"Typical. Well, that explains all the '*I miss you*' texts from him."

In about half an hour, they reached the neighbourhood of Sunnyside in Queens. Sharad pulled up in front of one of the houses towards the end of one of the lanes. Even before the car was parked, the front door of the

---

[54] *Hindi/Marathi term for maternal uncle*

house opened and a bunch of people filed out, rushing forth to welcome them.

"Daadu...." Varg was the first one out of the car as Shyam picked him out from the baby seat and swirled him around.

As soon as he was put down, Varg looked around curiously.

"Hey, kiddo. What's up?"

"Abhi chachu, don't call me kid. I'm a big boy now." Varg said seriously as the adults around him chuckled, except Abhi.

Scrunching up his face in mock seriousness, Abhi asked after a few minutes of contemplation, "How about buddy? Does that work?"

Varg's whole face crinkled with a huge smile as he rushed toward Abhi.

"Yes, we're friends!" He hi-fived Abhi and turned towards Gayatri. "Mumma... did you hear? I'm old enough to be Abhi chachu's buddy now."

Abhi laughed and enveloped Varg in a hug before perching him on his shoulders and running around declaring, "Who's a big boy?"

Varg didn't take even a second to respond, "I am!"

"Thank God you're here, Gayatri. I'm going crazy dealing with the Agarwal men all by myself." Radha said, hugging Gayatri.

"Oh dear! Please tell me you didn't scare off Nalini already." Gayatri asked Abhi, receiving a raspberry blow in response, which was immediately imitated by Varg.

"Gee, great! Thanks for that." Gayatri landed a punch on Abhi's shoulder. "Such big boys I see."

The whole lot of Agarwals, Kulkarnis, and Nalini, walked into the house with the luggage and stroller, in which Varya surprisingly lay sleeping, undisturbed, despite all the commotion around her.

As soon as they entered the house, Gayatri gasped, taking in the elaborate decor. String lights were hung up across the hallway and on the bannisters of the stairs leading to the upper floors.

There were streamers on almost every wall in the living room and the kitchen.

"Somebody would think there's a wedding happening here." Gayatri remarked, taking it all in.

"Umm, hello? How dare you insult our hard work like that! I was going for something grander here." Abhi said, hand on heart.

Uma chuckled, while Radha declared, with her hand on Gayatri's shoulder.

"Don't say that, dear. This is so much bigger than any wedding."

Tears brimmed her eyes and Gayatri could only hug the older woman; drawing as much consolation from the gesture herself as Radha.

It was only then that she noticed the banner behind the television in the living room. It covered almost the entire wall. Gayatri's breath hitched in her throat as she read the text on it.

Nalini was the first one to notice Gayatri's reaction and nodded her head in acknowledgement and reassurance.

"It was Abhi's idea of course." Nalini explained, whispering in Gayatri's ear once the hug was broken and everyone got busy shuffling the new luggage or preparing meals.

"Congratulations Gayatri - The Shero of Kulkarni and Agarwal Family"

Gayatri took in the banner again, sighing deeply while moving her hands over it caressingly.

"I wish I could hold on to you tightly, Aru," she murmured.

"Gayu, come. Dinner is ready." Abhi called out and Gayatri quickly wiped away the tears, walking toward the dining table to join her family.

As the night drew to a close and Gayatri snuggled up in bed next to Varg, she found herself getting cold feet. Sure, she'd been nervous before in life. But not about this and never when she was so well prepared.

"It's going to be alright." She whispered reaching out to rock Varya's cradle when she heard her cooing.

With her two kids by her side, she knew she'd be alright. That one thought finally put her to sleep, bringing forth a smile – a heart-warming one, as opposed to the one she'd been faking all evening for her family's sake.

***

"Mademoiselle, may I have your autograph please?"

Gayatri was at a Target store with Sharad, Nalini, Abhi and the kids to buy some groceries. A few posters of the coming event had been put up inside the store premises and Gayatri was just looking at it proudly.

She turned around in surprise and disbelief on hearing the familiar voice.

She squealed and hugged the person, still in shock.

"What are you doing here?" She finally managed to ask, breaking free from the hug.

"I live here remember? I got married and moved here a few years back."

"Yes, I know that Simi. But New York is a big city and we haven't really been in touch."

"And whose fault is that Gayu?" The hurt in Simran's voice broke Gayatri's heart.

"Hey, Simi. What a surprise!" Sharad barged in, enveloping Simran in a hug.

"Hello, Sharad. Another Kulkarni who has forgotten the Shindes." She greeted, landing a punch on his shoulder.

"Guilty! But I'm sure you know how it's been for the Kulkarnis." Sharad retorted.

"I'm sorry." Simran replied meekly, looking as if she wished the earth could swallow her up.

"It's okay." Gayatri and Sharad replied unanimously.

"Hey guys. Varya is getting cranky and…" Nalini rushed up to them and tugged at Sharad's sleeve urgently.

"Mummmmaaaaa…" Varg ran towards Gayatri, with Abhi right behind.

"I thought we were buddies now." Abhi quickly caught up with the little guy and gathering Varg in his arms, twirled him around.

"No complaining to mumma, okay? Now hand over the car keys or no PS 5 for you tonight."

Varg contemplated this for a few seconds, and stretched his hand out. His lower lip jutted out adoringly, and Abhi chuckled while snatching the keys and perching his tiny form upon his shoulders.

"Are they yours?" Simran asked, taking in the retreating figures of Abhi and Varg, with Varya's stroller beside them.

"Thankfully, only the smaller two are. The elder one is my brother-in-law." Gayatri replied with a warm smile.

"I'm sorry about…??"

"Varun.. yes. It's okay. I have the kids, She Rose, and my girls Ayesha and Nalini…" She nodded in Nalini's direction.

Nalini smiled awkwardly not knowing how to be a part of this conversation.

"Oh, sorry. This is Nalini. My girlfriend." Sharad quickly butted in, sensing Nalini would kill him if he delayed the introductions any further.

"My soon-to-be fiancée." He added on receiving a deathly glare from both Gayatri and Nalini.

"So, when are you coming to India next?" Gayatri asked Simran as they began to move towards the checkout counter.

"I'm visiting India next month. The Shindes have planned a grand celebration for Aarav, my son's first birthday and Arya, Kartik's daughter's second birthday."

"Hey, that's wonderful. I would love to meet your son. I'm sure him and Varg can be good friends."

"Why don't you all come to the birthday party?"

"Hey, why don't you come to our engagement?"

Simran and Sharad asked at the same time, causing everyone to laugh.

"Nalini and I are getting engaged in two weeks. We'd love it if all the Shindes could be a part of our special day. I'll call up Kartik too. It's high time I reached out anyway." Sharad said and Simran simply nodded, her eyes tearing up.

Once they exited the store, the group chatted a bit, exchanging numbers. Sharad ensured he had Kartik's in-use and correct contact details.

"I'll see you tomorrow." Simran whispered in Gayatri's ear while hugging her and before parting ways to walk towards her own car.

"You know Kartik is divorced, right?" Sharad asked Gayatri slyly as soon as they were all seated in the car, minus Simran.

"You know I'm 28, a mother of two and very much capable of making my decisions without you butting in, right?" Gayatri retorted.

Her phone rang and the name on the screen instantly changed her mood.

"How are my darlings? I miss you guys and so wish I was there."

"We miss you too, love. But you're always here in spirit." Gayatri and Nalini responded, with hands on their hearts.

"The drama never ends." Sharad snickered.

"And it never will…" chimed three voices in response, drowning him out.

It was true though, Gayatri realized as she, Nalini, and Ayesha got lost in their chatters, catching up with each other, completely oblivious to everything and everyone.

Her girls were always with her in spirit.

The drama would never end.

And that's all Gayatri needed.

For now. Forever. As long as she could have it.

***

Kyun na bole mo se mohan kyun

Hai roothe roothe mohan yun

Kaise manaaun haai kaise manaau

The woman dancing to the song had everyone mesmerized by her movements on stage. She was dancing gracefully no doubt. But it was the way she was able to communicate her emotions through her moves that left each person watching her, spellbound.

"When they said she was the best dancer India had seen in a while, I had my doubts. But seeing her live, I can say that's a false claim."

"What do you mean? Do you think she's not good?"

"Are you crazy? Just look at her! I meant it's false because she seems to be the best dancer *the world* has seen in a while."

The applause that followed at the end of the performance could surely hold a record for being one of the longest and loudest. Most people in the audience were on their feet as they clapped. The woman bowed in gratitude, acknowledging the audience as the curtains slowly fell.

"That was Gayatri Kulkarni from India, representing **She Rose,** a platform that makes women creatively independent. With that we come to the end of today's event. Please give a huge round of applause for all the wonderful women who made *Women Can '26,* an event we will remember for a long time."

The emcee paused for a while as the filled-to-capacity, Schimmel Center, fulfilled her demand.

"I would like to call all the women who have performed for us today on stage now before we disperse. Keep the applause on as the ladies join us one final time."

All the 30 women walked to the stage one by one while the emcee continued, "These women represent the performing arts from across the world and what sets them apart is what they have done with their skills. You can know all about them in the January '27 edition of *Women Can* where we'll be featuring their individual stories. Thank you all for joining us tonight. And always remember…"

"WOMEN CAN!!"

The crowd shouted out in response, completing the emcee's statement. Their applause continued till the curtains closed again and the stage was enveloped in darkness.

***

The *Love & (Mellow) Drama* Map

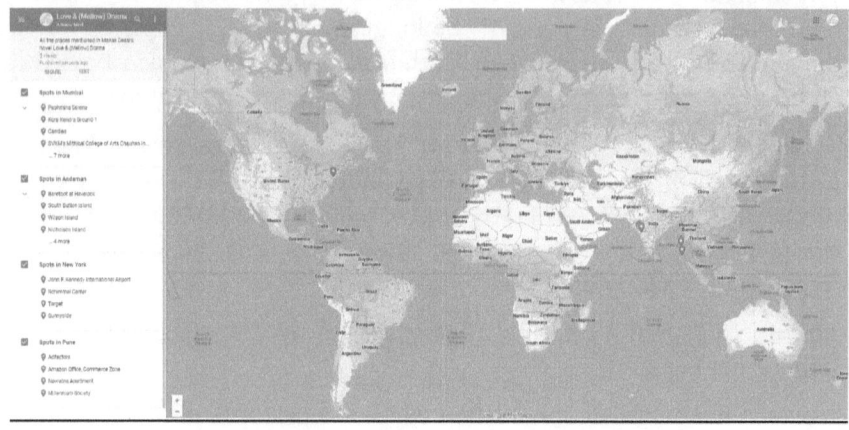

Take a virtual tour here

The *Love & (Mellow) Drama* Playlist

Song Name	When and Where it appears in the story
Dilwale Dulhaniya Le Jaayenge Theme music	Multiple times across the book
Pinga from Bajirao Mastani	The song that Gayatri performs to at *Dance Beat*
Aashiq Surrender Hua from Badrinath ki Dulhania	One of the songs that Gayatri choreographs for Rishi's wedding
Gallan Goodiyan from Dil Dhadakne Do	One of the songs that Gayatri choreographs for Rishi's wedding
Do Me A Favour Let's Play Holi from Waqt	The song that Gayatri and Abhi sing during their double date
Tainu Leke from Salaam-e-Ishq	One of the songs that Gayatri choreographs for Rishi's wedding
Tamma Tamma Again from Badrinath ki Dulhania	Gayatri's caller ringtone during the chapter *Festival of (True) Colours*
Shendur Laal Chadayo from Vaastav	Ganpati aarti from the chapter *Deva Shree Ganesha*
Mujhse Dosti Karoge title track from Mujhse Dosti Karoge	The song that Varun hums while exiting from Kora Kendra in the chapter *Dance,*

	Romance
Dil ka Rishta title track from Dil ka Rishta	The song that Gayatri refers to in the chapter *Deva Shree Ganesha*
My Dil Goes Mmm from Salam Namaste	The song that Gayatri uses as a response to Varun's text in the chapter *Dance, Romance*
Mera Dil Bhi Kitna Paagal Hai	The song that Varun uses to begin their texting conversation in the chapter *Dance, Romance*
Balam Pichkari from Ye Jawani Hai Deewani	The song that play during Holi festivities at Pashmina Serene in the chapters *Absence Makes the Heart Go…?* and *Festival of (True) Colours*
Kya Khoob Lagti Ho from Dharamatma	The song's lyrics *Pyaase dil ko aaj mila hai sagar* that comes up in Varun's mind in the chapter *Absence Makes the Heart Go…?*
Samjhawan from Humpty Sharma Ki Dulhaniya	Avni's caller ringtone during the chapter *Absence Makes the Heart Go…?*
Meri Khawabon Mein from Dilwale Dulhaniya Le Jaayenge	The song that Gayatri sings during the chapter *The Little Things (In Big Countries)*
Tip Tip Barsa Paani from Mohra	The song that plays during Holi festivities at Pashmina Serene in the chapter *Festival of (True) Colours*

Maula Mere Maula from Anwar	The song that Varun hums while looking at Gayatri's damp hair in the chapter *Locked Down*
Ek Zindagi from Angrezi Medium	Gayatri's caller ringtone in the chapter *Locked Down*
Bang Bang title track from Bang Bang	The song that Gayatri and Abhi perform to during their fresher's party celebration
Dilbaro from Raazi	One of the songs from Gayatri's solo performance in the chapter *Before & After (The Happily Ever After)*
Makhna from Drive	One of the songs from Gayatri's solo performance in the chapter *Before & After (The Happily Ever After)*
Nachde Ne Saare from Baar Baar Dekho	One of the songs from Gayatri's solo performance in the chapter *Before & After (The Happily Ever After)*
Tujhe Dekha To from Dilwale Dulhaniya Le Jaayenge	One of the songs from Gayatri and Varun's couple's dance performance in the chapter *Before & After (The Happily Ever After)*
Rang Saari from Jugg Jugg Jeeyo	One of the songs from Gayatri and Varun's couple's dance performance in the chapter *Before & After (The Happily Ever After)*

Kesariya from Brahmastra	One of the songs from Gayatri and Varun's couple's dance performance in the chapter *Before & After (The Happily Ever After)*
Shubhaarambh from Kai Po Che	Gayatri's bridal entry song from the chapter *Before & After (The Happily Ever After)*
Ruk Ja O Dil Deewane from Dilwale Dulhaniya Le Jaayenge	The song that Varun hums at the end of the chapter *Deva Shree Ganesha*
Dil Se Re from Dil Se	The song that Gayatri hums at the end of the chapter *Deva Shree Ganesha*
Diva by Beyonce	The song that Gayatri performs to during the ice-breaking session on her first day of college
Dekha Hazaaro Dafaa from Rustom	The song playing in Varun's car in the chapter *Kissing the Pain Away*
Pretty Woman from Kal Ho Naa Ho	One of the songs from Abhi and bridesmaids group performance in the chapter *Before & After (The Happily Ever After)*
Desi Girl from Dostana	One of the songs from Abhi and bridesmaids group performance in the chapter *Before & After (The Happily Ever After)*
Drama Queen from Hasee toh	One of the songs from Abhi and

Phasee	bridesmaids group performance in the chapter *Before & After (The Happily Ever After)*
Mangalayam from Saathiya	Varun's groom entry song from the chapter *Before & After (The Happily Ever After)*
Aankhein Khuli from Mohabbatein	The song from which the monologue for Varun's solo performance is used in the chapter *Before & After (The Happily Ever After)*
Saajanji Ghar Aaye from Kuch Kuch Hota Hai	One of the songs from Varun's solo performance in the chapter *Before & After (The Happily Ever After)*
Mujhse Shaadi Karogi title track from Mujhse Shaadi Karogi	One of the songs from Varun's solo performance in the chapter *Before & After (The Happily Ever After)*
Chicken Kuk-Doo-Koo from Bajrangi Bhaijaan	The song that Ayesha refers to for teasing Varun in the chapter *Not-So-Well-Begun*
Do Dil Mil Rahe Hai from Pardes	The song that Ayesha refers to for teasing Varun in the chapter *Not-So-Well-Begun*
Nagada Sang Dhol from Goliyon ki Ras Leela Ram Leela	The song used by Gayatri to teach Ayesha and Varun garba in the chapter in *Dance, Romance?*
Jute do Paise Lo from Hum Aapke Hain Kaun	The song that Varun uses as a reference in his note along with the gifted footwear in

	the chapter *Women, Woes*
Aas Paas Khuda from Anjana Anjaani	One of the songs from Gayatri's performance in the chapter *She Rose*
Mein Jahaan Rahoon from Namastey London	One of the songs from Gayatri's performance in the chapter *She Rose*
Bhare Naina from Ra-One	The song that Gayatri performs in the chapter *(Not) The End - Epilogue*
Tohfa Tohfa Tohfa from Tohfa	The song that Varun refers to in the chapter *Finding Foot(ing)*

You can listen to this exclusive playlist on YouTube, Amazon Music, and Spotify.

Note: Some songs aren't accessible on Amazon Music and Spotify so the complete playlist is only available on YouTube (a total of 46 songs)

Glossary of Terms/Phrases

Term	When it appears in the book and its meaning
Jaa Simran Jaa….Jee le apni zindagi	A dialogue from the Hindi movie *Dilwale Dulhaniya Le Jayenge* which appears in the epilogue, and the chapters, *Goodwill or God's Will* and *The Little Things (In Big Countries)* It roughly translates to "Go live your life to the fullest, Simran"
Bade bade deshon mein aisi choti choti baatein hoti rehti hai	A dialogue from the Hindi movie *Dilwale Dulhaniya Le Jayenge* which appears in the epilogue, and the chapter *Goodwill or God's Will*. It roughly translates to "Such trivial things keep happening in big countries (and one should learn to ignore them)"
Bura na mano Holi hai	A phrase used by Abhi in the chapter *Absence Makes the Heart Go…?* In India, people say this while celebrating the Holi festival and applying colors or spraying water on each other. It roughly translates to, "Don't feel bad. It's Holi after all."
Pyaase dil ko aaj mila hai sagar	A phrase from a Hindi song that comes up in Varun's mind in the chapter *Absence Makes the Heart Go…?* It roughly translates to, "Today the thirsty heart has found the sea."

Pyaar dosti hai	A dialogue from the Hindi movie *Kuch Kuch Hota Hai* which roughly translates to, "Love is friendship"
Koi bhi ullu ka patha sirf kuch dates pe leja kar tumko mujhse nahi cheen sakta ... tum meri ho, sirf meri.	A dialogue said by Varun in the chapter *The Little Things (In Big Countries)* which is a replica of a similar dialogue from the movie *Dilwale Dulhaniya Le Jayenge*. It roughly translates to, "No idiot can snatch you from me by taking you on a few dates.. you're mine, only mine"
Aai	Marathi term for mother used by Gayatri and Sharad to address Uma throughout the book
Baba	Marathi term for father used by Gayatri and Sharad to address Shishir throughout the book
Maa	Hindi term for mother used by Varun and Abhi to address Radha throughout the book
Papa	Hindi term for father used by Varun and Abhi to address Shyam throughout the book
Mummy ji	Hindi term used by married women to address their mother-in-law
Thoda vishwas thev	Marathi phrase used by Shishir to motivate Gayatri throughout the book which

	roughly translates to "Have a little faith in yourself"
Kichu ēkaṭā bala	Bengali phrase used by Ayesha in the chapter *Kissing the Pain Away* which roughly translates to "What nonsense you're saying"
Bhai/Bhaiya	Hindi word for (elder) brother used by Abhi to address Varun throughout the book
Bhav	Marathi word for (elder) brother used by Gayatri to address Sharad throughout the book
Mama	Marathi/Hindi word for maternal uncle used by Varg to address Sharad in the chapter *(Not) The End*
Chachi	Hindi word for paternal aunt (paternal uncle's wife) used by Varun to address Meera in the chapter *Moving On (or Holding On?)*
Chacha/Chachu	Hindi word paternal uncle used by Varun to address Ashok in the chapter Moving On (or Holding On?) and by Varg to address Abhi in the chapter *(Not) The End*
Maushi	Marathi term for maternal aunt used by Varg to address Ayesha in the chapter *She Rose*

Vada Pav	Vada pav also known as wada pao, is a vegetarian fast food dish native to the Indian state of Maharashtra. It consists of a deep-fried potato dumpling placed inside a bread bun and is generally accompanied by one or more chutneys and green chili pepper.
Gadadhari Bheem	In the Hindu epic Mahabharata, Bheem is the second among the five Pandavas. He is often associated with the emotion of anger/temper and his weapon (a club). The term Gadadhari Bheem is used to refer to someone who is in battle mode, extremely angry, or in the mood to fight/argue.
Chor ki dadhi mein tinka	A popular Hindi saying that roughly translates to, "A guilty conscience needs no accuser."
Jaisi karni waisi bharni	A popular Hindi saying that roughly translates to, "As you sow, so shall you reap."
Bheek mein diye hue	A Hindi phrase used by Gayatri in the chapter *He Said, She Said* which roughly translates to, "Given in alms"
Atithi Devo Bhava	A Hindi phrase used by Avni in the chapter *Absence Makes the Heart Go…?* which roughly translates to, "A guest is akin to God."

Vicks ki goli lo khich khich door karo	A Hindi product tagline for Vicks candies which roughly translates to, "Take a tablet of Vicks and get rid of irritation/hoarseness of throat."
Alvida Kehnse se phir milne ki umeed marr jaati hai	A Hindi phrase used by Avni in the chapter *Absence Makes the Heart Go...?* which roughly translates to, "Saying bye kills the hope of meeting again."
Khup chan distes	Marathi words uttered by Uma to compliment Gayatri in the chapter *Dance, Romance?* which roughly translate to, "You look very beautiful."

Other Books by This Author
Love (Try) Angle (Love Trials I)

Ayesha has just moved to the 'City of Dreams' with her parents. She befriends the charming Viren, who helps her find her footing in Mumbai. Though she is slowly adjusting to her new life, what Ayesha is most excited about is pursuing B.A. (Hons.) Political Science from a reputed college. Things don't go as smoothly as she had thought though. Because Abhi, her senior, seems hell-bent on making her life on the campus difficult from day one. Just when things seem settled, Viren joins the college as an Ad-Hoc lecturer. Is there more to Ayesha's friendship with Viren, and her frenemity with Abhi? It seems there's a love triangle blooming around the corner or will it be a Love (Try) Angle? Because Ayesha is not sure if it's love at all.

Mindful Musings & Peaceful Ponderings

Anxious

Conflicted

Nervous

Confused

Safe

Complete

Jubilant

Confident

Do these sound familiar? You may not have experienced these *feelings* lately or maybe not at all. But if you have, you aren't alone. The 50 poems in this book are a reflection of you, me, and all of us. They are the mindful musings and peaceful ponderings of human experiences that make us smile, laugh, cry, and wonder with emotions, that unite us all.

Under the Mistletoe & Other Stories

Diana is all set to welcome her loved ones for Christmas. An unexpected (and uninvited!) guest shows up at her door, spoiling her festive mood. All her attempts to thwart Dylan's intrusion go in vain as he keeps dropping in, again and again, insisting that she join his family for Christmas Eve dinner. Against her better judgment, she finally gives in, just to get him off her back. As they stand under the mistletoe after the dinner, Diana and Dylan know things have changed for the better for both.

A group of passengers is stranded at the airport together on New Year's Eve. Their plans were to celebrate the last day of the year and then ring in the new year with their loved ones by their side. But a delayed flight mars their plans and their happiness. They end up talking to each other, exchanging their New Year's Eve plans and how they celebrated it these many years so far. As they all welcome the new year together at midnight, their combined resolutions are to stay in touch with each other. They also resolve to make the best out of whatever life throws their way. Because as they have seen and experienced, not all things go as planned, always.

Samantha is visiting her native, Benakatti, after many years. Even though it's Christmas time, it's not a happy occasion in the family. As friends and family drop in for a visit, Samantha recalls the many winter breaks she spent in this village as a child. An unexpected guest shows up one day, bringing forth a cherished memory they had made on a foggy winter day many years ago.

These and 10 other stories encompass this festive special anthology. These are stories of hope, love, healing, new beginnings, acceptance, and everything that the holidays represent.

The Art of Being Grateful & Other Stories

Aashna receives a mysterious phone call in the middle of the night. The caller is a girl who says she has been kidnapped and will die if Aashna doesn't help her. Before Aashna can get details about the girl and her whereabouts, the phone gets cut off. Who was she and why did her voice sound eerily familiar? Will Aashna be able to help her?

Maanvi's life has always been about making everyone around realize that she is worthy too. From her test grades to her body type, everyone always had a piece of advice to give or some judgement to pass. How does Maanvi get affected by these? Does she manage to prove her worth to the world?

These and six other stories in this collection, cover a range of genres including romance, mystery, horror, thriller and much more. Delve in for a delightful reading journey!

The Untold Stories

Have you wondered about the events that happen around us? Do you think about the kind of lives people we come across everyday lead, and how they came to be what they are today? Our life is our story, but what about those little everyday incidents which create the anecdotes filling up the chapters of our life story? 'The Untold Stories' shares tiny anecdotes from people's everyday routines which go on to make remarkable chapters in their life stories. These anecdotes range from incidents around contemporary social issues and events such as terrorism and environmental imbalance to those circling around relationships.

A Rustic Mind

"We never think about the effects or repercussions of our everyday actions or even the things we come across on daily basis. Through 'A Rustic Mind' I aim to provide a thoughtful take on such actions and incidents. Poetic in its expression, these words will strike a chord which is not only deep but relatable on many levels. "

Ten Tales

This is a collection of short stories by authors across the world. The stories have been handpicked and selected based on their quality. The stories cover all genres in fiction.

Manali's story in this book is titled 'I'm Glad I'm Not Beautiful'. It spins a story around the much needed to be curbed issue and social stigma of acid attacks. The story circles around two school-going teenage girls, Abha and Vidhya, who are best friends, but are opposite in nature and appearance, and how a few incidents on a particular day turns their lives upside down.

Zista

"Zista represents Culture, the hub of which lies in India."

This title holds in its pages the very essence of India, its people and its culture, conveyed through a selection of short stories by few of the best authors of India.

Manali's story in this book is titled 'The Walls Have Ears'. This story helped her bag the Best Script Award. It talks about a young girl's day out in the infamous Kamathipura aka The Red-Light District of Mumbai.

Petrichor (compiled and edited by Manali Desai)

14 writers

7 short stories

9 poems

Who doesn't hold a special love for the rains? The smell of wet soil when the showers hit the surface of the Earth, opens up so much for us, emotionally. In this magical collection, we have some of the most special monsoon stories from a bunch of talented writers across the world. The contributors of this anthology traverse from 8 years old to 30 years old. What's common between them? Their love for monsoons of course! Because love for the rains is not age bound, right? This anthology is an attempt at bringing together writers from various walks of life. Each story or poem in this collection will make you rekindle your love with this most beloved season. It will be hard not to reminisce about your many romances with Indra over the years. The pages within this book will evoke nostalgic feelings in every reader. So, grab a cup of your favorite beverage and cozy up in your reading nook as you delve into Petrichor.

About the Author

Manali Desai

Manali Desai is a full-time freelance writer and editor cum blogger. Currently, apart from her ad hoc writing and editing assignments, Manali runs a blog where she shares poetry, personal essays, and book reviews. In her authoring journey, Manali has published six solo books and has helped new and aspiring writers get their books published. She has been a multiple-times bestselling author on Amazon with all her books ranking in the top ten in many categories. Her short story, ***The Walls Have Ears***, helped her bag the Best Short Story Award in 2019 at ***Stories from India*** by **Ukiyoto Publishing**. She has also won the Best Author: Fiction Award at ***Cherry Book Awards*** , and the Book of The Year title by ***BeTales Magazine*** in 2021 for her debut novel, ***Love (Try) Angle***. Her short story titled, ***The (Un)Blind Date***, which is a part of her Christmas special anthology, ***Under the Mistletoe & Other Stories***, won the best story prize in an online contest, before the book's release in December 2021. ***Love & (Mellow) Drama*** is her seventh book and second novel. It is a spin-off from her award-winning debut novel, ***Love (Try) Angle***. She can be found on all socials under her pen name, ***A Rustic Mind***.

www.ingramcontent.com/pod-product-compliance
Lightning Source LLC
LaVergne TN
LVHW041929070526
838199LV00051BA/2762